Beyond the Bleeding Heart

A Tale of the American Civil War

by

Jessica and Alexandra Elam

D1452560

TELEMACHUS PRESS

Cover designed by Telemachus Press, LLC

Cover art:
Copyright © iStockPhoto/147532276_JayBoivin
Copyright © iStockPhoto/491944471_Wilsilver77
Copyright © iStockPhoto/992815966_Mikehop
Copyright © iStockPhoto/1266438268_Wicki58
Copyright © iStockPhoto/1306467616Corey Macri
Copyright © iStockPhoto/1318596668_Julija Kumpinovica
Copyright © iStockPhoto/1331660100_Willard

Song Credits:
"Sweet Hour of Prayer" (W.W. Walford, 1845)
"Stand Up, Stand Up for Jesus" (George Duffield Jr., 1858)
"Siúil a Rún" It is unclear on the original writer of this song or of the date. It is believed to have been written in the 1800's.

Publishing Services by Telemachus Press, LLC
7652 Sawmill Road
Suite 304
Dublin, Ohio 43016
http://www.telemachuspress.com

ISBN: 978-1-956867-46-6 (eBook)
ISBN: 978-1-956867-47-3 (Paperback)

Library of Congress Control Number: 2022919785

Version 2023.02.21

Introduction

Dear Readers,

Have you ever wanted to travel into history and experience what life was like back then? We certainly have, and this is the way we did just that.

As young teenagers, we became very enthusiastic about the American Civil War. We read many Civil War books together and watched movies set in that time period. We were so inspired by the soldiers who fought in the war and their devotion to their country. We visited Gettysburg, Pennsylvania multiple times with a desire to get a closer glimpse into the history of this battlefield and the lives of the heroes who fought there.

Our novel is set around historical events. At times we may mention people who really fought in the war or who lived during those times. For example, the character "John Barnes" is based on the true historical figure "John Burns" who was the constable of Gettysburg during the Civil War Era, but we altered his name for the character in the novel. General Ulysses S. Grant is also mentioned in the novel. However, the majority of our characters are fictional. Also, the escape from the prison camp in Chapter 39 is based off of an escape from Libby Prison in Richmond, Virginia which occurred in 1864. Over one hundred officers escaped out of a tunnel, nearly half of them were recaptured. For the purpose of our book I needed an escape to happen in 1862.

As you read, you will notice along with the title of each chapter is the name "Elizabeth" or "Amy." This designates from which sister's perspective you will be experiencing that chapter. The sisters alternate every chapter. Jessica writes for the character Elizabeth and Alexandra writes for Amy's character.

We hope this novel not only inspires you to take a deeper look into the past, but causes you to cherish the present and change the future. May you never forget where you came from, and the men and women who served our nation so that you can be free.

Pleasant Reading!

Jessica and Alexandra Elam

Acknowledgements

To our Lord and Savior, Jesus Christ: Thank you for entrusting us with this talent of writing, may we always use it for your glory and to inspire others and point them to you.

To our parents, Kurt and Anna Elam: Thank you so much for the time you took to read, discuss and edit our book with us, for the long discussions about the causes of the Civil War and many other related topics, and for always encouraging us and believing in our dreams. We love you!

To our dear friend, Laura Huber: Thank you for your guidance through the process of writing and publishing this novel. Thank you for giving us suggestions and feedback, and for always encouraging us in the work.

To our publishers at Telemachus Press: Thank you for making this dream a reality ... something we can hold in our hands. It has been a pleasure and joy to work with you, we look forward to many more years in partnership with you!

To our wonderful Friends, Family, and Coworkers who have given us encouragement, support, and guidance during this work. You are our inspiration!

Dedication

To our Grandpa, Gustavo Zapata

You came to this great country full of hope and lived the American Dream ... a life of duty, honor and determination. Thank you for supporting and encouraging us to live our dreams. We love you.

Table of Contents

Beyond the Bleeding Heart

A Tale of the American Civil War

Live to bless, not to impress! ♡

Jessica [signature]

Life's Hard, not to impress. ♥

The Encounter
Chapter 1

Elizabeth

July 1859

Dearest Daughters,

We apologize for not writing sooner. We have been ill for several weeks now. While staying in this town, an epidemic of cholera swept the area. We know that once you receive this letter, you will try to come to our aid and nurse us in this time of sickness, but you must not. We beg you to stay in Gettysburg. For if you come to us, you will most certainly become ill as well. If we do not recover, we want to tell you how much you mean to us. You girls mean everything to us! Grow up to be strong and courageous women, but also be "gentle and quiet spirits," as it says in God's Word.

We love you more than you will ever come to know,

Father and Mother

And with that … my sister and I were on our own.

April 1860

THE OLD COBBLESTONE cracked and crumbled under my feet as I made my way through the streets of Gettysburg, Pennsylvania. The awful tidings of that message kept ringing through my mind. Shaking off the tormenting thoughts, I turned my attention to the heavy basket hanging on my arm.

Peeking under the light, checkered cloth, I smiled at the vegetables, meat and warm rolls concealed there. The preparation of every meal had fallen to me because my sister, Amy, had the unfortunate habit of destroying every meal she attempted to create.

The day was quiet, except for a soft breeze that stirred my hair under its bonnet. Out in the distant fields, farmers were building wooden fences and tilling the fresh, moist soil of early spring.

Determined to get home and set before my sister the meal I was designing, I was unaware of what lay in my path. Unbeknownst to me, a young blacksmith, carrying a carton of tools, was passing in my direction also absorbed in his own thoughts. The two of us, not watching our steps, collided, sending everything sailing into the air. Directly in front of me was a young and handsome face framed by coal black hair. The young man wore a white, long-sleeved shirt that was hurriedly rolled up to his elbows. His arms, as well as the shirt, were smudged with black soot in various places.

Staring at my ruined meal scattered in the dirt, a sudden flush of anger rose in my cheeks and I turned on my assailant. I was shocked to find that the young man had jumped to his feet, scrambled for his tools and was darting quickly down an alley way. Abandoned in the dust, I sputtered at a loss for words, staring incredulously for several minutes as the figure disappeared from sight.

Eventually finding my voice, I snapped under my breath, "The nerve of that man! Who does he think he is? Intolerable!"

Dusting the soot and dirt from my new dress and snatching up my basket, I shook my head in disgust and hurried home.

* * *

Along Emmitsburg Road, situated apart from the bustling town, stood a two-story brick house, complete with a navy-blue roof, shutters and wooden door. Many windows of glass dressed with lace curtains decorated the front. To the left of the house stood an oak tree, its leaves emerging from the branches. Hanging on one of its limbs, from two thick coils of rope, was a wooden swing waving softly in the breeze. Leading away from the door was a path made of red bricks outlined with rich soil. Behind the house was a large garden, where many delicious vegetables would soon be growing. To the right of the building stood a small stable where the horses were kept.

It was to this house that I came. I had lived here all my life. I remember Mother asking Father if we could move to a warmer part of the country at one time, but Father had responded so adamantly that we must stay in this house, that we never ventured to ask again. Now my sister and I lived in it all alone since our parents had died from the cholera epidemic nine months ago. It was hard getting along without them. Their absence was dreadful, even though it created a closer bond between us. At the age of twenty-one, I felt the weight of responsibility for my younger sister.

Still trying to wipe the dust off my dress, I approached the familiar building. Walking through the flowers on the brick path, I reached for the brass handle. The familiar creaking of the big door alerted Amy of my arrival. She stepped quickly down the stairs.

"Elizabeth! Your home! Finally! I'm so hungry," she said as she peaked in my basket. The mention of the food brought the whole incident of the morning sweeping into my mind.

Rolling my eyes, I mumbled, "You still have to wait for me to cook it."

"What's wrong with you?" she asked.

I sighed, "I'm sorry, it's not your fault. It's just that … I was on my way home from the market and this tramp on the street wasn't looking where he was going and ran into me. He just left me there too!" As we walked into the large kitchen, Amy began to laugh.

I turned on her and scolded, "It was not the least bit amusing! It was downright rude and … and horrible of him!"

My sister suppressed a smile, "Of course, I'm sorry."

Nodding slightly at her, I let her know it was all right, then concentrated my frustration on churning the butter, hoping to never see that scornful man again. And yet ... one thing I owe him: since that day there was never such creamy butter in all of Pennsylvania.

Looking Back
Chapter 2

Amy

A GENTLE BREEZE blew through the school room of tense students busy about their work. Every head was bent, eyes on the old worn books before them. The smell of oak pews and chalk dust filled the air. Old wooden floorboards creaked as I made my rounds among the long benches.

A few children glanced up from their slates as I passed. I smiled and nodded at them to go on. The sounds of chalk scratching on slate along with the rustling of my skirts were the only noises in the room. Reaching my own desk, I sat down, waiting for the children to finish. I loved teaching with all its responsibility. It was hard, but worth the time and effort. Some of the boys were bigger than me and were bullies, but I dealt with them sternly, although they were hardly three years my junior.

Two years ago, Mother and Father had greatly encouraged me when I informed them of my plans to teach. I had known I would need something to keep my mind off of Kelsey, though it continually drifted to him between the days I received a letter. My heart would pound with uncontainable excitement as the envelope was placed in my hand. Lately though, the letters had slowed considerably and I tried to tell myself he must be very busy. I was continually scolding myself for feeling so neglected when I hadn't received a letter on time.

Then there was Mrs. Denny, the town gossip, who was continually interrogating me whenever I stopped by her bakery. I would have avoided her altogether if my dear sister Elizabeth had not specifically asked me to stop by her shop. Mrs. Denny always asked about my letters from Kelsey, and knowing the general prejudice against the Irish in the town, I wouldn't dare tell her that he had not written to me in a long time. No doubt, the next day I went out, I would hear all kinds of stories. It was amazing what fruits of scandal she could produce from such simple facts. So I tried with all my might to guard our engagement closely from such public slander as Mrs. Denny could devise.

"I've finished," a high, squeaky voice pierced through the vivid daydream. I glanced up from my seat to where Clarence Brown stood. The thin, gangly boy beside my desk squinted down from behind his filth-covered spectacles. I took the paper from his bony hand.

"Very well, Clarence. You may take your seat."

Clarence bowed awkwardly and turned to trip over another careless student's foot. The class roared with laughter. I was instantly up out of my chair banging on my desk for order.

"Quiet, class, quiet!" I struggled to be heard above the noise.

Clarence was quite a spectacle sprawled in the aisle. His long, lanky limbs tangled amongst the other students and their seats. Luke Stone grinned smugly from where he sat, then slowly drew his foot back behind the desk. Luke, as my oldest student, was taller than me and he was constantly bullying Clarence. I approached the bench where he sat.

"Luke Stone, will you please go to the blackboard?"

The boy turned up an innocent face, "I didn't do nothin', Miss Matthews."

I placed a clenched fist on my waist. "I didn't do *anything*," I corrected. Then finished, "I know you all too well for that, Luke. To the blackboard!"

Spitefully glancing back at Clarence, he rose from his seat, glared down at me, and then moved away muttering, "Can't help it the clumsy little runt tripped over my foot." He sneered at the boy still on the floor.

"Luke," I scolded, "to the board." I watched the boy swagger over to the blackboard giving one last hateful glance at Clarence.

"You will have plenty of other duties this year 'til school is let out," I finished and saw the anger rising in Luke's cheeks, but it did not frighten me in the least. I was all too angry at the bullying that was carried on here.

Someday Luke would get a taste of his own medicine from someone bigger than he. How I longed for that day, but for now, all he received was my indignation over his cruel pranks.

The noon break soon approached and the children hurried out of the building into the sunshine to eat their lunches. Sarah, my good friend and assistant in the classroom, sat beside me on the porch steps watching the younger children playing tag. Wagons and horses passed in the street kicking up dust and the smell of the bakery floated lightly on the breeze.

"Smell that cherry pie," I breathed in the fresh aroma and closed my eyes, feeling the warm sun on my face.

"Mrs. Denny must be busy getting ready for the barn dance," Sarah stated, then glanced down at her boots in thoughtful silence.

I noticed her sigh, "What's wrong? You are going, aren't you?"

"Oh, I don't know. I'm not much for social gatherings."

"Sarah … You'll end an old spinster if you continue like that," I teased.

The younger girl laughed, "Well …" she turned to me shyly, "Is Elizabeth going? I shouldn't be half so nervous if she was there."

I thought quickly, "I believe she is. She hasn't told me otherwise."

"That's good! At least I'll have people to talk with," she smiled glancing away and letting her brown locks fall a little in front of her face.

"You know, Henry Sims has asked about you a couple times when I've been by the lumber yard." I watched to see if the younger girl would blush.

"Oh, Amy, stop it! You're just teasing me; no one ever inquires after me." She paused, then suddenly burst, "Oh! I almost forgot something! Mr. O'Conner caught me on my way and said he thought you would like to have this." I was handed a letter.

"From Kelsey," I sighed, "Finally," I whispered half to myself.

"You're so lucky, Amy, you've known who you would marry since you were little. I don't know that I'll find anyone here I really want to marry," Sarah watched me finger the envelope tenderly.

I tried to repress a smile, "It's been so long, I don't know if it will ever happen. Sometimes I forget what he looks like." I sighed, sorrowfully, "What if he's not the same …"

Turning away to the little mountains surrounding the town, I tried to imagine the day Kelsey would return after so many years.

"Certainly, he will not look the same, Amy, so you mustn't worry yourself over that."

I glanced over and smiled, "I suppose not, it would be a bit odd if he didn't change. I guess I'm just afraid things won't be the same."

"Amy, a friendship as close as yours wouldn't dissolve after only a few years apart," Sarah's hand was on my shoulder. "My father says, 'Though life's trials may take friends far apart and perhaps even change them, a true friend will always come back to you'." Reaching up, I gratefully squeezed her hand. "I know he'll love you just as much as he did when he left."

Our eyes met, "How do you know?"

"No one who has seen you two together can doubt the strong bond between you," she gave an encouraging squeeze of assurance.

"Of course," I dropped my hand into my lap, ashamed at my doubts. "I can't let my fear get the better of me."

She rose from my side, "He'll be back before you know it." I stared up at her, but the grateful words did not come, so I merely smiled and watched her go.

Then rising to my feet, I rang the bell for school to resume. The children plodded past me like an unwilling herd of cattle.

As I watched them, my thoughts returned to Kelsey with a quickening heartbeat. Surely when he returned he would be changed from living in a big city. He would no longer be the carefree farm boy that had left us five years ago. When he returned from the United States Military Academy West Point he would be ... a soldier.

* * *

Breathing in the fresh spring air, I traveled along Emmitsburg Road homeward. A crystal blue sky hung over this land I had called home from my earliest years. Fields of turned soil lay in patches around farmhouses, and the welcome aroma of spring floated along the breeze. Dark blue mountains commanded the horizon as far as the eye could see, and then drew near, stretching their sylvan arms to encircle Gettysburg. The din of the town faded as I passed to the outskirts. Long fences stretched for miles in the open countryside. Cows grazed, peacefully swishing their tails. Far in the distance, I could glimpse our home standing like a speck in the vast fields. A lone wagon moved down the road in my direction, the old mare kicking up the dust of the road into the wind.

I remembered when I was seven, riding down this road on the back of Kelsey's pony as he ran alongside me, holding the lead to make sure I was safe. He loved horses so much and was always teaching me something new about them. I used to believe he could really hear them talking to him. Smiling, I remembered my first lesson with him when I was only six. He weaved the leather reins around my fingers, gazing up at me with dark brown eyes, saying as he did so, "Hold the reins gently to show you trust him."

Kelsey was a better teacher than I could ever hope to be. He was always patient even when I was frustrated. I always had trouble staying mad at him for very long, when he spoke so gently and calmly in that Irish accent that I simply adored. He had called me "Lassie" from the first day I met him as a toddler. I was so nervous on the first day of school that I held Kelsey's hand all the way into town. Elizabeth was up ahead with her friend chattering about dresses.

"You'll be all right, Lassie, school's fun. You'll see," the gentle voice soothed me all the way to school, the same way it calmed a nervous horse. Kelsey never shied away from being seen with me, even when the other children teased us as we entered the schoolhouse.

Mr. McCarthy had worked hard to raise their farm, taking charity from no one, not even from my father. He made it clear that he would start their home with the sweat of his own brow and finish it the same way. He was a big sturdy man, but gentle as a lamb. A strong bond of friendship developed quickly between our two families. As I grew older, I noticed that some of the townsfolk hated the many immigrants that had started their own communities in Gettysburg. I asked Father about it one day and he shook his head, sighing and saying how some people were so prejudice against anyone different. It was easy to forget the prejudice out on our country farms, far away from the disgusted glances we received whenever we rode into town with the McCarthy's. I couldn't understand them and it angered me whenever the townspeople would turn up their noses and refer to them as "Those Irish Folk."

Even some of the other Irish townspeople looked annoyed when they saw us together. Mr. McCarthy had worked hard to get his family away from the big cities where most of the immigrants lived as laborers, working in factories or at any job they could find. He wanted to farm, and so he pushed his little family west. Kelsey, on the other hand, was bound for the northeast. When he grew older, he declared he would one day go to West Point and become a soldier. Mr. McCarthy had laughed and ruffled Kelsey's sandy hair, thinking it was just a passing phase that little boys went through. But Kelsey was full of determination and meant to accomplish his goal. And so, the day came and much too soon, when our young farm boy would leave for the northeast. Rain poured from the sky as we gathered together on the deck waiting for the train that would take him. He would finish school near his uncle's home where he would reside for the first two years. Then he would enter West Point Military Academy for four years. I had protested the idea when he had laid out his plans before me, but his willfulness soon made me see that it was useless to argue. So, deciding it was better to part on good terms, I tearfully consented, and Kelsey gratefully clasped me in his arms. Then, in the parlor of our home, the young fifteen-year-old dropped to one knee and made a request of me. Glancing down at the delicate silver ring that signified our engagement, I smiled to myself at the memories that were still so clear. Father had given his consent to Kelsey with the knowledge that we would have to wait until Kelsey returned from West Point, which was a span of six years. It was a long engagement, but Kelsey wanted it that way before he left, and so had I.

Five years had passed, and I had begun to feel like a widow without ever having been married. We all waited anxiously for the day he would ride home dressed in his uniform, a young soldier of our country. Sadly, Father and Mother would not live long enough to see Kelsey return. Staring down the road to our farm house, I sighed. It all felt like so long ago, like it was only a dream to which the ending would never be revealed. Then, hope filled within me. Only one more year ... only one ...

The Barn Dance
Chapter 3

Elizabeth

WARM LIGHT GLOWED out from the windows of the large barn. The noise of the fiddle and laughter could be heard within. Amy and I hurried quickly toward the building and walked through the open doorway. I was glad to have this opportunity to escape the repetitive nature of cooking and keeping house. These times were rare opportunities for me. Smiles from the town folk greeted us. People stood in little clusters or along the wall chatting happily.

The annual spring barn dance had come once again. My heart tightened as I remembered the last barn dance well. I had been sitting in a corner with the other unfortunate ladies who had not found partners and was watching as my sister danced with a young man and father partnered with mother. It always seemed that there were not enough young men in the town with whom to dance. Then father had come and extended his hand to me, "May I have the honor of dancing the next with you, Miss Elizabeth?"

A spoon clattered against the punch bowl. The image before me disappeared. Flinching, I looked around and sighed. The memories of our parents came more frequently as the time of their death elapsed. Everyday seemed to drag me farther away from their presence, from the times of laughter and happiness. Trying to forget, I approached a group of young lady friends from town, but was suddenly cut off by a large, jolly woman.

"Mrs. Denny, how good to see you," I smiled and took her hand.

"Never mind, my dear girl, never mind." The fidgety woman led me over to some chairs along the wall. "Have you heard the latest news?" I was suddenly assailed with all the latest gossip and rumors from town. When the plump woman finally stopped for a breath, I took the opportunity.

"My that punch looks delicious! Shall I get you some, Mrs. Denny?" Before she could answer, I was at the refreshment table spooning the red liquid into the cups.

"Miss Matthews," a voice nearby caught my attention. Turning, I saw a young acquaintance from town. "Could I have the pleasure of the next dance?" Smiling, I began to answer when the face of a man several feet away took my notice. I stopped short, seeing the young blacksmith I had encountered on the street earlier this week. I stared at him, forgetting the kind young man in front of me. Suddenly the mysterious blacksmith glanced up. Flinching under his sharp stare, I quickly snatched up the cups of punch and hurried over to Mrs. Denny. The woman must have seen the flush in my cheeks, for she pulled me down beside her and promptly began to speak in hushed tones.

"My dear Miss Matthews, I couldn't help but notice you seem to know something about this secretive newcomer to our community." It was more of a question than a statement, for someone like Mrs. Denny would not settle for a simple "yes" or "no". Her eyes darted back and forth, searching mine and then watching the blacksmith. I knew there was no escaping her.

"I really don't know him, or anything about the man. It's just that we had an unfortunate encounter on the street the other day." I paused, my fingers moving to brush nervously above my eyebrows, as was my habit whenever I encountered an awkward situation. Glancing back at him, I whispered, "Not a gentleman, that's for certain. Why he knocked me over and didn't even bother to help me back up."

Mrs. Denny's eyes widened, "No, indeed! You don't say! You poor girl!" After watching the young man for a minute, she turned back, leaning closer, "He seems suspicious to me." There was a pause. "Speaking of suspicious things … have you heard of the bank robbery down in Maryland? Rumor has it that after a gunshot was heard, a stranger to the town was found in the bank, with a gun strapped to his belt." Mrs. Denny leaned closer and closer, her excitement growing with the tale. "There in front of the man was the banker, shot dead!" She nearly shouted, her eyes widening. "Blood dripped—"

"Mrs. Denny, please!" I exclaimed, cutting her off from any further violent detail.

"Well," she stopped short, seeming offended, "I was just starting conversation." She sat back and scanned the room. Suddenly her eyes narrowed, resting on the blacksmith and she resumed her thoughts on that matter.

"Yes …" she mused, "this young stranger seems to have something to hide." Another pause, "But, what do I know? Better to leave the poor man to himself." She stood up and waited a few more minutes as if contemplating something. Then, patting me on the shoulder, said, "I shall speak with Mr. Denny about this. He may know something more …" the stout woman wandered off still mumbling to herself. Looking up, I found the cold blue eyes watching me. Starting, I quickly fixed my gaze back on the floor. When I finally found the courage to look up again, he was gone.

The Soldier's Arrival
Chapter 4

Amy

THE MUSIC CAME to a stop and everyone, nearly out of breath, laughed and applauded the fiddler. Merry glances were exchanged among the couples as they moved off to the side to get some refreshment at the tables. Catching sight of Sarah, who stood alone in a corner, I approached her.

Unable to contain my smile I stated, "I love dances."

Sarah laughed, "I can surely see that. You've not missed a single dance all night."

"But I see you standing off by yourself most of the time, Sarah. You must partake of at least a few dances," I encouraged. My friend seemed to dread the idea as she frowned and nervously squeezed her gloves into a tight, thin rope.

"I prefer to watch. I haven't the knack some possess for dancing."

She's afraid, I decided. *She had always been afraid to attract attention, make mistakes. I should have known.* I continued to persuade her that her fears were trivial.

"Well, you would instantly catch on. I have no doubt of that," I stated, watching her blush. "You just need the right partner." I glanced around, surveying the room for any possible options. My eyes rested on the young carpenter. "I've noticed Mr. Sims hasn't been able to tear his eyes from you," I whispered to Sarah.

"Oh, Amy, stop making things up," she wrung the poor gloves even tighter. Suddenly the young man, seeing we were discussing him, made his move, taking large strides toward us.

"May I have this dance, Miss Phillips?" he asked, offering a hand.

My friend shrunk back, "I'm afraid I'm not a very good dancer, Mr. Sims. Perhaps you would care for a more suitable partner."

"I don't mind, Miss Phillips, I believe you're doing yourself a discredit," he coaxed.

"Really, I'm not very good at all," Sarah shook her head more sternly. The young man's countenance fell and he forced a smile before turning away disappointed. I watched him go then turned instantly to Sarah.

"Sarah Phillips!" I hissed, "You've broken his heart!"

Sarah waved a hand, warding off my protests, "Oh, Amy, stop it, I've never broken anyone's heart. Besides, even if I did break his heart, I've saved his feet." Our eyes met and I found a spark of humor in hers.

"Oh, Sarah!" I laughed, though still disappointed for the young carpenter she had turned down. Another dance began and couples swept over the floor again. I spotted Elizabeth gliding elegantly, her long skirts rustling as she danced. She needed this social life every so often. After mother and father had died my sister seemed to carry their responsibilities on her own young shoulders. She worked tirelessly sewing, cooking, and taking care of the horses, while I was teaching. She was strong-willed and I was proud of her for it.

"Amy, did you see him?" Sarah's brother, John, was suddenly beside me.

I glanced around quickly, "See who?"

"The blacksmith," he whispered. "He was here. Stood in the shadows. I noticed him watching Elizabeth closely, so I kept an eye on her." My skin was crawling. I had never seen the blacksmith, but I'd heard enough about his mysterious appearances in town.

"Did he leave, John?" I asked anxiously.

"I dare say he did, some of the other young men and I decided to confront him, but when he saw us comin' he disappeared."

"You probably frightened him off," I suddenly felt remorse for my prejudice against such a lonely man. "John, you shouldn't have made him feel unwelcome. He may be a lonely stranger with no family and that's all the more reason to welcome him into the community, not frighten him away."

"Well, I didn't like the way he was eyeing Elizabeth," John grumbled angrily.

I smiled at his concern, "I know you meant well, John, but you should not have frightened him off."

"He didn't have to run away ..." he muttered under his breath. "Only cowards run when they've got somethin' to hide." Sarah shot me a glance, her eyes twinkling at her brother's unforeseen wrath. A few of the older students in my class had joined the party. I smiled as two of the girls spotted us and waved. Mr. and Mrs. Denny danced past us, blocking our view. Sarah jabbed me in the side.

"I've never seen the Denny's dance before," she whispered in my ear and giggled. Watching the mismatched couple, I guessed the reason why Mr. Denny had never asked his wife to dance. The big woman looked nearly twice the size of her partner, but leaned back all the same, as they swung around the room. John smiled and coughed as they swooshed past us, and I had to fix my hair from the breeze.

"John," I hissed trying to bite back a smile.

"What's this gathering all about?" Elizabeth approached.

"We were just admiring the couples, Miss Matthews." John answered Elizabeth, who eyed me critically. Sarah nodded eagerly, confirming our innocence.

"Hmm," Elizabeth mused over the situation. "Sometimes you three act just like children again." Sarah and I laughed at Elizabeth's scolding, but I noticed a look of hurt in John's eyes.

"And when did you outgrow our little company, Miss Elizabeth?" I retorted.

Elizabeth shook her head and Sarah put in, "It used to be five of us making mischief, remember? Elizabeth, John, you and I ... and Kelsey!"

"Yes, I remember," I stated softly. Everyone seemed to get quiet as we remembered our happy school years together. The fiddle broke through our silence.

"Would you like to dance?" John asked, offering his hand to Elizabeth.

"Thank you, John, I would."

Glancing over at my friend, I offered my hand likewise, prepared to move on from memories that seemed to bring me sorrow.

"You must honor me with a waltz, Sarah," I declared.

She hesitated and I began to persuade her, "Come! It's very smooth and easy."

"Well, if you insist," she consented.

Sarah caught on, just as I suspected she would, and we were soon giggling over who would play the part of the boy. As we spun around the room, I suddenly caught a glimpse of a very familiar face. As I turned, I saw Clarence Brown about to make his way toward us. He tugged on his dirt-stained gloves, pushed up his spectacles and cleared his throat.

"Oh no," I breathed at the sight of my clumsy student.

Sarah glanced back, "What, what is it?"

I gulped, "I think Clarence is going to ask to dance with me." My friend drew great delight at the thought. "Imagine, *a waltz with Clarence*," I whispered to her, "Oh, how do I hide from him …"

"Amy," Sarah broke in, "You don't want to break his heart!"

I stared at her, "Sarah, you couldn't break Clarence's heart with a hammer and chisel. He wouldn't give up. He's the clumsiest boy I've ever seen, but by far the most determined."

"True," she smiled, "He's admired you since he was old enough to wear spectacles."

Suddenly someone broke into our dance. With dread, I turned, expecting to see Clarence squinting happily up at me. Trapped, I turned to face my doom. But to my surprise a tall, striking soldier stood before me. Dark, sandy hair crowned his handsome brow and as the deep brown eyes searched my face, a content expression spread over him. A tender smile played at his lips.

"May I have this dance, Miss Matthews?" he asked, gently taking the hand I surrendered in a daze. Sarah stepped back in surprise, her mouth opened, but no words came. A strong arm slipped around my waist and I was suddenly swept away by this young soldier who ... *I knew ... I knew him, but how?*

Staring up into the gentle face so close to mine, I couldn't set my mind to it. Confounded, I gazed almost stupidly up at him.

"Well?" he said after a long pause. "Surely ya haven't forgotten me after only five years, Lassie?" A hurt look came over his once satisfied countenance.

The Irish accent, could it be? Lassie ... dare I hope? The voice is deeper, fuller ... there was suddenly no doubt about it.

Gasping, I cried, "Kelsey! Why I ... I thought you were in ... how did you ... and like this!"

He grinned, "I knew ya would regain your memory, though it may take some doing' ta untie tha' tongue."

My hands clutched tightly to him, afraid he would disappear like a phantom of my imagination. I couldn't have hoped for a better rescue from Clarence Brown! For a moment I was unable to find words to express my emotions.

"Why didn't you tell us you were coming home so soon?" I asked laughing from pure joy.

"Oh, just wantin' ta surprise ya," he gave a slight shrug.

"You certainly did," I looked down at the uniform fitted perfectly to him. "It suits you well." The buttons shone in the light and the single bar of a first lieutenant lay on his shoulder.

My eyes widened, "Oh! Kelsey McCarthy! Lieutenant! You never said!" He grinned sheepishly as I admired the bars.

"Thought I'd just show ya instead. Ya might not have believed me if I wrote it," he teased.

"You know I would have! I'm so proud of you. We all are," I tilted my head and stared up at him realizing for the first time how very tall he had grown.

Clapping filled the room again and Kelsey took my hand to lead me away from the more rowdy dance that was beginning. I moved away with him as if in a dream, still afraid to believe it was all true. How I had hoped for this day and imagined it in so many different ways. The words, what I would say and do. But now that it had come ... the joy, the excitement was even more wonderful than I had imagined. Oh, how I longed to feel the strong arms around me, to know that now everything would be all right, now that we were together at last. But such a show of affection would not be proper even among old friends. What a time Mrs. Denny would have spreading rumors all around the town. No, I would not damage our engagement in any way. It was delicate, especially since Kelsey was Irish. People were just waiting for a wrong move. But how my heart was bursting at the seams with joy!

"I stopped by ta call, but ya were gone. So I went home and my parents told me about the dance," he said, halting near the doorway.

"Have you had any rest then?" I asked concerned. He shook his head and I saw the weariness in his young eyes. "Perhaps it would be best if you went ..."

"No," he cut me off. "It's not only the trip that wears on me."

"What then?" I asked eager to share any of his troubles.

"Nothin' ta worry your pretty self about. Just the nonsense that goes on in the ci'y. Or should I say in Washington," he paused thoughtfully, a troubled look on his face. "Things already seem better being back home again. The dingy ci'y life can never amount ta the beauty of the country." He paused to study me intently, "And you're a sight for sore eyes, Lassie."

"Grab you a partner and get out here folks!" The fiddler called out into the mass of people standing around.

I stepped back to let a couple, who had just arrived, into the room. Everyone began shifting around so that it became cramped where we stood. Kelsey noticed and led the way outside. A few others had found their way out to chat in the more solitary environment. We walked along the fence rail and stopped just where the light from the room faded into blackness. Music and laughter drifted out into the night and sailed away on the spring breeze. The sky was filled with bright stars and the moon hung so low as if resting on the tips of the trees. Kelsey, leaning on a fence rail, breathed in the night air. Watching him, I realized suddenly the effect the years had on us. Kelsey was now much taller and the outline of his face showed a handsome young man of twenty. The brown eyes that stared out into the dark field beyond seemed as though they had seen so much more than anything I had known in this little town. The city life had changed him, I was sure. I had known when he was leaving that it would and it hadn't bothered me then, but now ... I turned from him, suddenly afraid. Glancing back into the barn I wondered, *What if he's outgrown me, the little country girl from back home?* He'd seen so much more of the world than what our little town had to offer. Surely this gathering was much smaller than anything he had gotten used to in New York. I could just imagine it: the fancy ballrooms, fine ladies and grand halls of West Point Academy. I saw Elizabeth dance past the doorway chatting with John. *We are such a small community. How could he possibly be happy here in this little town after seeing such grand sites? No doubt with his assignment he will have to take his leave once more, called away to a higher duty. Would I be left behind, a married woman living with her sister while her husband trekked off to unknown parts of the country? Or would I be left unmarried still? What if he had found someone else, someone more exciting? Surely there had been many elegant ladies clamoring to make this handsome young lieutenant's acquaintance.* My heart sank. These thoughts had not come to me earlier and I fearfully realized the possibility of their reality. Kelsey now hung his head, the wind tossing the sandy hair. I would not disturb him now with my questions of the future. Perhaps another day when he was rested.

"How has teachin' been for ya?" Kelsey suddenly awakened from his dream-like state, half asleep with exhaustion.

"Very interesting," I leaned my back against the fence returning my thoughts to the present, "I love it, yet it sometimes seems so difficult. Hour after hour trying to pound the same thing in, day in and day out. But then ... when they understand and the fire lights up their eyes, it all seems worth it."

A smile spread on his face, "Bet ya make a good teacher. Haven't been overworking those kids though, have ya?"

"No, not anymore than they need it," I smiled sheepishly.

"It's so good ta be done with West Point, but ta come out as a lieutenant, feels even better."

"How did you get out so soon?" I asked leaning closer.

"My uncle has a good friend who helped get me in sooner so I could get home a year early. I won't lie, it was rough at first, being the youngest of all my classmates, but I got through it all right," he grinned.

"I'm glad your back," I said smiling up at him.

"I am too, Lassie." He studied me and a sheepish look came over his face, "You know I barely recognized you."

I laughed, "Oh good … I thought I was the only one."

"No … you've changed so much, Lassie." He smiled then turned to stare into the darkness and I saw a troubled look come over him again, "Feels like I've been gone for ages."

I dropped my gaze to study the ground, feeling a tightness in my throat that made me uneasy. A wagon creaked past us and rolled bumpily down the road.

"Seems the gathering is breaking up," relieved for some distraction I observed a group coming our way.

"Looks like," Kelsey said replacing his hat.

"Did you happen to see Elizabeth?"

"I did. I said hello ta her. She's changed. I suppose, after what happened, takin' on so much responsibility would affect her greatly."

"Yes …" I said softly, "I feel for her. The work doesn't allow her much spare time to socialize, or even time to just be a young woman."

Kelsey's voice was hushed and he raised an eyebrow, "She hasn' got any sui'ers then?"

I glanced over at him, "No, and don't go asking questions of her. You sound exactly like Mrs. Denny," I hissed playfully.

Kelsey grinned, "Merely wonderin'." He became serious again, "It's a wonder she hasn't been snatched up by someone … pretty, sweet tempered Lass that she is."

We rode home under the bright starry sky, merrily discussing the events of the evening. Kelsey trotted his large blue roan beside us until we were safely home then, tipping his hat, cantered the stallion away into the night.

"It's wonderful to have Kelsey back, isn't it?" Elizabeth said folding her gown and laying it gently across a trunk. For a moment, I simply studied the way she fluttered about the room preparing for bed. Always busy yet so organized and precise in every movement, just like mother.

"Yes. It was such a surprise I can hardly believe it's true." I began absentmindedly brushing through my thick long curls.

"You should be quite proud of him. He's become such a gentleman, and soldier." She paused and glanced at me thoughtfully, "And he is *quite* handsome."

"Oh Elizabeth!" We both giggled at my sister's impudence.

"I'm sorry, I've made you blush." She teased, winking at me.

"Elizabeth, really, I didn't come here to be teased. I would like to talk with you … seriously."

She straightened and sat down beside me, keeping a stern look on her face, "All right, what is it?"

Clearing my throat, I organized my thoughts, "When Kelsey was gone I always dreamed of the day he'd return. Well, whenever I looked to the day of Kelsey's arrival I imagined everything would be perfect. We would have our lives planned out, knowing what the future held. I knew things would be different, but not in the way I feel like it is now. I thought … well Kelsey would be older of course, we both would, but we would be the same. We would know everything about each other, the best of friends just the way it was before. And now …"

"You're not sure of the future … he's changed." Elizabeth laid a hand on mine and met my gaze, "and so have you. Mother and Father aren't here to help anymore. We must make our own decisions, and follow where God leads. Even if we can't see where we're going." Sighing, she lifted her eyes staring at the ceiling, "You and Kelsey are starting fresh. You need to find out how you've *both* changed and grown. The path may be different than what you had planned, but I'm sure of one thing," she paused and whispered tenderly, "he still loves you as much and more than he did the day he left." She smiled and I saw a tear in her eye. "And where there is love, there is understanding … and patience. It may take some time, Amy. Even married couples are still learning about each other. Whether you get married in a few months or years … if your love is real it will remain, because love … is forever."

I wrapped my arms tightly around her as the tears welled up in my eyes, "I love you, Elizabeth. I don't know what I would do without you always there to help me."

I knew she was smiling as she spoke, "Oh, you don't need me … you're a lot stronger than you think, little sister." I knew she was trying to give me confidence, but I couldn't help feeling like a little girl as I held tightly to her.

The Mysterious Stranger
Chapter 5

Elizabeth

IT WAS STILL dark when I opened my eyes. The town was quiet this morning. Sitting up on my bed, I gasped a little as my bare feet touched the cold, wooden floor. Flipping the covers off and wrapping a shawl around my nightgown, I slipped quietly over to the window. Leaning against the sill, I pressed my face against the cold windowpane, watching my breath gather in little water droplets on the glass. Streaks of pale gray painted itself on the horizon. All was quiet. Stepping silently over to my brightly painted, wooden chest, I opened the creaking lid to pull out a fresh gown for the morning's work. I paused as a framed photograph caught my eye. Reaching down for it, I polished the glass with my sleeve. The picture was of our parents' wedding. Mother looked so beautiful in her silk, white gown, and Father so tall and handsome. Father had been twenty-two when he moved here from the South to study at a university. It was in this town, a year later, that he met our mother. Mother was from a wealthy abolitionist family. They had lived here ever since. I sat for a few minutes longer, thinking about our parents and watching the sunrise. The wedding picture sent a wave of frustration coursing through me. I remembered at the barn dance the other night, overhearing two women whispering about young ladies who hadn't been fortunate enough to marry yet. They had glanced my way and whispered even more quietly to each other.

By the age of twenty-one, young women were expected to be married, or at least engaged. However, with Mother and Father's passing, I had little time to concern myself with such matters. I had a house to keep, a sister to care for, and money to manage. If it was God's will, and marriage was in my future, I would welcome it with joy. But if it was not in my future, then I knew God had another plan and that there was much to do with this life I was given. A life well lived is a life with purpose and a vision. Ever since I was young, I had longed for adventure in the world. I wanted to use this time in my life to do something worthwhile. The townsfolks' comments and insinuations annoyed me. Sighing, I shook off the thoughts and, deciding it was time to start the day, shut the lid and hurried downstairs.

"Remember, we need to take the dresses and pies we made to the market today," I told Amy at breakfast. Money seemed to always be an issue, and I hated it. I tried to think of ways to earn some, such as sewing dresses and baking pies to sell at the market. Small ways for us to be able to live comfortably and keep our land and farm animals. "Every little bit of money we can scrape in helps. Goodness knows we need it ever since ..." my voice trailed off.

"Since father and mother left us ..." Amy finished softly.

I glanced over at her, "Yes." Our smiles quickly disappeared.

I didn't like the silence that came upon us when they were mentioned. I remembered the day they departed for their trip in the West. It seemed as though it was yesterday when we cheerfully hugged them good-bye. We were so excited to be keeping house while they were gone. Every so often we would get a letter from them saying what a fine time they were having. Then one day the letters stopped. We began to worry that something had gone wrong. Days later another letter arrived. We knelt down near the fireplace and read it together. Sure enough, it was from our parents, telling us they were ill and begging us not to come, for fear we too would contract the illness. Shortly after we received this letter, news came that our mother and father had died. Then came the horrible silence that lingered over the house and the weeping that seemed to constantly echo through the halls. After the town had been sanitized from the sickness, we left Gettysburg and arrived there. We had a funeral for them, and the preacher's short sermon reminded us of hope. Later, we had revisited the small church cemetery and laid flowers next to the cold gravestones.

Wanting to escape these thoughts and seeing that my sister desired to be alone as well, I laid my hand on her shoulder and whispered, "I'll be outside."

Snatching a book I had almost finished and tucking it under my arm, a breeze welcomed me as I slipped out the door. Sighing at the greeting, I wiped at a tear that stole down my face.

Passing through Mother's flower beds, I made my way out into the big, open fields surrounding the town. They stretched for miles before me, embraced by the distant dark blue hills. The fields were dotted with wooden fences and cattle cropped at the fertile grass. As I was walking along, a movement in the distance caught my eye. Far off, across the fields, I distinguished the blacksmith riding a horse into the trees of Seminary Ridge. *So that's where he lives. I wonder what he's doing here. I didn't see him in church on Sunday. I wonder why he keeps to himself and is so secretive.* Mrs. Denny's gossip slipped into my mind. *He does act suspicious ...* I reflected as I resumed my walk in the opposite direction. Coming to the slope of the little, barren hill cluttered with boulders, I picked my way to the right, losing myself in the midst of the trees until I had reached the summit. Locating a large tree that overlooked the far-reaching landscape below, I relaxed under its branches.

I smoothed my hand over the title of the book I held, *Uncle Tom's Cabin.* There had been much debate and anger over this piece of work. It was a story of slavery and revealed the evils of it. Yet, it also showed that in the states north of the Mason Dixon Line, as well as those south of it, there were people who disliked slavery and there were people who approved of it. Not all those in the South were inhumane, brutal slave holders as some seemed to think. In fact, there were people who owned slaves that spoiled them like children.

Reading this book helped me to see how important it was not to judge people as a group. It infuriated me to hear the talk in town about how "those Southern people are so wicked for holding slaves" or on the reverse, "I don't consider it an issue, the negro is beneath us. Why shouldn't they serve us?" For indeed, not all were abolitionists in the north, as some might think. To be sure, some of the Northern people did care and feel strongly about the evils of slavery, but there were also those who did not care, and even had a prejudice against the African man.

I knew, from reading papers and hearing talk, that the land was in a state of unrest and it seemed that the very ground of our country trembled uneasily and a strange feeling pervaded the air. I had never really thought much of it until I read this book and started paying attention to what I was hearing in town. Recently though, I felt the uneasiness, and it seemed to be seeping through the country and growing stronger day by day.

Words From the Past
Chapter 6

Amy

"OH! I ALMOST forgot about the potatoes! Elizabeth would ya hand me that cloth there, Lass!" Elga McCarthy rushed about the kitchen in a panic, her dark auburn hair slowly falling out òf the neat bun.

"Here, let me do that," Elizabeth offered extending a hand.

I smiled to myself, watching the two women fussing over supper. In my opinion, two women in a kitchen is too many. My sister was a thin daintily built woman, but the older Irish woman looked frail in comparison, though both were strong-willed and full of energy. In character, they were very similar. They were two of the dearest and most respected women I knew. Elizabeth winced as she burned her finger on the stove. Mrs. McCarthy took it tenderly in her hand to fuss over it with motherly care. Elizabeth, of course, protested against such attention "over nothing" but Mrs. McCarthy refused to let my sister win.

"Why, that looks a might bad there, Lass. Amy, fetch my ointment," Elga McCarthy called, leading Elizabeth away from the stove.

Since childhood I had become acquainted with the McCarthy's home and knew it as well as my own. We had spent so much time together. We had become like family, especially since neither of our blood relations lived close by.

"I'm all right, really," Elizabeth insisted.

Elga shook her head, "No, no, you sit right here and let Amy tend to you. You'll find she's a splendid nurse. You've helped me enough already. The surprise party will be a success."

Elizabeth smiled at Mrs. McCarthy's back, seeing her protests were futile against the stubborn woman. Continuing her preparations once more, she bent over the blazing fire, stirring various pots.

While dressing Elizabeth's wound, I sniffed the air, "It smells so good!"

Elga chuckled to herself, "My lad's favorite potato soup. Special recipe." Her eyes twinkled as she glanced back at me then continued stirring, "It's been so long since I made this for him. I could teach ya how to make it."

"That would be nice," I imagined the scene. Kelsey entering our very own house, asking what was for supper as I leaned over my own kitchen stove. Blushing at the thought, my daydream melted away. "I'm not a very good cook," I murmured, trying to laugh.

"Well, lucky for you Kelsey once told me he would survive on potato soup alone if I knew nothing about cookin'."

"When is he expected?" Elizabeth asked and flinched as I wrapped a bandage around her hand in the dim light of the kitchen. Glancing out the window, I saw how dark it had grown.

"About ten more minutes," Mrs. McCarthy answered. Suddenly Mr. McCarthy appeared in the doorway. His big frame crowded the room. The robust farmer wiped his hands on the dirt-stained trousers he wore in from the field and removing his hat, he caught his little wife around the waist.

"How's the supper comin', Lass?" he asked in his booming but gentle voice.

"Ah! Tomas, release me at once! We have guests present! Ya don't want them seein' what a heathen ya are!" The sharp eyes of Elga McCarthy turned on her husband as she slapped playfully at his hand.

"Guests?" Mr. McCarthy glanced about the room and cast a wink at us, "I don't see no guests, just our two little lasses over here. They're family though, aren't they? Or soon ta be!" He grinned at me and I felt the heat rising in my face.

"Tomas! You ought not to make the lass blush so!" Mrs. McCarthy scolded.

Her husband displayed a look of innocence, "What did I say that wouldn't be true with a little more time?"

Mrs. McCarthy shook her head in frustration and threw up her hands, "I've tried! I really have tried to civilize this man."

Elizabeth and I giggled as Mr. McCarthy was victorious over his wife once again. Some of my first memories in this house were of Mr. McCarthy teasing his wife. He loved watching her throw up her hands in distress. The husband and wife faced each other a moment. The sweet glance of a friendship passed between them and Elga shook her head to hide the smile.

"Now then, help us put out some of these plates here, me husband." Elizabeth and I rose to gather the meal and carry it into the dining room. The farmhouse was made of gray stones and near the fireplace in the parlor hung a tapestry with Irish stitching by Mrs. McCarthy. I glanced at it as we passed. It was a masterpiece and I always loved to gaze at it in awe. The rough wooden table stood in the center of the dining room, decorated with the special silverware Mrs. McCarthy only used for certain occasions. She had packed it away and brought it all the way from Ireland. On the windows hung dark green drapes tied back with a golden cord. A red Irish setter laid near the hearth snoring lightly as her paws twitched. Her soft, glossy hair reflected the fire light. Everything was set neatly on the table and Mrs. McCarthy stepped back to examine it proudly.

"There, all we need is a couple candles now," she bolted for the kitchen with Elizabeth following quickly at her heels, skirts rustling over the wooden floor. Mr. McCarthy chuckled as he watched them. Running a hand through his thick, sandy hair speckled with bits of grey on the temples, he smiled at me.

"Watch those two go, Lass, fussing over things the way they do. But then what would we do without them?"

I nodded, "They enjoy it, making preparations, pleasing their guests, cooking."

"That they do, Lassie," Mr. McCarthy poked at the fire and laid another log upon it.

"It's getting late. When do you suppose Kelsey will be here?" I asked, feeling a bit anxious as I glanced at the grandfather clock in the corner.

"Oh, I'd say just about now," an answering reply came from directly behind me.

Spinning on my heel, I faced Kelsey who stood just inside the doorway. He was neatly attired in his uniform, save the hat. His hair was wind-tossed like it used to be when he was younger, which strangely made him look more handsome. He glanced about the room as I stood frozen before him.

"What's goin' on here, Lassie?" he asked, seeing the bountiful feast laid out.

"Oh Kelsey! Your mother wanted to have a party for your coming home!" I burst with excitement at last. Behind me Elizabeth and Elga McCarthy shot out of the hallway.

"Well, I suppose it's no use shoutin' surprise!" Elga laughed and rushed forward to take Kelsey in her arms. Watching the little woman wrap her arms around her son's thin waist, I realized how difficult his absence must have been for her. Kelsey squeezed her tightly.

"Welcome home, my lad!" She smiled up at him and motioned us all to take our seats so she could begin her serving.

Mr. McCarthy said grace. As the dinner began, Elga proudly presented each course, reminding everyone how Elizabeth had helped her. Finally, she raised the plate of rolls and declared cheerfully, "And Amy volunteered to make the dessert!"

Kelsey, looking a bit shocked, glanced quickly over at me, and raised an eyebrow, "You made the rolls?"

"Indeed, I did," I declared, quite pleased with myself. I hardly ever got a chance to bake or cook at home. Suddenly, I caught Kelsey shifting uneasily in his chair and watching me closely as if I had just threatened him.

"Why do you look at me so, Kelsey? You haven't even tried them!"

Kelsey cleared his throat, "Well, it's just that … remember that time you made the apple pie?" I thought for a moment as the horrendous scene unfolded in my mind and I realized what Kelsey was leading up too.

I waved my hand, "That was years ago." Everyone's eyes were upon me as I tried to laugh off the old memory. Fear had suddenly entered the room. There was a long pause.

"Maybe we should pass on the rolls," Mr. McCarthy suggested nervously. An awkward silence proceeded, then he suddenly roared with laughter and pounded the table. "I'm just kiddin' Lass! What are you all waitin' for? Dig in everyone!"

"Perhaps you'll be surprised at these rolls, Kelsey," Mrs. McCarthy tried to sound encouraging as she passed the plate to her husband.

"That's what I'm afraid of," Kelsey murmured to himself. Mr. McCarthy pulled off the cloth to reveal the shrunken rolls. Shocked at the sight, I rose to my feet.

"Why! They were fluffy as could be when I took them out of the oven!" I declared in distress.

Mr. McCarthy covered his mouth pretending to cough, "Well, let's have a go at them, Lass. They can't be too bad."

Miserably, I sunk down into my chair next to Kelsey. Everyone took a roll, but no one took a bite. Instead, they looked them over as if they would find some sign of danger upon them. Kelsey took his, suspiciously squeezed it a little, broke it and took a bite. Everyone waited breathlessly. He chewed, nodded, paused, and chewed a little more. Then it happened, his eyes began to water, he coughed, rose from the table and rushed for the kitchen. We listened to the water pump and the sound of Kelsey coughing. I sunk in my chair. Disaster had struck again. I dared not meet Elizabeth's eyes. Kelsey returned wiping the sweat from his brow, his face was still a little red.

"Lassie, make sure you double check your labels, especially when using cinnamon," he sat down with a cough.

All was quiet for a moment then Elizabeth burst out laughing and was soon joined by all of the McCarthy's. Mr. McCarthy pounded his fist on the table again. Kelsey gripped his side laughing and coughing at the same time. I sat watching them all for a moment, then caught Kelsey's eye.

"Well, you're all a sight," I stated, laying my napkin on the table, which caused another round of uncontrollable laughter.

* * *

The dishes were cleared and the fire was dimming as we sat around in the parlor listening to Mr. McCarthy telling the tales of old Ireland. Since childhood, I could remember the way the images and landscapes would appear before my eyes. The heroes and heroines of tales were as real to me then, as my own mother on whose lap I had sat. We had all sat around the fire. I in mother's lap, Elizabeth near father, Mrs. McCarthy serving mugs of hot tea and Kelsey sitting near his father gazing up with excited eyes as the scenes of battles were told with great enthusiasm and energy by Tomas McCarthy. The warmth of the cozy Irish home seemed to cast a spell on everyone listening to the stories. No one dared speak a word. The smell of tea mixed with the aroma of the burning logs created a wonderfully mystical world about us. The stories went on late into the night, occasionally interrupted by a song in which everyone joined in. Sometimes Kelsey would play beautiful, melancholy tunes on his violin. The one I loved the most was when he played "Siúil a Rún," and I would sing along with it.

> I wish I was on yonder hill
> 'Tis there I'd sit and cry my fill
> Until every tear would turn a mill
> Is go dté tu, mo mhuirnín slán

It was a beautiful but sorrowful song. Kelsey had never tired of playing it for me and always seemed to enjoy it most when I sang along. The hours would tick by and then Mr. McCarthy would finish up one of his most exciting tales. I would start to drift off and then I would catch Kelsey staring at me, grinning at my drooping eye lids. He would wink and I would fight to keep awake, but somehow I always drifted off to find myself being carried up the stairs to my room in father's strong arms. The sweet memories had drawn a tear forth without my knowledge. I wiped at it while another fell into my lap. A hand touched my arm lightly and I glanced over at Kelsey.

"You all right, Lassie?" he whispered so the others would not take notice.

I smiled, "Yes."

He studied me closely with compassionate eyes, "Ya' sure?"

I nodded, "You know what I would like more than anything right now, Kelsey?" He waited, ready to take the command, and a grateful feeling swept over me.

"Siúil a Rún … It's been ages since I heard you play it."

A smile spread across his face, "I should have guessed."

I knew he was thinking of the endless requests. He rose from his seat and disappeared. Mr. McCarthy finished his story and Elizabeth and Elga laughed accordingly.

"Why where'd Kelsey disappear to?" he asked suddenly. The two ladies glanced about.

"He went to fetch his violin," I answered.

"Oh!" Elizabeth exclaimed, "How wonderful! It's been so long!"

Mr. McCarthy grinned, "Let me guess, ya wanted ta hear 'Siúil a Rún?' Am I right, Lass?"

Elga laughed, "Oh, I remember those days! How wee y'all were!"

Kelsey returned carrying the fragile, beautiful instrument in his hand. Everyone waited anxiously while he tuned the strings. Then all became silent and the first touch of the bow to the strings sent a thrill through the entire room. No one made a sound, even the chairs knew better then to creak. Closing my eyes, I drank in the heavenly music and cherished every verse that went by. The atmosphere was so still, peaceful and enchanting that it transported me back in time. The sad voice of the violin sang gently to us all.

> I'll sell my rock, I'll sell my reel
> I'll sell my only spinning wheel
> To buy my love a sword of steel
> Is go dté tu, mo mhuirnín slán

The Constable in Town
Chapter 7

Elizabeth

July 1860

THE BUCKSKIN GELDING arched his neck and gazed at me with soft brown eyes as I touched the velvety muzzle affectionately.

"Hey, Shadow," I murmured, "You want to go for a ride?" He stuck his nose in my hands feeling for any sign of treats. "You've had enough, dear," I patted his neck and heaved a side-saddle up on his tall back.

Soon I was riding down Middle Street past the clustered, little shops of Gettysburg. After a long day of sewing dresses, cleaning the house, churning butter and baking pies to sell, I needed a breath of fresh air.

Wiping the beads of sweat off my forehead, I gazed down at the dark blue, calico gown I had just made. It was trimmed at the sleeves, neckline and hem with lace. A row of buttons fell daintily down the center from my neck to my waist. I was jerked out of my admiration when Shadow suddenly jumped to a halt. Looking up, I saw a young man seated on a sleek, elegant horse right in my path. He wore a fine, black suit and his blonde hair was combed neatly to the side. His face was thin and well-proportioned and there was an expression of kindness about his countenance.

"Pardon me, Ma'am," he said with a southern drawl. "I don't mean to alarm you. I'm a constable from Maryland and I'm trying to find a dangerous criminal who may be hiding out in the vicinity. We have reason to believe the man is tracing his way up north. Do you have a sheriff in town I could speak with?"

Startled, I answered him quietly, "Yes, yes, we have a constable. Shall I show you the way, Sir?"

He smiled charmingly, "Please," motioning for me to lead the way.

We rode quietly down the street for a while, but not being able to suppress the curiosity within me, I asked suddenly, "May I ask who this criminal is? For what crime is he wanted?" My mind unconsciously flashed back to my thoughts earlier this week. *Was it the blacksmith?*

Suddenly I saw the subject of my thoughts crossing the lane and heading for the carpenter's shop. He glanced my way and stopped dead in his tracks. His stare was directed at the man next to me. I looked at the constable as well but noticed he did not see the blacksmith. The blacksmith's tanned face grew pale and his limbs stiffened. Then, turning quickly on his heel, he disappeared into an alley. All this passed briefly before my eyes and then the stranger responded to my questions.

"Well, he goes by the name of Nathan Tyler, last time I heard. He may have changed it though, as is the habit of escaping criminals. He's wanted for murder." I inhaled sharply at the words and clenched my reins until my knuckles turned white. *A murderer ... near our town?* Chills ran up my backbone. The young man, seeing my reaction, tried to console me.

"Please don't worry yourself, Miss, we'll catch him soon enough." I looked at him gratefully but fear still held me in its grasp.

Out of curiosity, I stayed in the office of our constable, John Barnes. I listened as the stranger showed Mr. Barnes his papers and began speaking earnestly to him about the criminal.

"... You see, Sir, he murdered a banker down in Maryland and made off with the money," he reported.

John Barnes sat at a little desk near the prison. The room was small and dim and had a musty smell about it. Mr. Barnes' steely eyes shifted as he mused over the predicament. Finally, he rested his gaze on the desk in front of him.

"I'll gather a group of men and scout the area for anything suspicious in the morning. It's growing too dark to see anything anyhow," he said sullenly. The stranger and John Barnes had a few more words and then the young man asked if there was a place he could stay while in town. I snapped out of my rushing thoughts and told him of the little inn down the road.

He held the door as we walked out into the dusky street. The sun was just beginning to disappear behind the trees to the west of us. Leading him down the darkening roadway, I realized we hadn't properly introduced ourselves and began the formalities. His name was Adam Carter. I showed the young man the streets he should take and said good-bye. He seemed like a very agreeable gentleman. A warm breeze blew gently as I directed Shadow toward home. However, scenes of the criminal still lurked in the back of my mind.

* * *

A search of the outlying areas near Gettysburg commenced in the bleakness of early morning. I lay huddled in my soft bed. Silence reigned in the town, except for the sound of the search party's horses below. Flipping the covers off and slipping a soft, woolen gown over my head, I snuck slowly down the stairs, but try as I might, I could not keep the door from its habitual creaking. The morning mist crept over the plains and rolled lazily over the silent hills. I crossed my arms and leaned against a fence rail several yards in front of our house.

I watched as the men cantered their horses through the fog and split into several groups. I could distinguish Adam Carter and John Barnes through the dim light. They took the direction toward Seminary Ridge and the thick woods that enveloped it. I gazed after them in suspense. *I think the blacksmith lives in that direction.* What would they find in that quiet solitude? Suddenly I feared that the blacksmith, if he was the criminal, in his attempt to escape would do harm to Mr. Barnes ... and the young constable. Nervously, I hurried to my room and began the day's cleaning. I was just about to wake Amy when I heard hoofbeats outside.

Jumping to the window, I watched as the men slowed their horses and gathered in a group on the dirt road below. Scanning the riders with my eyes, I did not see the captured blacksmith. No, there was no sign of him. I watched, perplexed, as the men met for a conference. Hastening down to the lower level of the house, I stood on the threshold, the door opened on its brass hinges. The men stopped their talking and turned to me. The color rose in my cheeks. *What did I mean by running to listen to their meeting?*

I opened my mouth and stammered, "Oh, um, I'm ... sorry, Sirs. I just ... wanted to ... I'm sorry," I began to close the door.

"Wait, Miss Matthews!" Adam leapt off his horse and came over to me. "You wanted to know what we found out." He smiled kindly, "Well, we found a little shack in the woods on that ridge to the southwest of town. I found some things that lead me to the conclusion that it is the criminal's hideout. Do you know who lives there?"

"Oh, yes, I've noticed a blacksmith that travels in that direction. I've seen him come into town to repair equipment for the townspeople, but he always leaves in a hurry. We were growing quite suspicious of him."

"Could you describe him to me?"

"Yes ... um ... he has dark hair, black really. He's thin, but strongly built ... I believe he has blue eyes." I racked my brain trying to remember the day we collided on the street and then seeing him the day of the barn dance. I shuddered at the thought of having run into him. Adam mused over my information in silence for a while and the group of men confirmed my description.

"Yes, that's Nathan Tyler, all right. Gentlemen," he addressed the group, "I believe we've found our man." The men murmured to each other nervously. Adam mounted his horse, "I'll send a letter out to the other law officers in the area informing them of this criminal. I'll stay in town a while and see if he returns." Saying good-bye to the group, I wished them good luck and returned inside.

* * *

Weeks passed and still no sign of the missing blacksmith. The sudden burst of suspicion and apprehension slowly subsided in our small town and all was at peace again.

"And so, you're sure everything is all right, Miss Matthews?" Adam asked kindly as he stood in our doorway one hot afternoon.

"Yes, Mr. Carter, everything is perfectly fine. However, it is very kind of you to check on us like this," I answered gratefully as I wiped my floured hands on my apron. Recently, Adam had come by every so often to make sure all was well with us. At other times, we met in the town and spent time conversing and laughing. I had become good friends with this amiable young man.

"Don't mention it. I always believe it is best to make sure people are safe, especially young ladies living alone." Amy came up behind me and greeted Adam.

"Any sign of the criminal coming back?" she asked eagerly.

"No, it seems as though he's run off again." Adam looked out into the streets. "I've traveled several hours through the countryside, but I still haven't seen him. I've also been back to his home occasionally, to see if he would return for anything, but he hasn't." There was a pause. "I regret saying it, but I believe it's time for me to leave. I had better help the other constables who are searching nearby counties."

Disappointment filled my voice, "We'll miss having you around, Mr. Carter. You've been such a good friend to us."

"Yes … do you have to go?" Amy added.

Adam smiled, "I'm afraid so." I felt my heart sink as we said our goodbyes and I slowly closed the door.

Hopeful Expectations
Chapter 8

Amy

THE WARM AUTUMN sun hung high in the noon sky as the breeze tangled in the treetops and the laughter of children rang on the open field. The weather was perfect. I toyed with my needle, pretending to mend a hem which Elizabeth had brought to work on, but she was obviously too busy helping some of the women set up their meals on a make-shift table. Today was the long-awaited annual church picnic, one of the greatest socials of the year. Children ran, playing tag in the fields, while the men stood around talking politics as usual. The McCarthy's always shared a picnic blanket with us. At present, Kelsey was leaning up against an oak tree next to me, his eyes half closed.

Mr. McCarthy suddenly rose to his feet. Tossing aside a broken piece of grass he had held between his fingers, he said, "Think I'll go see if Mr. Timothy needs a hand there."

I nodded, knowing this was his way of saying he was bored of just watching everyone. He was soon caught up in a conversation with Mr. Gustav, a close friend to us all. The families had all arranged their own spaces laying down their blankets and some tableware. My thoughts drifted to Elizabeth as I watched her trying to convince Mrs. Denny that the spoon she held was indeed her own, not a borrowed Denny spoon. I smiled to myself and set aside the needle that I had been holding.

"Ouch!"

I jumped at the exclamation and saw Kelsey jerk his hand away.

"Lassie, ya got ta be more careful with those needles o' yours!" He carefully pinned the needle to the hem I had been "sewing."

"Oh, Kelsey, I'm sorry. Here, let me see," I reached a hand forward to inspect the damage.

"I know you're hungry and all, but that's no reason to resort to cannibalism." He said as we both leaned forward to see the wound on the thumb. I glanced up at the dark eyes that were so close to mine.

"Why Kelsey McCarthy! What an awful thing to say!"

He grinned slyly, "Now, now, Lassie, don't get yourself all worked up." I sighed and shook my head. "What had ya so distracted?" he asked curiously, rubbing his hand.

I turned my gaze to Elizabeth, "Oh … how lovely Elizabeth looks today. Quite the image of Mother." Sighing, I lowered my voice and mumbled, "It's a shame Mr. Carter isn't here." I sighed and, shaking my head, caught Kelsey's eye. He looked suspiciously at me.

"Well," I hesitated, "She's very lovely today and I think it's time someone noticed!"

"Lassie … you're not planning on doing some … matchmaking, are you?" Kelsey seemed worried.

That word had not occurred to me, but it did sound like a very good idea now that it was mentioned.

"Yes, I think I will." I stated, pleased with the thought.

Kelsey covered his eyes with his hand and fell back against the tree, "Oh no!"

"Mr. Carter is a very nice young man!" I stated defensively.

"Hmmm …" Kelsey's answer did not satisfy me.

"He is, Kelsey. It was very kind of him to stop by and check on Elizabeth and me, to make sure things were well with us. He's very attentive. I think he cares for her. After all, he doesn't have to do those things." Kelsey opened one eye to stare at me.

"Oh, stop it!" I pushed him on the shoulder.

He laughed with me and leaned forward clasping his arms around his knees, "Ya know Lassie, I forgot how beautiful it is here in the autumn."

"Mmm," I agreed, closing my eyes. I felt Kelsey take my hand and gently kiss it. My eyes opened, and he was staring at me most seriously.

"I love ya, Lassie. Don't let anything ever make you forget that."

"Never," I breathed adamantly.

A rush of autumn air burst from the hill tops and across the field. Elga McCarthy and Elizabeth soon appeared with Mr. McCarthy to set up our meal. The Phillips laid their picnic blanket beside ours and after Mr. Timothy had said a blessing for the congregation, we all ate the delicious food prepared by the ladies, of which I had no part. A constant conversation was kept up by our families throughout the meal. Elizabeth produced an enormous apple pie. Admiring comments were made by all present.

"It's a beauty, Lass!" Mr. McCarthy laid it in the middle and sliced away while Elga handed out plates.

"You must have inherited your mother's gift for baking!" Sarah commented in her gentle voice.

I glanced down at the slice before me, discouraged. How come I never could get mine to turn out as well? When I looked up again Kelsey smiled, knowing my exact thoughts. Leaning over he whispered, "Don't worry, Lassie, you're an excellent seamstress!" I glanced down at the roughly sewn hem and shot an irritated look at him.

"Don't push me, Kelsey."

He chuckled to himself and turned away to eat his pie.

"This is delicious, Elizabeth," John Phillips commented. The nineteen-year-old blonde headed boy sat across the circle from Elizabeth.

She smiled, "Thank you."

Elga began a lecture on Irish baking and my eyes wandered about the circle. Mr. McCarthy and Elga sat side by side. They made a most adorable picture. The robust, tall husband sitting by his delicate, auburn-haired wife. Beside them, the tall gangly Dr. Phillips smiled gently as he sat with his daughter, Sarah, and son, John, who attentively watched Elizabeth as she told of her first collapsed pie. Dear John, with his soft blue eyes, calmly listening as the women talked over their baking. He was always so kind and attentive, ever since we were children … especially toward Elizabeth.

"Well, Kelsey, we can only hope Amy inherited her mother's talents as well," Dr. Phillips spoke up.

Kelsey smiled, "Well, cooking isn't everything." My face flushed, embarrassed at the thought of my baking and cooking "talents." "The way I see it, I'd rather have someone with good character than the many ladies that I've seen who can cook and have no character."

Dr. Phillips nodded as a smile spread across his face, "Well said." There was a pause and I met Kelsey's gaze with a grateful smile. "Here's to Miss Amy Matthews who will soon be Mrs. Kelsey McCarthy," Dr. Phillips raised a cup.

After a few minutes John asked, "When will that be, Kelsey?"

My face flushed red in embarrassment since no such date had been discussed between us upon Kelsey's arrival.

Kelsey hesitated, "Well, we haven't made a decision yet."

"Well, how about we make one now," Elizabeth added quickly, "Since we're all here, it seems a good time." I tried to stop her in mid-sentence, but suddenly ideas came pouring forth. Kelsey sat silent, courteously listening.

"October the 26th!" Elizabeth smiled at her suggestion.

"Elizabeth," my voice was choked, "Next month?"

"Please," Kelsey raised a hand to quiet the sudden burst of excitement, "If I may point something out." Everyone was silent, waiting excitedly. Kelsey smiled at their expectant faces. "I haven't even received orders. There are still too many things left uncertain." A strange cloud of solemnity covered his face, "I thank you for your enthusiasm, but it's a bit premature."

Elizabeth turned a disappointed face toward the dishes. An awkward silence came over our little assembly, most of all over Kelsey, whose countenance had become very thoughtful and distant.

"Perhaps we should clear the dishes away," Elga began her cleaning and Elizabeth and Sarah quickly pitched in. Mr. Timothy appeared and recruited Dr. Phillips and Mr. McCarthy for a game of tug-of-war. Kelsey rose to his feet and before I could say a word to him, he walked off toward a solitary grove of trees. While the other women were busying themselves, John helped me fold up the blankets. Every so often I would glance up to see Kelsey with his back toward us staring silently across the field.

"John," I began, "I'm worried about Kelsey."

The young man glanced over at his friend, then back to me, "What do you mean?"

"He gets very quiet and distant sometimes … especially when I ask questions. Whenever he thinks about getting his orders and future plans."

"The future sometimes makes a man feel uneasy, Amy, often unsure."

"No, it's more than that," my brow furrowed as I tried to convey my anxious thoughts to John. "He's seems worried. Something's wrong. He gets in a very dark mysterious kind of mood. I've tried to find out what it is, but he won't open up to me. I think he doesn't want to worry me. Would you try talking to him, John? He may open up to you."

John smiled, trying to reassure me, "All right, I'll try."

He squeezed my arm and placed the blankets in my hands. I watched him trod off to where Kelsey was standing like a statue. Laughter and shouting came from the games that had begun and seemed out of place in the solemn atmosphere that had suddenly surrounded me. A gnawing grew in my stomach as I turned away to join the others. *What was bothering Kelsey?*

Thunder on the Horizon
Chapter 9

Elizabeth

October 1860

NESTLED WITHIN THE low niche of a tree, I was so absorbed in my book that I hadn't noticed the autumn storm clouds slowly creeping up. I always read my books far away from the critical eyes of the townsfolk. It was not proper for a lady to read so much. Shadow was grazing peacefully beside me when his ears pricked at the sound of distant rumbling. A wave of thunder rolled over the horizon. Opening the leather bag latched onto the saddle, I stuffed my book inside. My feet in the stirrups, I urged Shadow into a smooth canter along Oak Hill. As we rode toward the ridge and to the left of the McPherson's farmhouse, the rain began falling in large droplets and the dark clouds began to defeat the blue sky with certainty. In a few minutes sheets of water began to pour down, clouding my visibility. I clasped Shadow's thin mane tightly. A lightning bolt struck nearby. Shadow jolted and paced quickly as the wind whirled around us. My drenched hair clung to my neck. The storm continued to grow even more threatening. With the trees waving rapidly and squeaking as they bent low to the ground, I turned in the direction I thought was accurate. After a while of riding in empty fields, I began to lose my sense of direction. Another bolt of lightning brought Shadow up on his hind legs in a frightened rear, and before I knew it, I was on the ground. Clamoring to my feet, I grasped Shadow's reins and patted his soaking neck.

"It's okay, Shadow," I said reassuringly, my hands shaking from the fall. Leading him on for several feet, I perceived we were now surrounded by trees. A dark object blocked my path. Stretching out my hands, I clasped a frame of cold, soaked wood. This must be the blacksmith's old shack. I had almost forgotten about him after he had been absent for so long. Tying Shadow under the little canopy that stood in front, I pushed the thin wooden door open, grateful to be out of the rain. My eyes adjusted to the dim light and I noticed a small cot in the back corner of the room. A stool and a makeshift table stood in the opposite corner. A little fire pit with an iron pot hanging over it completed the furnishings of the house. I sank with relief into the coarsely made stool. The storm clouds grew outside the little building and the wind threatened to overthrow the small structure. Water dripped through the ceiling. A flash of lightning brightened the little room and, to my astonishment, I noticed something I hadn't before. The iron kettle that hung over the fire pit had stew in it. I cautiously approached it. Maybe when the blacksmith was in such a hurry to get away, he left this stew in the pot. But as I leaned over it, the warmth of the food rose to meet my face. I drew back in alarm. *Wait, that means ...*

Just then I heard a noise on the outside of the back wall. It was a rustling noise and then all was quiet. I unconsciously held my breath. Suddenly the creaking of the door sent me retreating to a corner and a flash of lightning exposed a human form coming into the little shack. The blood drained from my face, as I realized, in horror, that it was the blacksmith. He had not seen me yet, as he had immediately moved toward the fire pit upon entering. How I wished I could escape, but the only way out was through the doorway which was very near to him. He lit a fire in the pit and paused, crouching beside it. His eyes stared intensely into the flames, the flickers of light reflecting off his handsome face. Yet this impressive visage was veiled with signs of determination and anxiety. Quickly calculating the risks, I darted from my corner past him and into the storm. I had only taken a few frantic steps outside the shack, when his footsteps caught up to me and a hand wrapped around my wrist, spinning me around. I began to yell as I attempted to twist my arm free from the tight grip, but the blacksmith had bound my mouth with his other hand.

"Who are you?" he asked sharply, slowly removing his hand from my lips.

"I'm sorry, I … I … got lost in the storm," I stammered, shaking as all the past rumors and reports of him flashed through my mind, "My name is Elizabeth Matthews. I live in the town." I wiped the sopping hair from my face, motioning back toward my home with a shaky hand. He eyed me carefully, his features showing signs of doubt, but the hand released my wrist.

"I'm sorry I intruded, I'll be leaving right away," I offered and quickly made my way to where Shadow was tied, not wanting to be in the presence of such a criminal one moment longer. Suddenly he moved back toward his shack, laying a hand on his head and running his fingers through his thick hair. When he came up to the little canopy, he placed his hand on the pole, his back turned to me and his eyes staring at the ground.

The storm was passing, yet the rain continued a steady fall on the earth. The surrounding trees and ground were gray with a gathering fog. Fumbling uneasily with Shadow's reins, I watched as the young blacksmith leaned against the far post that upheld the canopy.

"They sent you, didn't they?" he said suddenly, in a slightly angry way. I stopped what I was doing.

"Who?" I asked confused. He motioned with his head toward the town.

"Them. The sheriff … and the search party."

"No. No, I told you, I was lost," I replied honestly.

"Don't tell them I'm here," he said in a warning tone that frightened me.

Without thinking, I replied quickly, "I won't," and mounted Shadow as fast as I could. The blacksmith looked off into the distance, suppressing a strong emotion.

"They told you I'm a murderer, didn't they?" he asked sharply. I gulped, not knowing what to say. "It's a lie … all of it," he continued, "Carter lied … just to cover up. He saw a chance to get away with it and took it." I stopped, confused at his words. Then a wave of heat overcame me.

"Adam Carter is not a liar! I don't know what you're talking about, but I do know that Mr. Carter is only trying to keep people safe from dangerous criminals!" I burst out. His sharp, blue eyes met mine in a glance filled with resentment.

"Safe?" he repeated scornfully. He shook his head and stared back into the woods. "*He's* the one you should be afraid of. I know him." Before he could continue, I jerked Shadow's reins; wanting to get away from this unnerving conversation. Digging my heels into the horse's sides, I galloped off toward the town, leaving the blacksmith standing in the gathering fog of the forest.

Foreboding Warnings
Chapter 10

Amy

LEANING AGAINST THE fence rail, I tilted my head back to let the momentary sunshine warm my face. *It's like the kiss of God,* I could hear mother say. The past couple days had been nothing but clouds and storms, so this temporary noon sun was a welcome reprieve. Birds dipped in the autumn breeze. I could hear pots banging as Elizabeth worked in the kitchen. She hadn't seemed well since being caught outdoors in the last major storm. I had suggested she stayed indoors for a few days to rest. The delicious aroma of autumn hung in the damp air. Kelsey had come to repair the fence that the horses had managed to kick down. He worked steadily lowering the new rails into place.

"Hey, Lassie, could ya hand me the hammer?" he grunted.

"Sure," I placed it in his open palm.

He glanced up at me, "Elizabeth give you the day off or somethin'?"

"No," I glared at him, "I just finished my chores early this morning … some people know how to get things done quickly."

"Aye, and others know how to look for more after their done."

"Are you calling me lazy?"

Kelsey chuckled.

"For your information, Mr. McCarthy, I've had a room full of wild heathens all week I've been trying to tame."

"Excuses, excuses," he grunted under the weight of a heavy beam. I rolled my eyes knowing how he loved to vex me.

"I'm just teasin' ya, Lass," he gave me a half-smile.

"I know," I stepped over to where he was and leaned against the rail, testing the sturdiness. I paused and listened to Elizabeth's pot banging. "You know … She won't say a word about where she was when that last big storm came through …"

Kelsey held the hammer steady for a moment, "Curiosity killed the cat."

"She shouldn't need to hide anything from me, Kelsey. You know how close we are."

"I know, Lass, perhaps she just feels embarrassed about being caught out in it. She's not hidin' anything from ya."

"How do you know?" Furrowing my brow, I rested my chin in the palm of my hand.

"What would Elizabeth, of all people, have to hide?"

Suddenly a noise came from the road and we turned sharply. There, just a few paces away on a chestnut gelding, sat a man with coal black hair, charcoal dust smeared on his bare arms and face. It was the blacksmith! He had returned! A strange fear swept over me and I froze. Rumors of him being the criminal that Mr. Carter had been looking for had spread throughout the town after his disappearance. Kelsey, however, had determined not to judge anyone until they were proven guilty.

"May I help you, friend?" Kelsey asked calmly, stepping toward him.

The stranger watched us with a sharp eye as if considering whether to speak or journey on. Kelsey patiently waited, standing a few steps beyond me. After much examination, the young man on the horse spoke up. His low voice was edged with distrust and suspicion. "Do you know where the McCarthy's live?"

Smiling, Kelsey walked up closer to where the blacksmith sat, "Surely do, being one of them. What business do you have there?"

The blacksmith seemed to take offense at the questioning, "I have a job to finish with Mr. McCarthy," he answered defensively.

"Glad to hear that! Thought we'd never find a good blacksmith in town." Kelsey's voice was unaffected by the defensive manner in which the blacksmith spoke, "We've not been properly introduced yet. Welcome to Gettysburg, I'm Kelsey McCarthy."

Still the blacksmith eyed him warily. Remembering what John had said about his watching Elizabeth, I shivered under his cold stare as he turned his eyes upon me.

Kelsey continued, "Fine horse you have, three years of age? I believe he belonged to Mr. Dansport." Kelsey examined the gelding and patted his hand against the firm neck. I saw the blacksmith tighten his grip on the reins, his knuckles whitening.

"I bought him fair and square."

Kelsey glanced up at him, the gentle eyes meeting the cold steely gaze, "Right smart of you to go to Mr. Dansport. He's one of the finest horsemen in these parts."

For a split second the blacksmith seemed to relax until he caught sight of someone coming down along the fence. It was Elizabeth. She was carefully watching the bucket of water she carried, making sure not to spill it as she approached.

"I've brought you some water Kel—oh, I didn't know—" Elizabeth's voice trailed off the second her eyes caught sight of the blacksmith and her face paled.

A strange look passed between them and the blacksmith jerked the horse's reins, "I should be on my way."

Kelsey glanced from Elizabeth back to the young man, "Would ya like me to show ya the way? I'll be heading back shortly if ya care to wait while I fetch my horse?"

The blacksmith shook his head, "No, Sir, if you'll just point me in the right direction."

Kelsey nodded and pointed toward the McCarthy house, "Just down the road about a mile, the first farm ya come upon. Can't miss it."

The young man whipped his horse around, then turned back. "I only want to finish my obligations with Mr. McCarthy. I intend to leave again. No need to alert your so called 'constables' about my arrival. I'm no criminal."

Kelsey stared calmly, "No Sir. We have no quarrel with you. I wish you the best."

The blacksmith nodded his thanks, shot one last glance at Elizabeth, then took a fast pace down the road. We all stood silently watching him go.

"Seems troubled, that man," Kelsey began hoisting the box of tools, "I'm all finished up, Elizabeth."

My sister did not answer, but simply stared down the road at the distant horseman, "What was he doing here?" The rigid tone of her voice caught both Kelsey and I off guard. We stole a confused glance at each other. Elizabeth all but dropped the bucket to the ground letting the water splash out the sides, "I said, what was he doing here?"

She caught my shoulders in a firm grip and I stuttered in shock, "He just ... just wanted to ask some directions."

"Amy that man is dangerous! I don't want to see you near him," her eyes flashed as she shook my shoulders, "Ever!"

Kelsey's hands were suddenly upon hers, gently lifting her grip from my shoulders, "Elizabeth," he coaxed softly, "Easy, Lass."

She tore her hands from his grasp and then looked sorry for her sudden reaction, "I'm sorry, it's just that ... I know all about him and what he's done. I'd prefer Amy keep as far away from him as possible." I stepped toward Kelsey, too shaken to make any promises. Elizabeth stared me down determined to have an answer.

"What do you know for certain to make you so afraid?" Kelsey asked. "Besides all the rumors you've heard in town, nothing has proven him to be a criminal." He then asked, suddenly concerned, "Did he harm you, Elizabeth?"

Elizabeth shook her head violently, "No, never, but he has harmed someone else. And I wouldn't be surprised if he will harm more."

Kelsey stood, silent, assessing the situation for a moment. "He *may* have, Elizabeth. Nothing is proven," his brow furrowed. "How certain are you about all this, Lass?"

My sister shot a glance down the empty road, "Very."

Unveiling Truth
Chapter 11

Elizabeth

IT SEEMED AGES before the consistent rain storms finally slowed into a mist and the thunder relented and made its way over the horizon. I had spent the last week contained in the house with my sister who suddenly decided I was ill from being out in the storm. I didn't feel poorly, but obeyed her commands. It gave me time to think about what had passed at the blacksmith's shack. *What did he mean, 'Carter lied', that he was trying to 'cover up'? What did he mean when he said, 'I know him.' How did this criminal know Adam?* I tried to sort out the facts in my mind. At the moment, I was too afraid to tell anyone that he had returned because of the warning he had given me. Maybe he would leave soon, as he had said. I couldn't cover-up for a murderer though, I had to do *something*.

Cooking breakfast one morning, on opening a cupboard to retrieve some flour, my hand stopped on the handle. In the corner of the pantry lay Father's old pistols and rifle. Yes, I had to do something. I fingered one of the revolvers. *What was he trying to say? I could go back to that shack and hear his side of the story.* I would take a pistol for self-defense … just in case. *I don't know what I'll do after that, but it is better than sitting at home wondering.*

In the chill of the autumn morning, Shadow and I set out in the direction of Seminary Ridge. Another fog had settled in the shallow valley between the ridges and hills. The leaves had long since exchanged their leafy green for either a more subtle hue or a more vivid one. The wheat fields had begun to plead for a harvest.

I entered the woods, approaching the small shack once again. Hammering sounds reached my ears and led me to the back of the little building. The back shelter was attached to the room where I had previously taken refuge, and was only constructed of two walls and a roof attached to the back wall of the main room. Before reaching this opening, the blacksmith perceived my coming and walked out into the open. I hopped off Shadow and stood staring at him, trying to gather my scattered thoughts.

He stood, hammer in hand, his dark hair mussed and his brows furrowed in inquisitive expectation. His blue shirt was dirty and rolled at the sleeves in his usual manner. I knew how he must wonder at my unexpected return.

"Mister um," I hesitated.

"Nathan Tyler."

"Mr. Tyler, I came because … well … I want you to tell me your side of the story. What happened with you and Adam Carter?" There was a pause. He stared at me cynically, saying nothing. "Really, I just want to hear your side of it." There was another pause as he seemed to debate my honesty.

"Why do you care?" he questioned bluntly.

"I just need to know what is going on," I hesitated, "everything is too confusing." He looked at me a moment longer and then turned away, shaking his head in disgust. My blood boiled, "If you're so right, why won't you just tell me what happened? I want to know!" I raised my voice in frustration.

The young man turned and laughed bitterly, "No. You see, that's where you're wrong," his voice was sharp, as he pointed a finger at me, "You don't want to know the *truth*. No one does! I know what Carter's been telling you and everyone else in the town. But it's a lie. Carter is the murderer. He killed that banker and now he's trying to accuse me of it!" The blacksmith's face was colored in the heat of his anger. Touching the hidden revolver for confidence, I stood my ground.

"And how would he have accused you if you were innocent?" I asked, trying to keep control of my voice.

He shook his head, "No, I'm not going over this again. You're not going to believe me, and you know it! So why don't you just go back home and believe your lies." My face burned as the anger welled up inside me. Clenching my jaw shut, I spun around, as the blacksmith disappeared into the shadows.

* * *

Hot with frustration, I rode back into the town. Riding past the inn, I stopped my horse and tied him to the hitching post in front of the building.

Approaching the thin clerk at the desk I asked, "Sir, is there any way I can contact a man named Adam Carter? He was staying here in the summer. Did he leave any information?"

The clerk quickly thumbed through the pages scattered on the large desk. "Ah, yes, Mr. Carter. As a matter of fact, he just came back to town. Shall I get him for you?" My heart quickened, "He's come back?"

"Yes, Ma'am, he's just stopping for a quick rest from his search of the surrounding counties. I believe he'll be moving on in the morning." As he withdrew into the hallway, I dropped into a cushioned armchair. Before long, Adam appeared, his brown eyes shining.

"Hello, Miss Matthews! What a pleasant surprise." A smile came to my lips in spite of my anxiety to let him know about the blacksmith.

"How can I be of service to you?" he waited expectantly.

"Mr. Carter," I paused, "Please do not do anything to put yourself in danger."

He looked confused. "What is it, Miss Matthews? Is something wrong?"

"Well," I hesitated, "Oh, he told me not to say anything! Oh, Adam, I was so scared, but you need to know!" My voice choked.

"Who? Miss Matthews, what is the matter? Surely you can tell me," he said in an agitated tone.

I stuttered, "The blacksmith ... Nathan Tyler." I said under my breath. Adam stood up. "He said you did it, Adam," my throat tightened. "That murderer accused you of killing that banker. How could he?" I clenched my teeth.

"You spoke with him? Where? Miss Matthews, what happened? Did he hurt you?"

"No, I'm fine. He's come back to his home on Seminary Ridge." A strange look overcame Adam's countenance. Suddenly he began pacing about the room. He stopped in front of me and held out his hand.

"Stay here, I'll be back soon."

"No, Adam! Please get the constable, or someone to go with you!" The door slammed. "Please Adam! He'll kill you!" Heart throbbing, I stood blindly not knowing where to turn or what to do.

* * *

Minutes later, I was out of the hotel and racing toward the ridge. Approaching the woods, I could hear voices speaking in tense tones. Dismounting Shadow, I walked silently through the trees. Standing behind the brush, I took in the scene before me. Just outside the little building, about ten feet apart, the young blacksmith stood directly across from Adam.

"One day I will find the evidence against you. Then everyone will know the truth. I should have seen this coming. You always were one for cheating and lying," Nathan stated angrily. Adam had a look on his face I had never seen before. He began to smile scornfully.

"You'll never be able to tell anyone the truth. They all believe that I am a constable, I have the papers. They trust me. Why would they believe you? Look at you! A wandering, insignificant blacksmith," he scoffed. "They think you did it and would never dare to think it was me. And besides, you were the only one who *saw* me kill that banker." I sucked in my breath and a wave of dread swept through my body. *No! It must be a mistake!*

Adam continued, "No, not this time, Nathan. This time they won't believe you. Come on, I'm taking you back to Maryland. Start walking toward the horses." Nathan's handsome face had disgust and determination written all over it. But, he obeyed and started walking toward the waiting horses. I stood at a distance; neither of them had seen me yet. Just then

Adam cocked his gun and took aim at Nathan's unguarded back. I stepped forward, gasping involuntarily. The noise caused both Adam and the blacksmith to turn around. I stood, my face pale, with cold beads of sweat resting on my forehead.

"Miss Matthews, what are you ..." Adam started angrily. Nathan flinched as he caught a glimpse of the upheld and loaded pistol in Adam's hand. Adam glanced quickly back at his victim with a sinister visage, "Oh, no, you're not getting away this time!" He began to pull the trigger. I felt my hand wrap around the cold steel of my hidden revolver, pulling it from my waist. The blood drained from my face. Nathan dove to the ground and also pulled out a pistol, which Adam had not been careful enough to search him for. Shots resounded in the air. Darkness blurred my vision; all was still.

* * *

I cried out as flashes of regret, disappointment and utter shock flowed through my veins. My vision was clouded, but I perceived I was in a little room. I caught a glimpse of an old, wooden ceiling. Pulling myself dizzily from the ground, I staggered and clutched a chair to steady myself. I was in the blacksmith's shack. *How did I get here? What has happened?* A flash of remembrance painted the picture in my mind. I saw myself pulling the trigger of Father's pistol. My hand flew to my mouth as a small shriek escaped my lips. A violent tremor shook my body. *I killed him! Adam!*

Staggering out the door, I wandered blindly through the woods. Suddenly I came upon a fresh grave. Gasping, I fell at the side of the cold mound of earth. My mind in tumult, I simply stared at the freshly turned dirt. *The blacksmith must have buried Adam while I was unconscious.* Everything blurred around me and a knot in my throat choked my breathing. Digging my nails into the dirt, I agonizingly pulled at the grass.

"Why Adam? Why did you do this? I believed in you."

Suddenly a distant jingling noise reached my ears and pulled me out of my rushing thoughts. On a distant hill, I saw a horse saddled and packed with bundles. I discerned that its rider was the blacksmith. He stared at me and the cold mound of dirt across the distance that separated us, then, turning his horse, galloped out of sight into the western horizon. Suddenly my sorrow turned to an irrational anger.

"If you wouldn't have come here, none of this would have ever happened." I whispered in utter despair after the disappearing figure. Turning back to the grave, I touched the cold dirt as grief overtook me. I cried out and let my face fall to the earth in anguish.

* * *

Walking Shadow back through the fields, an autumn mist descended upon us. I wandered senselessly into our barn. *If I wouldn't have been there today, Adam might still be alive.* Suddenly, realization slapped me in the face. *But Nathan would have been killed! Justice within me is what caused me to pull that trigger. Adam was wrong. He was the murderer. It's true. Nathan was innocent.* I tried to convince myself. I tried to tell myself that Adam had done wrong and I wasn't wrong for saving an innocent life by taking this murderer's life. Nevertheless, at the same time I could not suppress the illogical resentment in my heart toward the blacksmith for being the cause of this whole predicament. Besides this struggle, there was a gnawing inside my heart. I had gotten to know Adam and he had been a friend to me. Tightly grasping the half-wall of the stall, I buried my face in my arm.

Suspicious Minds
Chapter 12

Amy

"ADAM ... DEAD," MY lips quivered as the words slipped from them. A trembling hand flew to my mouth. My mind blurred for a moment, then I focused on the tear-stained face of my sister. Trying to control my emotions, I asked bluntly, "What happened?"

Elizabeth shook her head. Her eyes searched the ground in front of her. Strands of her brown locks had fallen from their usually tidy position. Smudges of dirt shown on her face as she wiped a tear away.

"I went to the hotel where he was staying and I told him all about the blacksmith ..."

"The blacksmith? What about him exactly?" I asked, frozen in anticipation. Considering the rumors that had been flying through the town, I didn't know what to expect.

After my sister had related to me her meeting with the mysterious blacksmith, at which I was whole heartedly shocked, she continued telling of her conversation with Adam.

"He left so suddenly I couldn't stop him. I followed and when I reached the shack that Mr. Tyler lives in, I heard Adam say with his own mouth that he himself had killed the banker ..."

I was suddenly clutching my sister's shoulders, searching her tear-filled eyes. "Adam admitted that he killed him? Elizabeth! What are you saying?"

She slowly raised her eyes, conviction written in them, "Nathen Tyler is innocent. Adam ... is the murderer ..."

My grasp suddenly relaxed as I knelt before her, "Adam ..." was all I could manage. Then slowly I asked, "Did Nathan kill him?"

An unexpected sob burst from my sister with shocking force, "No, Amy! I did!" Her body shook with uncontrollable emotion, "I killed Adam!"

"What?" the word came as a whisper.

"Adam commanded Nathan to walk toward the horses, then pulled out a gun at his unguarded back, and I ... I ... shot him!" She fell forward into my arms and I held her for a moment too shocked to cry.

"It's all right," I soothed, stroking her hair, trying to make sense of it all. "It's done ... God has declared justice."

* * *

Staring down at the fresh dug earth, a sick wave crept over me. Elizabeth knelt before it wearily laying a hand on the mound. My eyes moved from top to bottom over the grave taking in the scene. It seemed like hours before either of us spoke.

"I thought he was one of the best men I knew," Elizabeth began in a hushed voice. "He was so kind and caring toward us. Somehow, I always seem to think just the opposite of a person's character. When I should be cautious, I'm not. When I should let go of my prejudice ... I ... I can't." She came to an abrupt ending, marveling at her own revelation.

A sigh escaped my lips, "Perhaps that's just the way life is sometimes. But Elizabeth, we all did what you did. Everyone thought highly of Adam and poorly of the blacksmith. It's sad, but that's the way men think sometimes. We judge people from the outside when we should be looking in. We judge even without taking more time to understand them, to hear them out, to find out who they are, what they believe in, why they act the way they do. We don't know Nathan. We may never know him."

"But I still ... I can't let go of the feeling," she struggled. "I can't help but feel angry with him. I don't know, perhaps I still feel like this is entirely his fault." A tear slid down her cheek, "If he wouldn't have come to town none of this would have happened!"

"I think it would have," I whispered softly. "Just not here. Not here, where it affected us." She stood up beside me and I slipped an arm around her waist while she stared at the grave. She glanced over and placed a hand on mine, her young face weary.

I continued, "You need to tell Mr. Barnes. He needs to know what happened. You cannot hide this, Elizabeth. It will soon be discovered." She lowered her head, tears streaming down her cheeks. Slowly she nodded, "I will … soon … I promise."

Slowly we left the woods, arms linked together. As I glanced back at the small shack and the fresh grave, it all seemed a painful reminder to me of how quickly life can be taken. Elizabeth would be scarred forever at having taken a life, even if it was justified. I pitied my sister, not able to imagine having ended someone's life, seeing them fall before my eyes … the sickening thud. Breathing in the fresh moist air, I decided I could not live with that guilt. I squeezed her arm as we headed for home.

* * *

Autumn was in full swing, the trees had long since exchanged their usual rich green color for various shades of reds and yellows. Storms seemed to gather up in piles on the hills and then pour forth their wrath swiftly. Today was just such a day. With the news of Adam's death, a terrible gloom crept into our house once more. In my distress, I wandered from it toward the McCarthy's, seeking refuge. I felt terrible for leaving Elizabeth, but she was sleeping and I thought it best if I didn't wake her from what little sleep she could get.

"Ah, what news has been flying around town in the paper," Mrs. McCarthy wiped her hands on her apron and placed an apple pie in the oven.

"What is it?" I asked curious.

"Things don't look too good. I don't know much, but I hear me husband Tomas and Kelsey talking. Things have always been tense between the Northern and Southern states," she paused thoughtfully before flouring her rolling pin. "Why can't folks ever see eye to eye on things. Well, I suppose there are some things that will always be in dispute. No doubt slavery is one of them. You'd think if the English could find a way to resolve the situation we, in the land of the free, could do the same."

I stoked the fire, "Elga, do you consider yourself an American or Irish?"

The auburn-haired woman straightened and stared at the wall in front of her, "I'm an American, but I'll never forget me beautiful homeland, the songs and tales I was raised on, the people. There's something special there for me and Tomas. But me lad, his roots are here. He was raised here. The things he loves the most, are here in this land." She smiled warmly and squeezed my hand, "His heart and soul are tied to America. He's got that stubborn Irish in him though, I know it. He'd fight and die for all he believes in and there'd be no changing his mind." I nodded and began helping with the second pie. Things grew quiet as we listened to the pattering of rain and concentrated on our baked goods. Mr. McCarthy was at a meeting of the elders, and Kelsey was out in the barn, leaving us women folk to our baking.

"You know, Lass," Elga hesitated, staring intently into her dough, "I'm a little worried about Kelsey. For a man who just got home on leave, he seems very … preoccupied. You think he'd relax and enjoy the comforts of home before he gets his orders." Her voice grew quieter and she glanced toward the door. "Sits up in his room scribbling away at somethin'. I hear him when I pass. Won't tell me anything about it though when I ask him. Brushes me off … playful like." My hands slowed, sticking in the lump of tough dough. I suddenly remembered the way he stared off into the night at the dance, the weary look in his eyes and the strange vague words he spoke.

"I was wonderin' if ya could get somethin' out of him. Prod around a bit, subtly. I know how close ya are, Lass. If he'd open up to anyone it'd be you. See what's troublin' him. Would ya?"

Pulling my hands from the dough, I wiped them on my apron, "I'll try."

Elga smiled satisfied, and went back to her business of slicing apples. For some odd reason I didn't believe Kelsey *would* open up to me. *Hadn't I already tried? Perhaps now was a good time to ask him about our marriage, if indeed there was to be one.* It seemed he was avoiding the subject intentionally. I pondered these thoughts on the way to the barn with fearful curiosity. The smell of fresh hay filled the air and a host of animals perked their ears as I entered into the dim yellow light of a single lamp. A barn cat purred around my legs and I reached down to scratch his fluffy neck. The atmosphere was peaceful and inviting, and I instantly relaxed. At the far end of the barn where the horses were kept, I heard the sound of brushing. Weaving around the piles of hay and sacks of feed, I spotted Kelsey crouching down as he ran his hands gently down a blue roan's legs. I watched him for a moment as he carefully felt the soundness of the bones. The stallion curiously locked his eyes on me and reached his nose forward, the soft eyes searching my face. Smiling, I held back so as not to disturb Kelsey's examination. Finally, he rose and patted the stallion's neck.

"Sound as a bell, Lad. You could march for miles on those sturdy legs of yours," he stated, his back turned toward me. Stroking gently along the dark gray neck, he whispered, "Cogadh tagann mo chara."

The Gallic words, though strange to me, sent a shiver down my back and there seemed to be some foreboding ring to them that echoed about me. The stallion's ears perked and he stared past me. His muscles tensed as if he had understood, better than any human, the words that had been spoken to him. Suddenly, I felt as if I had intruded, but the solemn atmosphere that closed in around me would not release me. So I stood frozen, waiting to be noticed. Kelsey turned a little and leaned his head on the stallion's strong neck, his eyes closed and he breathed deeply. After a moment, he straightened and suddenly turned upon me.

"Amy!" Startled, he stepped back, "I didn't know ya were there! You're quiet as an Indian."

I forced a smile, which came extremely hard after the strangely mournful scene I had witnessed, "I'm sorry I startled you."

"It's all right," he shrugged and closed the gate that screeched in protest.

"He's a beauty. What's his name?" I asked reaching out to stroke the long black mane. It was silky to the touch and shined in the dim light.

"Saighdiuir," Kelsey breathed, and his hand came alongside mine stroking down the stallion's neck.

I stole a quick glance at Kelsey, "What does that mean?"

"Soldier." The stallion shifted and pushed his large head up against Kelsey's chest. Kelsey smiled and ruffled the mane.

"Where did you get him?"

Kelsey stepped back and ran a hand down the broad back, "Richm—," he stuttered, "Rich ... Richard Busse, a man I met in Maryland. He breeds horses."

I nodded, pretending I had not heard him correct himself. We stood, rubbing the thick coat of the stallion for a moment.

"Kelsey, I can tell something is wrong," I whispered under my breath. We turned to face each other and I stared up at him. "Kelsey, remember the time George Fredericks was going to beat you up behind the school? You wouldn't tell your father, because you wanted to take care of it on your own to show you could handle it. You don't have to fight alone. Let me help," I felt his hand in mine. "After all that's what we're supposed to do, be there for each other, bear each other's burdens through life. Isn't that part of marriage?" There was a long sigh and I watched Kelsey's eyes searching the ground. He was struggling.

"Can't hide anything from ya, can I, Lassie?" There was a long pause, "I need time, give me more time." He met my gaze, "I have some things I need to figure out." Kelsey turned away and moved to the opposite side. My hands fell.

"This is something I must do alone, Amy," he turned his back toward me and his head hung.

A cold feeling swept over me, "What is it?"

He came close once more. While staring deep into my eyes, a strange look in his own, Kelsey answered, "You'll know when the time comes ... I promise, you'll know."

I nodded stiffly, staring at the soldier across from me, for indeed that was the most prominent look that had come over him. He had changed ... plans had changed ... life had changed.

* * *

"Yoohooo! Miss Matthews!" The loud calling of Mrs. Denny rang over the busy street. I turned on my heel. *Caught again* ... Sighing, I pulled on a smile and climbed the stairs to the bakery. I wondered if the news about the blacksmith and Adam Carter had come to light yet. Surely Elizabeth had told Mr. Barnes by now. I could only imagine what Mrs. Denny would have to say. But to my surprise, she said nothing about the case. Instead she waved an envelope in her hand. Could it be that something more important had come up?

"I believe this belongs to someone in your interest!" She smiled, "I was by the post office and thought I could be of help by getting it to you, since you come by my bakery so often."

Likely story ... I took the envelope, and with clenched teeth smiled, "Thank you, Mrs. Denny, but I can manage picking up our mail on my way to school."

Mrs. Denny laid a hand on my arm, "Oh, I know, I just thought this would be of great importance and wanted to get it to you as soon as possible. See it's addressed to your Kelsey McCarthy." With a chubby finger, she pointed out the written address. "Perhaps his orders? A very elegant hand those officers of West Point have, don't you think?" She stated stuffing the last bit of a pastry into her mouth. I stared down at the words: To Mr. Kelsey McCarthy. *If it was indeed from West Point wouldn't it be written to Lieutenant Kelsey McCarthy?* I suddenly felt very hot in the summer sun and pulled my bonnet closer to my forehead to shade my eyes.

"Well, thank you, Mrs. Denny, but I have to be getting on my way," I tried to turn, but Mrs. Denny caught my arm.

"Have you picked out a date for your wedding yet, Miss Matthews? We're all so excited to celebrate with you!" This question I was beginning to get tired of answering.

"No, we have not ... But you'll be the first to know when we do, Mrs. Denny. Good day." Quickly, I was down the stairs and on the road once more. In my hand I clenched the strange letter. I lifted it to my eyes again when I was sure to be out of Mrs. Denny's watchful gaze.

Suddenly I smelled a strange but lovely scent. *Perfume? In the middle of the street? It must be the letter!* I held it closer and quickly sniffed, yes, it was the envelope. *What a revolting smell! What am I thinking?* I sighed. *It's just a letter.*

Nothing to be worried about, probably from a friend at West Point, whose wife writes out the address … and then sprays perfume on the envelope. The paper felt rough and unpleasant to my touch and I quickly hatched a plan to place it back in the post office, so I wouldn't have to deliver such a letter myself. The postmaster, Mr. O'Conner, who had fought in the Mexican War, had lost his leg in a battle and seemed to have taken on a new perspective of life. His kind and gentle spirit was known to all and trusted. Father had always been ready to help him with his old house that needed much fixing up. Mr. O'Conner was very kind when he received the letter back and ventured no questions about it.

"How is your sister?" Mr. O'Conner asked politely, as he placed the mail in separate boxes.

"Very well, thank you."

"Say, could you go to that back room and pull out a box of stamps I have in the cabinet? I've been looking for someone to take on a few hours here, but no one seems to be interested in the job." I listened as I entered the back room and searched among the dusty cabinets.

"If you have any students that would be interested in the job, I'd be much obliged. This leg of mine is making it a might hard to get around these days. Ah! Kelsey! Here to pick up the mail?" I froze, my hand on the stamp box.

"Morning, Mr. O'Conner, what do ya have for me today?"

"Let's see." Hearing the elderly man search through the mail, I peeked out of the back to see Kelsey waiting at the counter. "Here we are." Kelsey was handed a stack of mail, which he searched through as if looking for something important.

"Nothing else?" he asked shortly, looking disappointed.

"Oh, wait, I believe there is!"

The envelope, which I had just delivered, was handed over. *I must act now.* I stepped out from the back room.

"Here are the stamps you wanted, Mr. O'Conner," I announced.

Kelsey's head jerked up, "Morning, Lassie." He sounded a bit flustered, "You start workin' here?"

I laughed, "No, I was just getting something for Mr. O'Conner."

"I see," Kelsey nodded and I saw the letter had somehow disappeared, "I'd better be getting home. Thank ya', Mr. O'Conner. Give me a holler if ya need anything."

"I sure will, Mr. McCarthy."

I followed Kelsey out the door. He glanced back at me, "Ya headed home, Lassie?"

I shook my head, "No, there are some things I wanted to get done at the school."

Kelsey grasped the reins and swung up onto the blue roan. Just as he did so, I saw the corner of an envelope appear tucked away inside his sleeve. *So that's where he hid it so quickly!*

"Don't over work yourself." He teased and backed the stallion, before heading down the street. Turning toward the school, I plodded back up the street with a sinking heart.

The Outward Façade
Chapter 13

Elizabeth

A BUSTLING CAME from inside the hotel. People rushed in and out through the swinging double doors, all of them in high excited tones. I glanced through the doors curiously. Suddenly Mrs. Denny came flying out at me and my sister.

Gently grabbing her arm, I asked, "Mrs. Denny, what's going on?" she looked at us in surprise and then a gleam of excitement came over her face.

"Oh! My dear girls! Haven't you heard? Something awfully suspicious has happened!" She pulled us close and whispered, "Do you remember the friendly, young constable? Well, he's gone missing! Disappeared in the dead of night, no doubt! When John Barnes went in looking for him today, do you know what he found? Well, do you? Money, that's what, my dears, money! Loads of it!" She smiled satisfactorily. "What do you make of that, my dears?"

I felt the familiar choke of distress return and without answering her, I rushed into the building, dragging Amy with me. The clerk, John Barnes, and many citizens of the town were gathered in the hallway and leaked into the crowd outside. Pulling myself and my sister through the commotion, I managed to get to the door of the room where Mr. Barnes stood scratching notes on a pad of paper.

"Mr. Barnes, what happened?"

He glanced up quickly at me from his work and then continued speaking as he wrote, "Well, I had come to pick up a note from Adam Carter. Upon his arrival back in town, he told me he would leave it in his room. Today I entered and didn't see it in the place he had indicated. Oh, nothing of importance, just an errand he needed me to run for him. However, I found this letter lying on the table and naturally assumed it was the note I was to pick up." He held up a page. "Once I read it though, I began a careful search and found these." There, in the corner of the room were two white, cloth bags with the words: "Bank of Rocky Ridge, Maryland". I took the parchment that was handed to me and scanned over Adam's handwriting.

My Dearest Cynthia,

I'm sorry I did not write sooner. After our night of laying out the details of the scheme, I went to the bank the next evening, as planned.

I shuddered as he explained the details of the robbery and murder. Scanning the page, Adam stated how Nathan had come upon him during the robbery and confronted him. However, Adam managed to escape leaving Nathan appearing as the one who had committed the crimes.

... I received news that the townspeople had thrown Nathan in prison for trial. Upon word of his escape though, I came back to the town and acted as a volunteer to help the constables search for him, knowing that Nathan would try to find evidence against me. I am now in Gettysburg, Pennsylvania. The people in this area believe and trust me. They are easily persuaded. Nathan Tyler was in this vicinity, living on the outskirts of the town. He's run away again, but I have all the constables alerted and on the search for him. Above all we can't let him make it back to Rocky Ridge, or he might find the evidence he is looking for. I know him too well to feel safe letting him go. He must be silenced ...

My heart dropped, remembering all too clearly Adam's attempted murder of Nathan. My eyes moved to the bottom of the page.

In hopes of seeing you soon, Ada

Seeing the unfinished signature, I realized that I was the one who had
interrupted his writing when I had come searching for him on that fateful
day. He had been careless enough to leave the letter on the desk in his rush
to find the blacksmith. My heart sank. I had been so deceived and blinded
to what Adam's true character had been. I handed the parchment slowly
back to John Barnes.

He took it and said in a serious manner, "I'll make sure the authorities
are made aware of this. We'll find Carter and question him. As for Nathan
Tyler, well, if he ever comes back, I think the people of this town should
give him a chance to explain his side of the story. I should probably alert
the constables that live near the address printed on this envelope and I'm
sure they will be able to find this 'friend' for questioning." He exhaled
noisily, "Well, I suppose we should arrange a search party to arrest Mr.
Carter." He stuffed the paper glumly in his coat pocket.

I choked and forced myself to speak, "I don't think that will be
necessary."

John Barnes turned to me, "What do you mean? Do you know
something about this?"

I looked down at the ground. "Yes … everything," I answered quietly.

He took me by the arm, "Maybe we'd better have a talk." I was led
into Adam's hotel room, where I told him how I had seen Adam try to kill
Nathan in cold blood. Then came the most difficult part … the tears stole
down my face as I told Mr. Barnes that I had shot Adam. I also recounted
how I had seen Nathan leaving town. It was a hard task for me, but I knew
it had to be done. The truth had been told.

The Lady and the Locket
Chapter 14

Amy

A DARK AUTUMN overcast sky covered the day and quickly slipped into night. Climbing the stairs to the McCarthy home, I paused before knocking. Perhaps I should not bother Elga with my worries about Elizabeth. But who else could I go to for advice? I wondered if they had heard of Adam's death and guilt? I hadn't thought to tell Kelsey when I had last seen him in town. Indeed, I had had other things on my mind that day. The door suddenly creaked open with the wind. *Someone must have gone to the barn to bring in the horses and forgot to shut the door all the way.* I stepped inside and closed it tightly behind me. The aroma of bread filled the atmosphere. I peeked in the kitchen where everything was swept and in its proper place. I closed the door and glanced about the empty house. It was dim with barely a candle lit. Pausing for a moment, I listened. I heard a murmur of voices in the rooms above. As I climbed the stairs, the strange silence of the rest of the house kept me from calling out to anyone. The curtains in the upper rooms hung down, and the glow of a fire crackled in the sewing room. I was about to step into the room, sure Elga was inside, when a strange figure of a man stepped from the room directly into my path.

"Oh!" I gasped. He wore a uniform and had neatly combed black hair. Kelsey suddenly appeared at his side with a confused, shocked look at the sight of me.

"Excuse me, Ma'am," the stranger said in a stern, cold voice.

"Amy?" Kelsey blurted out, "I'm sorry, Lieutenant. This is my Fiancée, Miss Amy Matthews." The lieutenant's gaze seemed to penetrate through me. I felt very small and out of place standing before the two soldiers. The lieutenant, who was in his mid-twenties nodded stiffly toward me, but said nothing.

"I'm sorry, Lieutenant ... I was searching for Mrs. McCarthy ... beg your pardon," flustered I tried to find my way out of the awkward situation.

"She's out visiting a sick neighbor," Kelsey put in.

The lieutenant shifted, glancing around, rather uncomfortable at this small talk. He rested a hand on his sword hilt.

"Did you need something?" Kelsey asked.

I tried to keep my attention on him so as not to stare at the mysterious stranger but my gaze kept shifting uneasily to him. "No ... no," I mumbled.

Kelsey turned toward the lieutenant, "The lieutenant is a friend from West Point."

I tried to engage in a light-hearted conversation. "I see. I hope you enjoy your stay in Gettysburg, Lieutenant. Have you ever been to our small town?"

The young man answered coldly, "No, Ma'am, I have not had the pleasure." Kelsey's friend did not seem the best conversationalist.

I cleared my throat, "How long will you be staying?" Now it was Kelsey's turn to shift and look uneasy.

The lieutenant answered directly, "Two days at the most."

"Are you headed to a post somewhere?" I asked a bit curious at the short and sudden visit the lieutenant was making.

He paused before answering, "No, Ma'am."

It suddenly dawned on me that he could be the bearer of Kelsey's orders. *Would Kelsey be leaving soon ... in two days perhaps?* Slowly I dared to ask the question, glancing first at Kelsey then at the reserved lieutenant.

"Did you bring orders for Kelsey?"

The young man glanced at Kelsey, "No, Ma'am."

Kelsey quickly put in, "Will you excuse us, Lieutenant?" The man nodded as Kelsey led me into the sewing room.

"Mum should be back in a moment, Amy. Would ya wait for her up here and I'll send her up when she comes back," Kelsey glanced over his shoulder at the young lieutenant waiting in the hall.

"All right, I'll wait up here." Kelsey disappeared down the staircase with his friend and I stood alone in the sewing room.

After looking over a few patterns Mrs. McCarthy had laying on a table, I strolled about the room and paused before the window. I leaned forward to look out and a board beneath me popped. It sounded strangely hollow. I knelt down and tapped. It was hollow. Glancing around, I made sure I was still alone before picking at a knot hole in the board. Suddenly it lifted. A sack was inside. This was like something out of Elizabeth's mystery books! I stared in amazement, then my fingers reached down and untied the string. An envelope fell out.

To Mr. Kelsey McCarthy

The same handwriting … and perfume … that was on the other envelope. My stomach turned over. *How can this be happening?* I quickly pulled out two other envelopes, all written by the same hand as the first. Suddenly, a small shiny object fell out and landed on the floor with a loud thud. Afraid it had been heard, I quickly snatched it up and listened for footsteps. Nothing. My eyes locked on the jewel. A solid gold locket hung on a fine golden chain. Elegant designs were etched onto the front of the locket. The detailing was incredible and I knew at once it was worth a great sum of money. My fingers pried open the two golden covers to reveal the image inside. She had lovely long curls that hung down around her delicate head, a fine pointed nose and gentle eyes with dark lashes. I choked and suddenly footsteps sounded on the stairs. Without thinking, I shoved the locket into my pocket and replaced the letters in their pouch before laying the board down snug in its proper place. Just as I rose, Elga McCarthy came through the door untying her bonnet.

Rumors of War
Chapter 15

Elizabeth

IT WAS NOW late November. The excitement and horror of the past months were finally starting to sort themselves out in my mind. It was hard to grasp that Adam had been a murderer. It seemed as though he was the only man I had become fond of, and then the unthinkable had happened. I struggled, thinking to myself, *had he really been my friend?* But even crueler than that was the tormenting thought of having killed someone … and not just anyone, but someone with whom I had become friends. I knew I had to shake off these thoughts and move on with my life. Try as I might, this tormenting thought was always lingering, even as I knelt down to ask God for comfort and peace.

Walking down the narrow streets of Gettysburg, I looked around at all the little shops and houses huddled together, preparing for another cold winter. I made my way into the mercantile, starting my busy day. No one was there at the moment, but thinking I heard someone in the back room, I waited patiently. Browsing around the little shop, my gaze landed on a freshly printed newspaper article. I scanned through it, my eyes catching a few words:

… Abraham Lincoln to be the next President of the United States!

… Tensions grow with the election between the slave and free states!

… Rumors of secession spread through the land!

I picked up the paper and glanced over it. Recently, the talk of the many differences between the states had become common conversation. *Would the slave states really try to break from the Union though?* I knew there was great opposition among the Southern slave states against a Republican being elected. There were even threats that they would secede if such an election should take place. Well, now it had happened, Lincoln was elected. *Would the Southerners go through with their threats? What could it mean if they did? War?* I shuddered at the thought. This same America that we called the Union, and that was the "Promised Land" to many, could end up fighting itself and tearing the land apart over its differences.

* * *

The padded snow crunched under my feet as I made my way along Middle Street. It was now Christmas Eve and I still needed to find a gift for my sister. As I passed the tannery, the idea came to my mind. *Of course! Amy needs new shoes!* I entered the low building and greeted the German tanner and shoemaker, Gustav. He helped me choose a fine pair of stylish new boots for my sister. As he began packaging them, he asked in a thick German accent, "Have you heard the news, Miss Matthews?"

"No, Sir, what news?" I inquired.

The older man looked up grimly, "South Carolina seceded from the Union since that Mr. Lincoln was elected. Rumors are that a good many other states will follow their example." I stood, shocked for a moment. *So, it has happened then.* A chill ran through me. He continued, "Southern Senators are resigning from the Senate and Federal troops in South Carolina are being threatened. Things are not lookin' pretty, my dear girl, not at all."

We said a few more words, and I headed back onto the street. A blast of cold air blew through the streets, whipping snow into my face. I traced my footsteps instinctively back to the house, my mind a blur with the recent news.

* * *

I left the turkey sizzling above the fire as I went to the closet to retrieve the large, worn, family Bible. Entering the family room, I found Amy near the stones that made up the large fireplace. She was fingering Father's initials that he had deeply carved into one of the big stones. She flinched as I came into the room, then gazed back at the carvings. I laid a hand on her shoulder and led her over to the couch. We sat down near the fireplace and took turns reading the Christmas story from the gospel of Luke. Then we hastened back and set the table. It looked like a picture; the turkey lay on a platter, surrounded by decorative leaves and cherries. Apple and cherry pies were steaming, sprinkled with sugar, alongside the rest of the food, all looking warm and colorful. Even though we had no company, my sister and I agreed to make the Christmas Eve dinner just as our mother had always done. The McCarthy's had invited us over tomorrow for Christmas Day dinner. After we had eaten, we went into the parlor and took turns playing the smooth ivory keys of the piano while we sang carols.

Christmas was bittersweet since the death of our parents. We talked late into the night, recalling many memories of them. I also mentioned the news I had heard earlier that day and we discussed it, wondering if it would mean war.

Intruder of the Night
Chapter 16

Amy

A COLD WIND whistled around the house howling as it fought its way under the door. The frame of the house occasionally popped and creaked, holding itself steady. I lay awake, eyes darting to the door whenever I heard the noises. For some odd reason I awoke in the middle of the night, startled by a peculiar feeling of something lurking outside. I shuddered, thinking of the dream that had taken part in waking me. Mother and Father had been there, so real and life-like that it gave me chills to think of it. When they had disappeared, frightening loneliness surrounded me, except for the sound of terrifying cries. The noise had become so deafening that I sat up in my bed sweating.

It must be the papers I had been reading of the possible war closing in around us that sparked these nightmares. I pulled the clean quilts tighter as an eerie howl echoed down the chimney. Perhaps it was the talk around town of the growing tension with the South that created these war-like scenes. Or was it the struggle inside me?

Reaching into a drawer, I pulled forth a small cloth. After it was unraveled, it revealed the golden locket. It was the most beautiful piece of jewelry I had ever seen. *Where had it come from? If only I knew.* My heart sank and tears clouded my vision.

"Why, Kelsey? Why?" I whispered through tears. *I can't understand why he doesn't love me anymore. When did I become replaceable to him?* I shoved the locket back into its hiding place and lay awake for a few minutes struggling with my thoughts. I knew I could not keep quiet for long with such a secret hidden in my drawer. *I must get the locket back somehow. Perhaps I could simply slip it back into its hole ... But the letters? No, if I take it back, I must confront him with it.*

Slowly sliding out from under the warm quilts, I crept to my sister's room. After listening to her slow, soft breathing, I moved quietly away. I stood at the top of the stairs staring down into the pit of blackness. The wind howled fiercely. With a little shiver, I descended the stairs, crossed the parlor and passed in front of a small window before reaching the kitchen, where I would make myself a pot of tea.

Outside I could see snowflakes whipping through the fields. The moon would randomly peek through to muse over the damage done below. I put on the water, then sat in the light of a single candle, sipping the warm liquid that soothed me. I had begun drifting into a light slumber, when suddenly the cup crashed from my hand down to the floor. I quickly snatched it up. Hearing no sound of Elizabeth waking, I placed it softly on the table and leaned back.

I must have dozed for a while, because I was suddenly awakened by a small thumping sound on the porch and I instantly sat upright. It continued until it stopped before the door. The pounding in my chest was for a moment the only sound I could hear. Then ... softly, slowly, the doorknob jiggled. Was I simply seeing things or was it true? The brass knob moved again more definitely. I was instantly on my feet flying up the stairs. Shaking Elizabeth furiously, I gasped to catch my breath.

"What? What's going on?" she yawned.

"Someone's trying to break in!" I whispered in a shrill voice.

Suddenly Elizabeth's eyes widened, but without a word she snatched up her shawl and shoes and pulled me into the closet. She left the closet door cracked in order to peer out. For a moment, there was silence. Then we both heard it, the creaking of the downstairs door as it opened to admit the intruder. Staring at each other in the dark closet, fear gripped us. We were trapped!

* * *

For what seemed like hours, we sat huddled in back of the closet. I clutched Elizabeth's arm as she held fast to a pistol. We listened to the sound of the intruder below. He moved from one room to the other, opening the doors to every closet and every desk drawer. Every inch of my skin seemed to crawl as he ascended the staircase. In silent agony, I waited 'til he reached the top and moved to a different room.

Elizabeth whispered in my ear, "We're going to run to the McCarthy's." Her eyes flashed in the dark as she touched the door, "Now!" She whispered hoarsely.

In a mad scramble, we rushed down the stairs not hearing the intruder run out of the room to watch us go. I launched a hand toward my shawl as we passed it and then was pulled out the door. Vapor clouded my vision as my lungs ached to bring in the frosty air. My feet went numb after a few seconds of running and I stumbled in the snow. Elizabeth pushed me on, never looking back.

"If we don't keep moving at a good pace we may get frost bite! Is he following?" I called to Elizabeth.

"I don't think so, but we can't turn back to look! Keep going, Amy!"

I coughed from the sting of the frozen air surging through my body. Every shadow we passed seemed to move to chase us, giving me the energy I needed. The moon that had guided our path suddenly hid behind a cloud. All was dark. Moments later, light became visible on the horizon.

The Hope of Christmas
Chapter 17

Elizabeth

THE WIND BLEW wildly. My hand shook as I pounded on the big door. Gasping for breath, I turned to my sister, "Are you all right?"

Amy nodded, her face pale.

The memory flashed in my mind. The footsteps wandering throughout the house. They seemed to be searching for something ... or someone. Someone had broken into our home and I shuddered to think the burglar could be following us. I continued pounding all the more, as chills ran up my spine at the thought of what had just happened. Lights began to flicker in the windows and footsteps could be heard within. Soon the door was pulled open. A tall figure covered the entrance.

"Oh! Mr. McCarthy! Please help us!" I cried.

"For goodness sake! What's the matter me lasses?" he asked in a concerned tone. Mrs. McCarthy soon appeared in the doorway as well. Kelsey stood in the background. I explained the situation, my voice trembling.

"Saints preserve us!" Mrs. McCarthy exclaimed, cupping a thin hand over her mouth. Mr. McCarthy and Kelsey jumped to action. Grabbing their guns from the mantle they disappeared into the snowy night. Mrs. McCarthy gently led us into the warm house, all the while fussing and muttering about how, "The poor dears don't even have coats on! And in this weather!" Amy and I were soon seated beside the fire. A couple of hours went by and Mr. McCarthy and Kelsey returned with John Barnes, the constable.

"We searched the whole house. No one was there. He's probably already long gone by now." The constable gave the report. "I'll go back with you next morning and you can check what's missing." We all sat down in the parlor and Mr. Barnes continued. "I think you were just the unfortunate target this time. Robberies like this happen occasionally, but I wouldn't worry. I doubt that you were picked out specially. No need to think the burglar will come back." The quiet assurance calmed me a bit. We were all silent for some time, when Mrs. McCarthy spoke up.

"Well then. Since all of you are already here, you might as well stay the night. I've got a couple guest rooms to put ya in. It's too frightful a night for you to go back out. No sense in goin' back to your houses when I'll be invitin' ya all back for the Christmas Day celebration," she smiled. I was grateful to the McCarthy's for allowing us to stay in their home. I had no desire to return to the house at this moment.

* * *

I sat up in bed, my forehead sweating. "We have to get out! He'll find us!" I yelled. Then, finding myself in a quiet, comfortably furnished room, I tried to sort out my thoughts. *We're safe. We're at the McCarthy's house.* Breathing a sigh of relief, I wiped my brow. Amy stirred in a bed at the opposite corner of the room. Waking her, we dressed and freshened up to go to breakfast.

Mrs. McCarthy made a splendid meal consisting of fluffy biscuits, gravy, eggs, sizzling sausages, ham, golden pancakes with sweet maple syrup, blueberry muffins, rich coffee and hot tea. We all gathered around the large dining table and Mr. McCarthy said a prayer of thankfulness for the meal and for the reason of Christmas: God sending His Son in human flesh to save the world. Mrs. McCarthy habitually made the sign of the cross over her chest as we all said, "Amen."

As we passed around the delicious food, I stated, "We were so thankful to see a light glowing from your house last night. It was so dark I don't know if we would've seen it otherwise."

"Ah, the candle in the window. 'Tis an Irish tradition. A symbol of welcome to Mary and Joseph as they traveled looking for a place of shelter," Mrs. McCarthy replied.

Mr. McCarthy added, "We leave the door unlatched on Christmas Eve night. It is also a tradition, so that Mary and Joseph or any wandering traveler may enter and eat the food left on the table. When ye lasses came a knockin' at the door last night, I almost thought ye were Mary and Joseph lookin' for a place to shelter." Laughter circled the room.

We spent the whole morning and early afternoon with the McCarthy's and John Barnes. It was a wonderful way to spend Christmas Day. We returned to our house later that evening. I followed Mr. Barnes into the house with a touch of apprehension running through me. Several things were knocked out of place, but it was, for the most part, in order. Quickly, Amy pointed to the lock box engraved with Father's initials.

I caught my breath, "Oh no, it's broken open!"

Amy dashed over to it and stopped short. All was still. "It's all there," she whispered and dropped into a chair, holding the box. Quickly she began counting it. Then her brow furrowed in confusion. "Only a few dollars are missing. He opened it, saw all that money, but only took a few dollars," her eyes slowly met mine. "How can this be?"

I stared, at a loss for words. The money was in disorder as though the burglar had dug through it in search of something else. I turned suddenly to the constable in pursuit of an answer. He was examining the box closely, with his arms folded and his dark brows contracted.

"Perhaps he stayed long searching for the money, then heard you and the McCarthy's coming so he just grabbed a little and ran off?" I offered.

John Barnes shook his head. "But why not just take the box as he ran off?" Several minutes passed by and finally Mr. Barnes spoke up again, "Ladies, since you live farther out of town than most of us, I am going to leave you with a bell to ring for any emergency you have. I'll have it hung up today." I thanked him, but still an eerie feeling remained with me and I could see that something was bothering Mr. Barnes. Father and John Barnes had been close friends and I sensed that Mr. Barnes felt especially responsible for our safety now that Father was gone. For there *were* other people in our community who lived farther out from the town and yet he had not offered them a bell to ring in a time of emergency. Glancing back at the money box, I was thankful that the intruder had not taken much, but noticed with a sinking feeling that it was not very full in the first place. What was I to do to earn a living here?

* * *

The pounding hooves tossed up the light, dry snow from the cold earth. It was February now, and the sun hung low on the horizon, shooting its colorful rays to the earth and painting the snow with its assorted hues. The cool breeze swept softly through the fields. We turned our horses up a rocky hill. I had no need to urge Shadow on as he cantered quickly up the acclivity and past Lady Ann. I smiled at her rider, Amy, as I went by.

She laughed, "I see, you want to race, do you?" As we reached the summit, we slowed our horses and stared out at the view, perceiving our small town in the distance. The trees were barren and we could see for miles. It seemed a peacefulness flooded over the landscape along with the scarlet rays of the dying sun. After a few more minutes of quiet, I broke the silence.

"Well, shall we press on, before we're left out here in the dark?" We nudged our horses and rode along the hills and fields until we reached Seminary Ridge. My body stiffened as my gaze met the cold marker of Adam's grave. I could feel my sister's eyes on me.

"Come on," she said softly. We rode a little further and came upon the old shack. Amy jumped off her tall horse. I dismounted as I saw that Amy wanted to investigate the place. I followed her quick footsteps into the small room. Amy waved her hand at the dust that arose upon our entrance. I smiled, and then remembered all the confusing conversations I had been a part of in this place.

"What is this?" Amy asked, surprised to see that her investigation had not been in vain. She held up an old piece of parchment. Very old, by the looks of it; it seemed as if it had been crumpled several times, but then unfolded again. It was also smudged with a fair amount of dirt and soot. I stepped outside to get a better look at it. My sister hovered over me.

"What does it say?" She asked curiously.

"You're acting just like Mrs. Denny!" I teased, as I scanned over the page. It was hard to discern through the grime and crinkles, but I finally managed to read it.

My Son,

    My heart is breaking as I recall the treatment of your father toward you. I write to tell you to come home. I am living with my sister in Hedgesville, Virginia. Come here and we will be together again. We can start a new life, Nathan. We can forget the past; your father will not search so far as Virginia for us. I know it will be hard to start new, but as long as I have my son with me, it will be a home.

With all my love, your Mother

My voice faded as I read the last words. I stared at the paper. *So, his father … threw him out of the house?* My sister watched the page in my hand solemnly.

Then she broke the silence, "How sad … poor Mr. Tyler," she sighed dismally. "Do you think his father … beat him?"

I glanced at her, "I don't know," I paused thoughtfully, "I wonder if he ever went back to his mother."

"Well, I surely hope he did."

I folded the paper and looked around, "It's getting late, we should probably be heading back." Placing the paper softly on the small table, I followed my sister out of the shack.

Nothing Honorable
Chapter 18

Amy

MY SWEATY FINGERS gripped tightly around the locket. *How could I do it ... what could I say?* I knew I had to give it back to confront Kelsey and yet it seemed one of the hardest things I would ever do in my life. I stood on the landing of the stairs, staring up the wooden staircase. Then slowly I ascended, feeling I was walking a plank about to jump off into the ocean of uncertainty. When I reached the hall, I heard someone in the sewing room. Mrs. McCarthy had told me Kelsey was inside and would be down in a minute. *Now was the time to confront him.* Silently, I stepped inside the doorway to find Kelsey kneeling on the floor with the board lying beside him. With his hand in the sack that lay in the hole, he searched for the locket. A lump swelled in my throat.

"Looking for something?" I asked. He jumped to his feet at my words. He had a strange look in his eyes, like a guilty victim caught in the midst of crime.

He didn't even speak and for the first time in my life, I was afraid of him, afraid to show what I held in my hand. This was not the same Kelsey who had left five years ago. My stomach turned and my fingers opened as if at some command to reveal the locket. Kelsey glanced down at it and then back up at me.

"Would you mind telling me where this came from?" I asked almost in a whisper as I turned the locket over in my hand.

"It isn't what you think," his voice was stern and quite different than I had ever heard.

"What then?"

His head dropped as he placed his hands on his hips, "Amy, there are things I can't tell you." He looked up, "it's complicated … I just need you to trust me."

"Things you can't tell me? Well I can't trust someone who won't be honest with me, Kelsey," I held out the locket again. "This and the letters, those are not things I can lay aside as if I had never seen them."

"You've seen them? What did you read?" He was suddenly upon me searching my eyes.

I stepped back, eyes still locked on his, "Why?" I asked slowly.

He shook his head and ran his hands through his hair in frustration, "I can't say."

"Kelsey, please, be honest with me. I will try to understand. Just tell me the truth." Silence followed and I held my breath, my whole body shaking. His eyes searched the ground and fell on the sack which lay on the floor, open and bare.

"This is bigger than both of us, Amy …." The words rang in the tense room. He took a step closer and spoke gently. "Amy, I've never pretended with you. My intentions are still true, still honorable."

"Honorable!" My anger flared, "Kelsey, there is nothing honorable about what I see here! Hidden secrets, deceptive lies. The boy who left home five years ago would have owned up to his mistakes, not hidden them beneath the floorboards."

"It's not what it seems, Amy," Kelsey caught my arm as I turned to leave, angry tears welling in my eyes. "What I keep from you is only to protect you!"

"How can I believe that?" Searching his eyes, I let the tears fall heavy upon my cheeks. "My dearest friend, I've trusted you, I've waited for you … I've loved you. And this is how you repay my love …" I tore the thin silver ring from my finger and shoved it into his free hand and pulled away. I could hardly see his face through the tears that clouded my vision, "I release you from our engagement."

I turned hastily to leave the room, but an arm caught the door frame barring my way.

"Wait, Amy, wait," Kelsey stared down into my eyes, a deep sorrow in his own. "I won't let you go like this."

"It's too late, Kelsey, I'm done."

Then slowly, Kelsey's arm dropped to his side and the way was opened again for me. I stepped from the room, descended the stairs and found myself on the road leading further out of town into the solitude of the forest.

* * *

April 1861

All was dark as I sat alone in the little school room. The morning was still and heavy with the threat of an approaching spring storm. I held my head in my hands wearily and waited for the patter of footsteps to come up the stairs at the front of the schoolhouse. After rising early, I had taken the lonely walk down Emmitsburg road into the sleeping town. Thick clouds were closing in around the fields, crawling down from the mountains. Clasping my hands together I glanced up with a heavy sigh to look around the room. A mixture of emotions swirled around me like an ocean drowning out any hope for the future. Pushing back my chair quickly, I rose to shove open a window. I peered out into the foggy morning ... *I will never trust another so deeply for as long as I live.*

"Miss Matthews?"

I turned quickly to the small red-haired girl who stood trembling in the doorway. "Yes, Eva, what's the matter?"

She dropped her lunch pail and books and ran toward me catching hold of my dress. "I heard something following me to school!"

I stroked the little head hiding in my skirts, "It was most likely just another student coming to class."

She shook her head violently, "I don't think so! It snorted real loud once!"

Puzzled, I knelt down in front of the girl, "Like a horse?"

"But after a while it got quiet, then it hid in the outhouse!" she whimpered.

"The outhouse?" I rose to investigate and Eva remained inside the school. A group of children greeted me at the stairs. As I approached the outhouse, I saw it rattle and shake. Someone was pounding their fist against the door. Then I saw two pieces of wood wedged in the door to keep it from opening. I rushed forward.

"Hello! Who's in there?"

"It is I, Clarence Brown!" Came a squeaky voice. Then the pounding became louder. *Clarence. I should have guessed. Most likely it's a trick of Luke Stone's.*

"Clarence, don't bang on the door! It'll make it stick worse. Hold on!" I bent down and began working at the trap.

"I shall have revenge!" Clarence shouted furiously.

Finally, after a struggle, I pried the door open and Clarence came bursting out. He straightened his jacket, pushed up his spectacles and marched up the stairs demanding to see his captor. I followed in a hurry. The whole class was in an uproar over the dilemma. But this did not stop Clarence. He marched directly over to Luke Stone who sat smugly in his chair snickering.

"It was you, you foul creature, was it not?" Suddenly, Clarence took a swing and Luke ducked, sending him off balance. An amused look spread across Luke's face as the opportunity of a lifetime came his way.

"You want to fight me, squirt? I'll teach you a lesson you'll never forget."

"Boys, stop it!" I shouted coming between them, "Fighting is no way to solve a dispute!"

The whole class held its breath as Luke and Clarence glared past me. Suddenly the sound of a galloping horse caught our attention. Someone was coming through the town. The bell began to sound with an alarming clang. I rushed to the door and, standing on the top step, peered out into the early morning. The children surrounded me, anxiously watching.

Suddenly a horseman appeared out of the fog, riding at top speed, "War! War! The Southerners have fired on Fort Sumter!" He was gone as fast as he had come, leaving a dreadful silence behind. The town bell alone clanged on continuously.

War ... it has come at last ... Someone tugged my skirt and I glanced down into round frightened eyes.

"What's happening?" whimpered little Robert. I reached down and took his hand in mine.

"It will be all right."

"I knew there would be a war!" Luke boasted triumphantly, "I just knew it!"

I shot an angry glance back at him, "This is nothing to be proud of, Luke."

His eyes narrowed and a smile played at his lips. "Fightin's the only way to solve a dispute."

A Matter of Pride
Chapter 19

Elizabeth

May 1861

IT HAD HAPPENED. Eleven states had seceded and were now called the Confederate States of America, with Richmond, Virginia being named the capital of the new country. Not only had the country been torn in half, but also the state of Virginia. Some of the counties wished to remain in the Union. Now there was a Virginia and a West Virginia. Yet not all the slave states had seceded. Four still remained in the Union, namely Delaware, Kentucky, Maryland and Missouri. It had all happened so quickly. On April 12th, a band of Southerners, Confederates, as they were now called, had fired on Fort Sumter, a United States Army post in South Carolina. No one had been killed, but it was considered an act of rebellion and of grave importance. Fort Sumter had surrendered. Many men we knew had gone off to accept the call to arms against the Confederates. States had seceded and now there were two countries where there had been one. Some people believed that nothing would come of this, that it would all blow over and we would be left with two countries. I felt there was more to it than that. Union and Confederate troops were gathering like dark clouds, and I wondered how long it would be before the storm.

* * *

The wicker basket grew heavy on my arm as I shifted it for the fifth time. Approaching the bakery I stepped inside, greeted by the smell of warm, fresh bread. Laying the basket on the counter, I sighed with relief. A timid, thin man with glasses came from the back room.

"Mr. Denny, how nice to see you. How is your wife?" I smiled, thinking of the many differences between the two. Mr. Denny nodded softly and adjusted his glasses as he inspected the pies I had set on the counter.

"Lovely pies, Miss Matthews. Strawberry … and peach, I imagine?"

"Yes, I was hoping to hurry home and make several more for tomorrow—" suddenly I was interrupted.

"I'm sorry, Miss Matthews, we cannot take more so soon. We have plenty as it is. Once a week is sufficient."

"Oh …" my mind flashed back to the quickly emptying money box as Mr. Denny dropped a few small coins into my hand. I hoped I would at least have enough to buy Amy a small wedding present when the time came. My heart ached as I wondered what would happen after the money box emptied. I knew for certain Amy and Kelsey would offer to let me live with them. However, I could not bear the thought of imposing on them as Amy's pitiable, unmarried sister. I hurriedly walked the streets toward the mercantile. A young man caught my eye. He was dark skinned, but not very dark; a young mulatto man. He wore ragged brown trousers, a smudged white shirt and a brown hat. Over his shoulder was slung a burlap sack and he carried a couple of peaches in his hand. As I came closer, and was about to pass, he spoke up.

"Excuse me, Ma'am. Would you be interested in some fresh peaches?" I involuntarily glanced from the peaches down to the man's bare feet. They were dusty and tinged with blood stains.

"Oh, no thank you. They look very delicious though."

The young man nodded, giving a small smile as he stared down at the peaches in his hand and then moved on. At the mercantile they had more dresses than they could sell, and so I left the shop with no more money than I had come with.

The sun shone warm on my face as I began the walk down Emmitsburg Road toward home, a soft breeze blowing through the loose hair under my bonnet. Looking down the dusty road, I noticed two figures approaching in my direction. Shading my eyes from the glaring sun, I recognized them as Mrs. Johansson and Mrs. Clemmons. They were sisters who ran various charities and orphanages in the surrounding areas. Seeming pleasant enough in brief encounters, these ladies were of a somewhat conceited and aloof nature.

"Miss Matthews, how are you this fine spring day?"

"Very well, thank you, Mrs. Johansson," I smiled and gave a small curtsy.

Mrs. Clemmons eyed me with a brow lifted and said, "I suppose you are looking forward to your younger sister's marriage quite eagerly." Her tone of voice struck me, but I quickly forced a smile.

"I am very happy for her."

Mrs. Clemmons gave a smug smile and added, "I'm sure it will be quite lonely in your home once Kelsey receives his new post assignment and she is gone to be with him."

"Yes, indeed."

Mrs. Johansson glanced at her sister and then gazed at me. "Miss Matthews, you cannot pretend with us, we know of your situation and would like to help you as best we can." I began to shift my eyes away from the interrogating women, searching for a way out.

Mrs. Clemmons took up her sister's statement. "Miss Matthews. Let me put this to you plainly. Seeing as how you have not the intention or means of marrying, we would like to offer you a job in our Charity and Orphanage Foundation. We need another woman to take charge of a nearby orphanage in Littlestown. We think you would be ideal for the situation since you have no connections here." With each hurtful word, I felt my blood rise.

Seeing my discomfited expression, Mrs. Johansson began again, "You really must consider this offer, my dear girl. You will be paid quite handsomely and therefore earn your way in the world." *Paid.* The word rang in my mind as the image of the emptying money box loomed up before me. The picture painted itself in my mind: working in an orphanage, cooped up night and day, never able to go out and meet new people, have new adventures ...

"I ... I can't," I whispered hoarsely. Tightly grasping my basket, I moved quickly away. *I can't stay here any longer ... I must get away from all this!*

* * *

July 1861

Streaks of pale pink painted themselves on the wall opposite the window. I closed my eyes against the light of the morning sun. Troubled thoughts had tormented my mind all night. Pictures of young men dying and screaming for relief on bloody battlefields etched themselves in my head. I had tossed and turned all night, these thoughts and pictures torturing me in my half sleep. The news of the first major battle of the war between the states had bothered me greatly. I had seen a sign posted on the mercantile window asking for women volunteers to help with the cooking, sewing and care of the wounded in the army. I had tried to keep myself occupied with the cooking and cleaning of the home, but there seemed to be no purpose to it anymore; Amy was to be married in several months and would be leaving to live with her husband. I gazed silently at the last coins lying in the money box. I hadn't told Amy about the matter, not wanting to upset the happy bride-to-be with my own bothersome troubles. Again, I felt a burning desire to go ... somewhere in the world, and do ... something. If I volunteered to help the army, at least I would have food and a place to stay. *I have to leave. I have to do something. I couldn't stand just living in an empty house, scraping for money and being pitied and patronized by the townsfolk.*

"Amy, I need to talk to you." I started quickly, setting down a plate of biscuits for the morning meal. "I've been doing a lot of thinking lately, what with the war and all, and I feel like doing *something*. I feel like everyone is getting involved in something very important, and I'll be left sitting here at home doing ... *nothing*." I finished, sitting down in a wooden chair. Amy looked at me and seemed to know my feelings. She said nothing, but waited for me to continue. Getting back up from the chair, I walked over to the window and stared out as the rising sun stretched its rays over the grassy fields.

A long moment of silence persisted, then I whispered quietly, "I'm going to leave ..." a few seconds passed. Turning slowly around, I looked at my sister. She sat, her hands folded in her lap and tears stood in her eyes. I stepped over to her and laid a hand on her shoulder.

"I feel I need to do this. You and Kelsey will be married in several months and have your own home somewhere. I need to make my own way. I'm going to volunteer to help the army."

Lieutenant Morgan
Chapter 20

Amy

GLANCING DOWN FROM the wagon, my gaze fell upon a long line of men all shifting about in the summer sun. The tables were set up with military officers standing by watching the crowds of men signing away their lives for their country. Many of them were young, about my age, and kept up a continual excited chatter with one another. As I watched the broad proud grins that spread across their faces, I wondered, *Do they truly know what they are getting into? How could they? War is but an exciting word to them, shouted from a passing courier, that stirred up their lives and sparked their imaginations with stories of heroism.* But this was real, it was brutal. It would invade our lives and change us, every one of us. The young men who were cheered as heroes going off to battle would soon be weary, hardened veteran soldiers. The horrors of war would surround them, walk with them in the day light, sit beside them in the darkness and haunt them in their sleep.

I had read enough accounts of war in my history studies to know what would take place, though it didn't seem possible in our beautiful country. Now I was watching the young men I had grown up with and gone to school with, heading off to war. My own sister ... devoting her young life to the welfare of strangers. Things were changing so fast.

"Have they sent for Kelsey yet?"

Quickly I turned my attention to John, who sat calmly beside me, guiding the team. We were both headed to the O'Donnell house outside town; John to drop off medicine and I to inquire over an absent student.

My throat tightened, "No ... not that I've heard." I stared at one of the countless posters around town tacked up on shop walls.

To arms! To arms!

Your country calls!

A bald eagle held a ribbon in its mouth with the words:

The Union—it must and shall be preserved!

"Did you ever find out what was bugging old Kelsey so much?" John's voice was lowered. "Couldn't get him to tell me a thing when I tried."

"No," I lied, my stomach turning over at the reminder. The sudden declaration of war had, up to this point, kept any questions of Kelsey at bay.

There was a pause, "You know ... I uh, signed up. I'll be heading out about the same time as Elizabeth." John ventured a quick glance at me, then turning away took a deep breath, "I, uh, thought we could travel out together. Thought you'd feel better knowing she's with someone you know."

A chill swept over me. *John was leaving too! Did his family know yet? Poor Sarah, they've been so close all their lives.*

"Oh," I choked. "That is comforting ... thank you, John. Please take care of her."

Quickly I turned to stare across the fields to hide the tears that were clouding my view. As I did so, a horse and rider trotted up opposite us. The rider's hat was pulled down low, his eyes shaded. He wore a dark coat and rode a black horse. The horse's sleek, black flanks dripped with sweat, as if he had been ridden far and hard.

Curiosity came over me and I squinted as they trotted past and a shiver crept up my spine. *Could it be? How odd!* I was almost sure that the rider was the young lieutenant I had seen at the McCarthy's house the night I found the letters and locket under the floorboard. He passed, glancing over his shoulder. As our eyes met, I saw it *was* the lieutenant!

* * *

"Miss Amy!" Mrs. Denny rushed on me and quickly pulled me through the doorway, closing it behind me. She peeked through the lace curtains, "You would not believe the strange happenings I've heard today! The oddest young man just left my shop. He was very quiet, wore shiny black boots and spurs and only asked for a loaf of bread." Laying my basket on the counter, I waited for the rest of her tale, a little impatient to be on my way. Her eyes grew wide and she spoke in a whisper, "Just last night the mercantile was broken into and some random articles stolen! But that's not all! In the same night, a pistol from the gun smithy was missing! What times! We're hardly safe in this town anymore!"

"Do they have any idea who the thief was?" I asked trying not to sound too excited that Mrs. Denny had finally stumbled across something worthwhile.

Mrs. Denny raised an eyebrow, "Constable Barnes says he has no suspects, but I have my own ideas."

Certainly, I wanted to say, but kept silent. She waved me over to the window and I was made to look outside.

"See there," she pointed across the street to the Gettysburg Inn run by some German immigrants. All seemed quiet. An old man hobbled in front of the inn past a black horse tied to the hitching post. The animal was tall and lean, beautifully built and looked as if he could run for miles. I wasn't sure, but I felt almost certain I recognized it.

"That horse out there is that strange young man's. He's staying at the inn. Now I don't want to start any rumors … but that man is a main suspect of mine. He's far too dark and mysterious for my taste," she intensely whispered.

Dark and mysterious … sounds all too familiar. Gettysburg is attracting far too many strangers these days.

As I walked down the street past the inn, I paused and glanced over at the horse tied before the entrance. *Could it be the Lieutenant's?* My curiosity grew rapidly. *It wouldn't hurt to drop by and pay a visit to the innkeeper. No, I won't be a Mrs. Denny!* Turning away, I fought with myself. Slowly my steps turned toward the inn and I stared up at it. The great brick wall loomed sadly above me. All windows were shut, save one, whose lace curtains were drawn outward laughing at the breeze.

Staring up at the curtains, I wondered if perhaps it was his room. *What would he want in a country town like this? The only connection he would have would be Kelsey.* Slowly I began to climb the stairs. The inn foyer was vacant and, glancing around, I began to ascend the stairwell that led to the second floor. The carpeted wooden stairs creaked and groaned with old age. Reaching the second floor, I was met by a long corridor that stretched out the length of the inn. Not a sound came from the apartments as I passed. Suddenly I felt a draft and saw one of the doors cracked ever so slightly. This must be the room with the open window.

Tapping lightly on the door frame I asked, "Is anyone in here?" The door creaked further open and I stepped a foot inside. *Someone could be hurt.* "Hello?" The room appeared empty; it hardly had a thing in it. The only items that announced any occupancy were a hat hanging on a hook above a single saddle bag. An envelope lay beside the saddle bag and caught my eye. After a quick glance back into the empty hall, I moved forward into the room. There was an arm around my throat in a matter of seconds and I reached up in vain to free myself. Not even a cry for help would come! *Let go!* I screamed inwardly. There was the click of a pistol cocking.

"State your business here!" A voice whispered in my ear. The grip gave enough for me to answer hoarsely.

"The door was opened and I thought someone could be hurt," I choked. I was then released and shoved roughly to the back of the room. Gasping for air, the room spun about me and I clung to a bedpost.

"Who are you?" the harsh voice demanded.

"I ... I," I stuttered helplessly. With the air returning to my lungs, I gazed up now quivering. The cold compassionless eyes that met mine were indeed that of the lieutenant's. "You're the lieutenant that was at the McCarthy's house, are you not?" Taking a step back, he sheathed his pistol and glanced back at me looking me up and down.

"Miss Amy Matthews," he said recognizing me. Surprised at his having remembered my name, I nodded. "Miss Matthews, do you usually roam the inn simply to see that no one is in need of help?" The lieutenant crossed the room and closed the open window, locking it tightly.

Swallowing hard, I answered, "No, Sir, I ..."

"I thought perhaps you had different motives," he turned on me.

"I knew you were staying here, Sir. I passed you on the road just a few days ago." At this the lieutenant looked surprised.

"You have an impeccable memory, for a woman." I felt insulted and complimented all at once. Feeling a little braver I ventured the nagging question.

"May I ask what business you have with Kelsey McCarthy?" The stone-faced look I received as an answer informed me that I had asked the wrong question.

"Your curiosity will only cause you trouble in the future, Miss Matthews. I suggest you restrain it now." *The arrogance of this man! He dared to question the concern a woman had for her fiancé?*

"Sir, I would like to know what your dealings with Mr. McCarthy are and I feel entitled to know since he is in fact my fiancé." There was an amused look on the man's face, as he took up his bag and slung it over his shoulder.

"Is he, indeed?" he asked and shifted his gaze down to my finger that no longer bore the silver engagement ring. My mouth went dry and I stood there gazing down at it. The piercing implication of his words felt like another knife driven into the open wound.

"Good day, Miss Matthews." I listened to the sound of his footsteps disappear down the hall.

Intruder by Day
Chapter 21

Elizabeth

October 1861

THE LAST NAIL was driven into the boarded-up window. Feeling a hand slip into mine and squeeze it, I glanced over at Amy, who was standing beside me. I forced a smile at her.

Mr. John Barnes approached me. "That was the last window, Miss Matthews. She's all boarded up and ready to wait for your return. Miss Amy will be fine to stay in it for a while until she's married though. After that, I'll stop by and keep up the appearance of the place for you."

"Thank you, Mr. Barnes, we are most grateful," I said sincerely.

* * *

After a walk in the town, Amy and I treaded down Emmitsburg Road approaching our house. The autumn wind brought a slight chill with it, and I pulled the shawl closer around my shoulders.

"I'm sorry I will have to miss your wedding, Amy. I would have loved to be there you know." I glanced at her uneasily. It seemed that every time I mentioned the wedding lately Amy would stiffen up and quietly acknowledge my statements.

"The next ferry down the Ohio River wouldn't come for a while yet," she started. "Please don't feel bad." There was a pause. "I will miss you very much though." I nodded and kept my eyes fixed on the road ahead, knowing that, if I looked at her, we would both lose control of our emotions. The rest of the way we had a more pleasant conversation and laughed at the latest news Mrs. Denny had informed us of.

As I approached the doorway to our home, I suddenly realized something was not right. The door itself was cracked open and the lock looked as though it had been broken.

"No …" I whispered hoarsely.

Amy caught my arm, "Maybe we should get Mr. Barnes."

Controlling my voice, I said simply, "We probably just forgot to lock it," but still grasped Amy's arm as I walked into the building. Dusk was settling over the area and the last bits of sunlight reflected off the top windows of our home with a dying brilliance. As I stepped over the threshold and walked into the parlor, I heard a scratching noise coming from the family room. Standing near the fireplace was the figure of a man. He seemed to be preoccupied. My foot stepped on a creaking board as I began to back out, too afraid to say anything. Startled at the noise, the man whipped around. I couldn't believe my eyes. It was the young mulatto man I had seen in town the other day. I turned and ran out of the house toward the emergency bell Mr. Barnes had set up. Amy followed close behind me. Grasping the thick rope, I pulled down with all my strength. *Bong!* The first toll broke the silent air. *Bong!* The second. Suddenly a hand yanked my arm from the rope and pulled me back toward the house. I felt the strong arms of the mulatto man tearing me from the bell.

"No! Let me go!" I screamed. For several seconds, I struggled in vain to loosen myself from his grip.

"Let her go. Now!" Amy's voice reached my ears, shaking, but strong. I raised my head to see her holding up one of Father's pistols, cocked and ready to fire. Just then the noise of pounding hooves fell upon us. I turned to look up the road and saw John Barnes riding a horse down Emmitsburg Road. The mulatto man shot one glance at the coming rider and then at our house. Releasing his hold on me, he took off running. Gasping from shock,

I dropped to the ground and stared at the disappearing figure. Mr. Barnes reined in his horse and was quickly at my side.

"Did he hurt you?" he asked hurriedly.

"No ... no, he only scared us." I replied, still watching the distant figure disappearing into the trees.

"Amy, are you well?" I asked as I walked toward the doorstep where my sister still stood, holding the revolver.

She nodded, "Thank you for coming, Mr. Barnes."

"I just don't understand it. Another break-in? I wonder if it was the same man," Mr. Barnes spoke as we followed him into the house. I led him to the spot where I had first seen the man. Around a stone in the fireplace, the one Father had carved his initials into, were marks and scrapes. It looked like the man had tried to bust through the mortar to take out the stone. A hammer and chisel lay on the hearth.

John Barnes stared at the stone for several minutes, then said, "Check the money box."

I obeyed, knowing there was not much there for a robber to take anyhow. Pulling out the drawer of the desk, I took out the box. Then it hit me. This had Father's initials on it as well. The last time our house was broken into, the money box had been opened and searched through and now it was left alone and unharmed. This time, however, a stone with Father's initials had been the object. Leaving the box, I told Mr. Barnes about the eerie coincidence. His eyes never left the markings on the stone as he mused over my words.

"Whatever this man is searching for is behind, or in, something with your father's initials on it. I don't know why or how, but that seems to be the case. I may take up this endeavor myself sometime. Maybe some dynamite would help," he laughed grimly.

We decided that, since I was leaving to aid the Union cause the next day, Amy was to stay at the Denny's house until the day of her wedding. I didn't like the idea of her staying in this house by herself when so many strange things were happening.

* * *

The autumn wind whipped around the house and howled down the chimney. It seemed each board creaked and groaned under the pressure. I lay with the covers wrapped tightly around me. A shudder ran through my body as I thought of the strange invader that had come earlier that evening. Then my thoughts turned in another direction. *Was I doing the right thing in leaving? What would happen to me once I left the safety of our home? How would I live in the vast unknown?* All my life I had been surrounded by those I loved and those who loved me. The fear inside told me to stay where I was, but a stronger urge prevailed. I could not stay here, living as a burden to my sister and brother-in-law, or living alone in this house with no money. I *had* to go.

"Amy, have you seen my old bonnet?" I yelled through the house the next day, digging around in a large drawer.

"Try my chest in the parlor!" She called back.

It had been a hectic day gathering my necessities for the long trip. Walking through our warm home, I gazed wistfully at the familiar surroundings: Father's old chair, the rug Mother had knitted. I swallowed hard. I would soon no longer be surrounded by all this. Fear of the unknown suddenly shook me, but I set my face toward the horizon and didn't turn back.

Fearful Expectations
Chapter 22

Amy

ALONE AT LAST, I stood in the neat little room above the Denny's bakery. At least it was warm, being directly above the baking area downstairs. My trunk sat at the bottom of the bed which stood in the center of the room with a nightstand beside it. Slowly I dropped father's leather sack in a corner. Light seeped in through the cream-colored curtains and spilled across the wooden floorboards and onto a rug. It was onto this rug I fell, clenching my knees to my chest, as I muffled the sobs into the skirt of my dress. Elizabeth was gone at last and I felt a terrible loneliness. I had lost the one person that I felt I could confide in about my situation with Kelsey. My last chance of sharing my sorrows with her was gone. It had been months since my ordeal with Kelsey. Everything became so revolved around the sudden war that I had not allowed myself to cry, but the wound stayed fresh. Thankfully Mr. and Mrs. McCarthy had gone away recently to visit Mr. McCarthy's aging aunt in Boston. I would have hated trying to avoid them for fear of the questions.

These were dark days with so many leaving. Lincoln had called upon seventy-five thousand troops to preserve the Union and put down the absurd rebellion. They were leaving town and headed for training camps. The town folks cheered them as they moved in a clumped mass down the streets. The officers rode with faces fixed ahead, not heeding the excited crowds, the weeping women, or the children, who ran alongside the men with big grins on their young faces. *Yes, they would be heroes, our courageous men in arms, but would they return?* My heart sank at the thought as I watched the processions. It was hard to picture the reality of war as the band played and the brass flashed in the sunlight.

Soon the town looked like a field harvested of its young fighting men, leaving behind some lame old men and a few scrawny boys. The town grew quieter and the streets were bare. Here and there a boarded shop sat alone on the sidewalk, creaking mournfully in the wind. One of the few buildings that seemed unchanged was the schoolhouse, although my students were being affected by the war as much as anyone. With growing sadness, I noticed many empty chairs. Some of the older boys had vanished, apparently to join the army. Indeed, I found it hard to join the children for recess, and to laugh and watch them at play. My tolerance for such gaiety had vanished. Instead, I sat alone in the school room, usually with a good thick book to drown out the world around me. Then I would rise to call the children back inside.

Just a week ago I had caught some of the children using sticks to play war and killing each other off with guns and sabers. The anger rose so violently inside me that I took a switch to four of the boys. They returned to their seats in the classroom with wide eyes as I leaned over my desk with my head in my hands. They didn't understand what crime they had committed, but the scene was more than I could bear. Images of the young men I grew up with charging through smoke and gun fire rose before my eyes. I had promptly dismissed the class after this incident.

It was Saturday and I sat alone inside the school building checking over papers. Rising, I wiped down the blackboard and began writing out next week's arithmetic problems. The school door creaked open and I spun around. An officer stood in the doorway.

"Can I help you, Sir?"

Stepping forward he swept his hat off cordially and held it in his hands, "Yes, Ma'am. I was told you might be able to help locate the whereabouts of an officer."

I laid the chalk down and wiped my hands. "I'll certainly try. What is the man's name?"

The officer stepped forward, "A Lieutenant Kelsey McCarthy."

My stomach turned, "I can tell you where the McCarthy's live."

The man raised a hand, "I've already been there, Ma'am. You see, Kelsey McCarthy was to report to the recruiting station with his orders, but he never showed up."

"I'm sorry. I don't understand ..." I leaned a hand on the desk behind me for balance as the room seemed to fade.

The man hesitated, "Lieutenant McCarthy has gone missing. We believe he is in hiding."

"You ... you mean you're after him?"

The man cleared his throat, "Yes, ma'am. He's charged with the violation of direct orders and if he's on the run, he's considered a deserter of the federal army. Therefore, it is against the law to harbor such a person."

I felt the blood drain from my face. *Kelsey, a deserter ... on the run ... what could this mean? What was he doing?* "I'm sorry, Sir, I do not know where he is. I haven't seen him for some time."

The officer seemed to be weighing my honesty, then he finally replaced his hat and nodded, "Thank you for your time, Ma'am. You *will* let us know if you see him?"

I nodded, unable to speak and watched him disappear behind the closed door.

* * *

Back at the Denny's that evening, I reached down, pulling the empty drawers open. I began mindlessly placing items inside as I pondered the visit from the officer that day. *How could Kelsey do such a thing? Become such a different person?* Pulling forth my small leather-bound Bible, I placed it in the drawer. I stared a moment then opened it, flipping to my favorite verse.

"I'm so confused about all this, Father," I prayed out loud as I turned the pages. A thick white envelope was enclosed among the pages. There was no address, nothing on the outside. I pulled it out, my curiosity growing. *Had Elizabeth placed it there before leaving?*

October 26th, 1861

My Dear Amy,

My heart breaks at the thought of having crushed your hopes and dreams for our future together or at having hurt you in anyway. How I have longed to return to you these past years. Even now I cannot bear the thought of leaving you again. The Lord alone is the one who holds me to my duty, without fear of what the future may hold and without regret of what the past has brought upon me.

How many times I have longed to tell you everything, but for your own safety, not mine, I would not allow myself. I can say no more on this subject.

Please know, my love, that my heart is and always will be yours 'til the very day of my death. Honor binds me to the course ahead. I stand alone with God as my witness to testify to my actions.

May God be with you.
With all my love,
Kelsey

P.S. I know they will come to you when I'm missed. I beg of you, burn this letter after you have read it. I believe with all my heart that we will meet again and when we do, I hope you will have full understanding of my actions.

A sick feeling welled up in my stomach. More confused than ever, I placed the letter back in the Bible cover and decided I could not destroy it yet, not until after reading it over and over. Torn and confused, I methodically resumed my unpacking. Suddenly something struck me. Lost in the words of the letter, I hadn't thought of it before. *How had the letter mysteriously appeared in my Bible? And dated yesterday!*

Army of the West
Chapter 23

Elizabeth

THE WAGON JOLTED and rumbled over the rough, dirt road, sending clouds of dust up under the wheels. I gripped the coarse, wooden seat, while holding my bonnet on with the other hand. A light breeze whipped my hair into my face and the late autumn sun glared its scorching rays into my eyes. It was now early November. I glanced at the man beside me and spoke over the noise of the creaking wagon.

"Is the camp far from here, Sir?" The man kept his eyes on the road and spoke through the pipe that was wedged between his teeth.

"Couple more miles," he sat for a while in silence, then turned to me, rubbing a rough hand over his unshaven chin. "You tired much, Missy?" he asked. I looked up meekly and nodded my answer.

It had been a long trip. From Gettysburg, John and I had taken a carriage to the nearest dock on the Ohio River. We later stopped at a small town called Aurora in the state of Indiana. I continued on my journey, but John stayed in Aurora for several days. He wished to visit with some very close friends who owned the lumber yard in that town. The coins Amy and I had left had paid for my passage on the riverboat. With my sister staying at the Denny's, I didn't have to worry about her being left with nothing to eat. I had boarded a steamboat and travelled down river until I came to a town in Illinois. From there I had taken this wagon and was now nearing my destination: the encampment of the United States Army in the West.

The army was, namely, the Southeastern Missouri and the Western Tennessee.

The only world I had ever known was our small town of Gettysburg. The states that now surrounded me had only been names. In these past days of traveling, I had seen more of the world than I had ever known.

Since July, when I had heard news of the first battle of the war, I had considered and deliberated with myself as to which cause I wanted to support. I did not tell anyone of this decision, as everyone in our area was expected to join the Union. I wanted to consider both sides of the issue however, before making my decision. As to the Southern cause, they weren't just "fighting to keep their slaves" as some people said. I saw it as a principle: they were fighting for the right to live as they wanted to live. Already, the Northern and Southern states had seemed to be two totally different nations. The North had its factories and immigrants that had settled there. The South had its agricultural society and a relationship with England; the English bought their cotton and the Southerners bought their cheaper manufactured goods. The Southerners didn't want other people looking at them with contempt for the way they lived. They wanted their freedom and I understood that. On the other hand, the Northerners were not just fighting to free slaves. They were fighting to keep the Union. If the Southerners were allowed to secede without a fight, then it could go to an extreme; where, every time a state didn't agree with something, it would secede until we were left with a squabbling group of little state-countries.

As to the question of slavery, reading *Uncle Tom's Cabin* had helped me to see that not all the Southern people thought slavery was right and not all the Northern people thought it was wrong. Most of the Northerners didn't even care about slaves. But reading that book made me see just how horrible it would be to live as a slave. Most slaves would consider death a better option than life in bondage. And even though I did agree to some extent with the Southerners, I could not support their cause because if they won, their new country would continue to be a country with slaves. And it was rather ironic that those people who were fighting for their rights to live freely, would in turn deny the rights of an entire race to live as free men as well. If only for that reason, I would have decided to support the Northern cause. But I also didn't want to see this great nation torn in two; I wanted the strong unified nation that the Founding Fathers had foreseen. As to the decision to come to the western army instead of the Army of the Potomac: I suppose I just wanted to get away ... somewhere far away and totally new, and so here I was.

From the height of a sloping, grassy ridge, I gazed upon rows of clean, white canvases, stretched out on the wide meadow, neatly ordered as soldiers on a battlefield. Occasionally, a larger tent jutted up amidst the smaller housings, designating officers' quarters. In the very center, standing in a little clearing, was the general's pavilion. About a mile beyond the encampment was a vast wilderness stretching as far as the eye could see, and beyond that, dark blue mountains rose in the far distance many miles away. A single wide wagon path cut through the wilderness, contrasting sharply against the diversity of dying colors in the November trees. A brisk wind swept suddenly through the tall prairie grass, tossing my bonnet playfully behind my head. I turned and watched the wagon that had carried me this far driving off down the winding dirt path; the last connection of return to my home. A small cloud of dust trailed behind it in the distance. Sighing, I gazed back at the army of tents that confronted me. *Well ... here goes ...*

Stepping lightly down the slope through the waving grass, I swung my small bag over my shoulder and fixed the bonnet back on my windblown hair. As I drew near the encampment, I began to discern figures in blue uniforms wandering through the maze of pavilions. Some stopped what they were doing and watched my approach. I was soon swallowed up by the enclosure of tents. Not knowing what else to do, and feeling rather embarrassed by all the attention I was getting, I directed my steps toward the large pavilion in the center. I unconsciously began counting my steps, trying to ignore the staring faces around me. *Aren't there other women in this camp?* I wondered nervously. As I approached the large tent my heart began to beat faster. I swallowed hard and approached a stiff officer standing at the entrance to the tent, his hands clasped a shining rifle across his chest.

"What can I do for you?" he asked quickly when he caught my eye.

I cleared my throat and answered, "I'd like to speak to the brigade general. I want to offer any services I can."

The man eyed me critically, then disappeared into the tent. Suddenly he reappeared, "Come with me."

White canvases and blue uniforms whirled around me as I hurried to keep up with him. Following through the maze of tents, I heard quiet whisperings around me and shot a glance at a group of soldiers. Seeing me look their way they laughed and shoved each other playfully. I suddenly felt very uncomfortable. *What am I doing here?* For a few seconds my mind flashed with ideas of how I could get out of here and go back to Gettysburg: to the house and my sister, where I belonged. The officer stopped abruptly and I, in turn, nearly ran into the back of him. In the center of the row of tents, a kettle was bubbling over an open fire. A middle-aged man stood before it, ladle in hand. The officer pointed him out to me and stated, "You can help with the cooking, the laundry ... and eventually with the wounded. A couple of the men have been doing all the cooking lately. But they have more important work besides fixing meals for the army."

The officer waved his hand at me, motioning for me to start helping, then spun around and disappeared into the rows of tents. I turned back toward the man who leaned over the kettle. He quickly dropped his head back to observe his stew and quietly continued stirring, not even glancing up as I approached.

The awkwardness was more than I could bear. I spoke up just to relieve the air, "A pleasure to meet you, Sir. My name is Elizabeth Matthews." He nodded, acknowledging my presence and managed a soft greeting, "Miss."

"Can I get you anything for that soup?" I continued. Receiving no reply, I awkwardly glanced around and spotted a small, open tent in which boxes and supplies were nestled neatly. Finding several small carrots, a few shriveled potatoes and a knife, I commenced chopping the vegetables into cubes. Several minutes later, I approached the silent man with my provisions. Without waiting for his consent, I dumped them into the pot and walked back to the tent. The man looked at me, but said nothing. Feeling that I made the man uncomfortable by my very presence, I busied myself organizing the storage tent.

Half an hour later, voices and the plodding of footsteps caused me to peek out from my hiding place. A group of soldiers were beginning to find their way over to the large soup kettle where the temporary chef was scooping the meal onto tin plates and handing them over to the hungry men. I watched silently from inside the storage tent as the men spread themselves over the thick grass and enjoyed their refreshment. A gnawing hunger suddenly tightened in my stomach. Feeling too shy to approach the kettle for my own meal, I scanned the tent for any remains. Finding a dried flour cake, I ate it quickly, brushing the crumbs off my calico gown. Shyly, I peered out of the little opening and into the dusky air of evening. The vanishing sun sent a reddish glow through the camp. Laughter and quiet conversation carried softly on the warm breeze. Here and there were small groups of men clustered together enjoying their evening meal. *Should I join them?* My insides shrank at the thought and shaking my head gently, I retreated deeper into the tent and leaned up against a large crate. My body sagged with weariness from the long trip. Closing my eyes, I leaned my head back against the wooden boards. *Lord, did I do the right thing in coming here?*

* * *

A bugle pierced the quiet air, sounding revelry. Jumping out of my sleep, I sat up.

"Amy?" I whispered, then realizing where I was, so far from everything I knew, the sickening feeling returned. I pulled back the thick canvas flap and looked out. Mist rose off the soaking grass and a steady drizzle persisted. Another blast of revelry sounded through the air. I shivered as a chill ran down my arms. Digging around in the bag I had brought, I pulled out a heavy shawl and wrapped myself in it. Suddenly a figure burst through the canvas. A middle-aged man with frazzled black hair stopped short in seeing me.

"Oh, I'm sorry Darlin', didn't know anyone was staying in the storage tent." He chuckled to himself and began pulling food out of a crate. "The men get hungry awful fast and it looks like no one else is going to do the cookin' and servin'. Daniel's not out there yet, so it looks like I'll have to do it myself." He laughed again and added, "Reckon I have to do everything around here!" With that, he sauntered out of the tent carrying an armload of food and dishware. I stared after him, still not excited about leaving my hiding place. The tent flap had been thrown back by the man, leaving me vulnerable to the outside. Suddenly the man, some distance away, called back to me.

"Say, would ya mind bringin' that large pot out, Honey?" My face reddened at the familiarity. Then glancing around me, I found the black kettle and heaved it up. *I suppose I have to go out sometime.* I stepped out into the descending mist and realized the camp had come to life despite the rain. Men were rushing about on foot or horseback. I approached the small fire pit in the center of the row of tents and set the pot down next to the talkative man.

"There we go, that'll do it." He said, pulling the pot effortlessly up and hanging it over the fire. "The rain can't stop us from cooking. Haven't seen you before. The name's Paul Hanson." He stuck out a hand and shook mine.

I couldn't help but smile, "Pleased to meet you. I'm Elizabeth Matthews."

Suddenly the man squinted at me, "Say, can you sew up busted shirt buttons?" Laughing I answered in the affirmative and it seemed to satisfy him. He began telling me of several men who had busted shirt buttons that were in need of repair. As we talked, Paul began the preparations of the morning's meal. Embarrassed, I realized that I was the one who should be assuming the responsibilities of cooking and cleaning.

"Please allow me," I offered.

Just then a horse and rider came up and stopped short. The stiff officer I had first met was in the saddle and shouted out, "Prepare to move out by evening! Your commanding officers will march you to the river where you are to board the ship." Digging his heels into the bay, he raced on to continue with his message to the rest of the troops.

"Looks like you got here just in time for the action, Darlin'." Paul said, as he watched the rider disappear into the next row of tents. "Might not be pretty either. I reckon you came to help with the wounded?"

"I'll help where I'm needed." I replied, but couldn't help feeling my stomach turn. I had never seen a battle before ... or hundreds of wounded men. That evening as the sun was reaching its destination in the west, 3,000 men boarded a ship that was to take them down the Mississippi. Walking up the gang plank, I followed other women and some surgeons who were to go along with the soldiers. I gazed out across the wide river as the sun danced and sparkled its fading light on the rippling waters. *Am I ready for what lies ahead?* I glanced back at the soldiers as they moved about looking for a place to settle down. *Am I ready to see these men battered and torn from battle? To help tend their wounds?* I watched them in wonder. *What must it feel like to know you are going into a battle? To know you may feel the sting of burning lead in your body ... or even die?*

Casualty of War
Chapter 24

Amy

"THERE IS SO much to do! So much!" Mrs. Randolph crowed as her knitting needles clicked, "The men need us! They really do! Why this war may last through the winter and they must have warm clothing or they'll freeze to death!" The ladies of the sewing committee nodded their agreement noisily.

Mrs. Denny had just stuffed another cookie in her mouth and the crumbs fell all around her as she nodded in full agreement, "Um, huh!"

"How much suffering and death this war may cause is beyond our comprehension, Ladies ..." Mrs. O'Conner shook her head wearily, "Oh what comforts we will soon have to be deprived of. What agonies we shall endure because of these Rebels!"

"What can we do? War is upon us as a thief in the night. We must gather our courage and aid our men!" Mrs. Denny gulped down a cup of tea as though she were dying of thirst on the battlefield. I could feel the irritation rising within me. Here we sat in a cozy parlor, hardly a sign of war about us, enjoying tea and cookies and lamenting of our impending "hardships." Mrs. O'Conner, a little woman with a furrowed brow, bent over her needle work, her spectacles slipping slowly downward as she worked, until they rested on the point of her nose.

Trying to concentrate on the simple scarf that was assigned for me to work on, I wondered how long it would be before I felt content to sit in a sewing circle chattering on about the evils of war, and the terrible hardships we would suffer. If indeed they would ever reach us, which I greatly doubted. *Was this all we could do for our men?* I wondered, as I glanced down at Mrs. Denny's crumb covered socks. Sighing, I reached for a spool of thread.

"It is a sad situation we're in, Ladies," Mrs. Randolph said as she broke the rare silence, "War changes so many things and people ..."

"You know," Mrs. O' Conner piped up, "I've been hearing rumors of a young girl who went missing just a week ago. She was believed to have been seen somewhere near the Pennsylvania border dressed as a soldier!" A gasp filled the parlor.

"What an indecent girl! What was she about?" The ladies were fanning themselves furiously, forgetting all about the cause and their sewing and knitting for the soldiers.

Mrs. O'Conner leaned forward, "She was bound and determined to join the army, that's what!"

"Oh!" Mrs. Randolph leaned back in horror, "What has the younger generation come to?" she lamented, dabbing her brow.

"The arrogance!" Mrs. Denny stated between nibbles, "As if she could do anything to save our country. Leave the fighting to the men, is what I say!" *Of course she would say that*, I thought, *since it would deprive her of her comforts and cookies ...*

"They say her family has had a hard time and is barely able to feed the seven children. I suppose it was an easy solution! Remove one mouth to feed ... and she will be getting paid ... she can then send some money home." Heads shaking and fans waving, the ladies considered the rumor.

"The things that happen when young people are not brought up properly," Mrs. Randolph stated. "No good can come of such decisions. She will most likely never make it home ... shot in the first battle or caught and tortured."

"Yes, who knows what brutalities those Rebels inflict on their prisoners! I shudder to think of a young girl in the hands of those criminals!" Mrs. Denny spewed.

"Oh my!" Mrs. Randolph was once again on the edge of fainting.

"Amy! Bring some smelling salts for Mrs. Randolph! I'm afraid the topic has exhausted her. She may have a spell!" Mrs. Denny demanded.

After reviving Mrs. Randolph, the ladies continued on the same subject about the cruel Rebel criminals, and how they would never have allowed their daughter to sneak away to join the army. They would go after her, and stop at nothing to keep her from the dangers. How courageous and angelic they appeared in the tales they concocted. I fell into bed and stared up at the ceiling utterly exhausted. I had finally finished all the socks and scarves the ladies had left undone. The wild rumors of the day had nearly exhausted me; tales of rebel sympathizers in our town, of spies, robberies, kidnappings, scandalous far-away battles … and a girl … who joined the army. I sighed and rolled onto my side. The night was pitch black and my window, which faced directly west, showed flashes of lightning far off in the distance. A slight rumble followed and a storm loomed. It appeared as a battlefield to my eyes and I wondered … wondered if Elizabeth was in the middle of it.

* * *

"It's an embarrassment! Our trained troops are retreating in the face of those … those Rebel scums!" Lawrence Howell, Mr. Timothy's hot-tempered nephew, spewed like an angry volcano. He was quite the opposite of his soft-spoken uncle. "Cowards! All of them! When I get my hands on a musket, you won't catch me runnin' from no Reb."

"It's an easy thing to talk about, while we sit here safely in our houses," Mr. Philips passed a plate of biscuits around the table. "Sometimes a retreat is necessary in order to save lives."

"Retreat is never an option, Sir," Lawrence's eyes flashed. "That battle at Manassas should have been our victory! And ended the war this past summer! Now they're all raving about their hero, that Stonewall Jackson!"

"Stonewall Jackson?" I asked confused.

"A Major General from Virginia," Mr. Phillips said, leaning over to enlighten me, "They say another Confederate, General Bernard Bee was inspired by Jackson and called out to his men, 'Look, men! There is Jackson standing like a stonewall! Let us determine to die here, and we will conquer!'"

"What courage," Sarah stated, dabbing her mouth with her napkin. Lawrence Howell scoffed, but remained silent and for once I had to agree with him. Men, like Jackson, were dangerous.

"Courage indeed, Miss Phillips," Mr. Timothy began. "All must find their courage in times such as these, whether on the battlefield or in the home, even as we wait anxiously the news of our loved ones."

Surrounded by friends and neighbors, we ate together in the Phillip's parlor. I felt lonely once more, the deep void of family … and Kelsey.

"Manassas was a great loss, but we must keep up hope that this war will end soon." Mr. Timothy searched the room with tender eyes.

"Not before I can get in it," the seventeen-year-old Lawrence Howell grumbled, "and get a chance to kill some Rebs."

Mr. Phillips shot him a stern look, "This is no game. Killing is not to be thought of in such a manner, young man. All life is precious and valuable in the sight of God. Never kill out of anger, only to protect and for a cause greater than any selfish ambition. We fight to preserve our country, to keep it whole and make it free for all men. No man should be in chains or brought low by his brothers simply because of the color of his skin. If you fight, you fight for your country, for your fellow men. Many will give their lives for that cause."

"Amen," Mr. Timothy whispered. The room grew quiet as we all contemplated the words of Mr. Phillips silently. *To fight for each other.* The idea had not occurred to me in this way. *Yes, fighting for each other against those Rebels. Let it end soon,* I prayed, *Let it end soon.*

"I should be getting back to the Denny's," I began to rise. Everyone was up in an instant.

"So soon?" Sarah asked, touching my arm sorrowfully. *She's nearly as lonely as I am.* I saw the strain of worry in her young eyes.

"I'll visit tomorrow," I smiled and took her hand.

"I'll get your coat," Mr. Phillips stated, always so attentive. He scooted his chair out to escort me to the Denny's which was just a block away.

"Oh, please, you needn't see me home. I'll be quite all right. The sun is only just beginning to fall behind the trees."

"Are you sure?" he asked concerned.

I nodded, "Quite."

"Very well."

The setting sun painted a picture of fiery splendor upon the clouds that stretched across the sky. Breathing in the crisp air, I started down the quiet street. The wagon station was lonely and eerie as I passed. I paused to stare across the platform. I could see myself just over two years ago standing there watching and waving as mother and father had pulled away for the last time. We stood on the deck and waved happily until they disappeared from view. *It was just yesterday, wasn't it? Or was it a lifetime?* It seemed like a lifetime since I had seen their smiling faces, kissed their cheeks ... felt secure in their arms. They would be home as soon as possible they promised. Yes, they'd promised just as Kelsey had. Promised that after he returned, everything would go as planned. We would be married. It was not to be ... his heart had been stolen from me ... too many years away.

I sighed heavily and heard a moan. I froze and listened closely. There it was again, a deep, long pain-filled moan. I searched the platform with my eyes, too afraid to move. Suddenly, I spied a slumped form on the other side of the deck. Someone lay helpless on the floor. I rushed forward.

"Sir! Sir! Do you need help?" I knelt on the floor and tried to turn the body over but this task proved difficult, for he was a man of considerable size and muscle. "Sir ... Henry Sims!" Sure enough, it was the young carpenter. "Henry!" I tried to wake the soldier, gently shaking him by the shoulder. *How did he get here?* He left for the army four months ago. He moaned and as I shook him I suddenly felt a warm wetness on my hand. *Blood! He's bleeding to death!* I lifted my blood covered hand and choked at the sight of it. A pool of blood lay under the young man's wounded shoulder. "Henry!"

The eyelids fluttered a little, "Help me ..." a soft whisper came from his lips.

"Henry, it's Amy, I don't want to leave you." *If only I had something to bind his wound!* Acting quickly, I took my scarf and began tearing away the blood drenched cloth. *Flesh, raw flesh ...* I turned away to lose what contents were in my stomach. I forced myself back to the wounded man, gripping my stomach and began tightly wrapping the shoulder.

"Amy … Amy … where …" Henry began opening his eyes, they were glassy and dazed.

"You're home, Henry, you made it to Gettysburg," I tried to soothe as I tied a tight knot.

"Gettysburg … Gettysburg," he murmured.

"Henry, who did this to you? What happened?"

He swallowed hard and winced, "They came like ghosts." He coughed, "… Out of the dark … never saw them … Rebs."

"Rebs, up here?" Fear seized me at that dreaded word.

"I don't know … don't know where they are … coming home on furlough …" He coughed, "came out of the dark … I panicked and shot at them."

"You've bled too much. I have to get Doctor Phillips!"

"No! Don't leave me!" There was a sudden urgency in his voice that I had not expected. Fear filled his wide, bloodshot eyes.

"Henry, I must! You'll be all right," I began to rise and he caught the hem of my skirt.

"No, Amy! You don't know them like I do! They're everywhere! They'll burn the town and kill us!" He was suddenly sobbing and clinging to my skirt with his good hand, "You can't see them … only hear …" He coughed harshly, "I don't want to die!" I stood horrified and awe struck by this poor hysterical creature who clung like a terrified child to my skirt. "I'm afraid, Amy," he suddenly released me, having exhausted himself. His face paled and he turned staring up into the sky.

I fell down beside him, "Henry, look at me." The eyes remained fixed, but there was still a pulse. I searched his face.

"Don't let them find us, Amy," he whispered closing his eyes and breathing deeply. I stroked his hair off his brow, tears filling my eyes, "I won't, Henry, I won't …" A long sigh came from him, heavy like a summer breeze, then silence. Gently I rocked back and forth too afraid to rise.

"It'll be all right … it'll be all right," I repeated over and over to myself. Darkness crept over the hills and I sat alone with the soldier lying still before me, his head in my lap.

* * *

How my heart longs for you ... simply to know you're safe would be a comfort, but alas the letters from the west are slow at arriving, and I hear rumors of Rebels just west of our little town. Perhaps this is the reason for the delay. Oh, Elizabeth please write soon so that I know all is well with you. My heart grows increasingly anxious. We have already buried several bodies that have returned home in rough wooden coffins. I don't know how I shall bear this war without you ...

I stared down at the words of the letter I had written to Elizabeth. Suddenly they were crushed in my palm. *She has enough problems to be sure, enough sorrow and death around her. She will send a letter soon and I will write another day when I have something joyful to tell of.* I rose from the desk and stared out the window. *Should I have gone with her? I feel so useless, so trapped. If only I could do something more, more than knitting and sewing socks and scarves.*

* * *

"How fleeting is life, how like a vapor is man ... are we not told that we are here for only a little while? But life is over in the blink of an eye." Mr. Timothy raised his eyes up to the sky. The four coffins lay before him shrouded in wildflowers. "We send these souls up to you now, Father, knowing that they died with honor, with hope in their hearts. And now we wait ... wait eagerly for the day when we meet again. Help us to remain strong ... let us make them proud. We will not cower or give into fear, just as they did not. This war will end. The day will come when victory will spread over the land and also peace ... peace. Yet, the heart will continue to ache, and loneliness will remain, but let us take comfort that these men: fathers, brothers, sons ... did not die in vain." Slowly the coffins were lowered one by one into the six-foot graves. Flowers were thrown in, prayers whispered and tears shed.

The Wounded Soldier
Chapter 25

Elizabeth

November 7, 1861

WE HAD ARRIVED early in the morning, landing three miles above Belmont, Missouri, and had begun attacking the Confederate garrison stationed at Belmont. I had been told this battle was part of the general's plan to capture the Confederate stronghold at Columbus, Kentucky, just across the river. Confederate General Leonidas Polk, who was in Columbus, had troops stationed at Belmont, but on hearing the battle across the river there, he sent in reinforcements from Columbus. Our general, General Ulysses S. Grant, had sent a detachment up to Paducah, Kentucky in the hopes that Polk would believe it to be the main attack and Belmont only a diversion. Polk however did not buy Grant's trick, but sent more reinforcements into Belmont. Five Confederate regiments arrived at Belmont just as Grant ordered his men to get back on the boats. We headed back to Cairo. It was truly an inconclusive result, yet both sides claimed some kind of victory.

* * *

The unearthly screams and groans of the wounded and dying came echoing through the camp. The sound grew ever louder as the wounded came dragging themselves in from the boat, or leaning on the arm of a friend. My hands shook as I wrung out yet another rag in the basin of boiled river water and handed it to the surgeon beside me. After caring for the very seriously injured on the boat ride back to Cairo, we quickly set up a hospital just outside the main encampment. I found it hard to believe this miserable scene was the same place I had come to only a couple days before. As the evening dusk crept over our makeshift hospital, I lit candles under the low canvas and set them in different areas of the large pavilion. They seemed to shiver as they tried to give some dim light to the darkening surroundings. As I took a candle to a nearby table, a hand reached out and took hold of my apron.

"Please ... Miss ... water ..." a weak voice whispered. I turned and saw a young man, his face bloody and bruised by the butt of a rifle in hand to hand combat. All within me wanted to tear away from him and run outside to get away from the horrors of war. Bracing myself, I laid a hand over the one that still clung to my skirts.

"Of course, Sir," I said in a shaky voice and, dipping a ladle full of water, held it to his lips. I lifted the young man's head up as he drank.

"God bless you ..." he whispered as I hurried away, trying to keep myself from surrendering to emotion.

The surgeon came up to me, "I need you to bandage a man's hand for me. I must tend to the more seriously injured." He walked quickly to his business. Nodding mindlessly, I unwound some bandages from a roll and approached the area that the surgeon had pointed out. A young man sat on a low table holding his right arm. Shrapnel was lodged under the skin and blood seeped from the wound. I grimaced. *I didn't know I was going to have to remove the pieces. Didn't the surgeon know I had never done anything of this sort before?* The face of the young man was hidden by the dim light and his dark hair blended into the surroundings. I reluctantly reached for his hand, but drew back as the young soldier looked up. Cold blue eyes met mine in complacency, but then widened as recognition dawned on the soldier. My lips moved but no sound came. I fumbled with the bandage in my hand and stepped back in utter disbelief. The young soldier was none other than the mysterious blacksmith from Gettysburg!

Nathan began to stand, his eyes darting for a way out. Wincing, he fell back into his seat. My eyes travelled to his leg where a steady flow of blood trailed from the knee to the ankle. The surgeon had not noticed the bullet in the leg. Old, forgotten memories and emotions rushed upon me. The confusion, the unnerving conversations, the irrational anger, the image of my finger pulling the trigger of Father's pistol and Adam's form falling to the ground rushed through my mind in the blink of an eye. With my hand flying to my mouth, I began moving backwards slowly, shaking my head. Spinning around, I flew out the opening, throwing the canvas flap aside. The surgeon grabbed my arm.

"Miss Matthews, you must tend to the wounded. I know this must be hard for you as it is your first time seeing a battle scene, but you must help those who are fighting for the cause." He didn't understand. I did want to help. I just could not face *him* again. The surgeon shoved the bandages back into my hands, "Tend to that wounded man."

I stood frozen in my tracks. I lifted my hand toward the surgeon as he walked away, opening my mouth saying weakly to no one, "I … I can't …" A minute passed, then taking a deep breath, I turned back around. I had thought these feelings and emotions had passed with time. Seeing him again took me back to all those confusing and irrational emotions once again. Yet, I had to go back inside the tent. If I didn't now, I would spend the rest of my time here hiding from those sharp blue eyes.

I forcibly moved one foot in front of the other, unconsciously twisting the bandage in my hand. Looking up, I saw Nathan sitting as he had before, staring intently at the ground: his mind most likely flashing through the same memories. As I approached, he glanced up and flinched, then watched me steadily. Avoiding his gaze, I carried a basin of water over to where he sat and set it beside him. Reluctantly, I reached for his wounded hand. As I did so, Nathan stood up and, grasping whatever support he could, began moving away.

"Mr. Tyler, your hand needs care," I said softly, but rather hoping he would go.

Nathan turned, "I'm fine. Take care of those who really need it." After saying so, he proceeded moving toward the tent opening. Another surgeon stepped in his way.

"Now young man, you sit right back down. You're not going to do any good for your country this way." Grasping Nathan's broad shoulders, he began turning him back toward me. My insides twisted during these uncomfortable seconds.

"No, I said I'm fine." Nathan spoke sternly and pushed the surgeon aside with his good hand. Trying too quickly to get away, he stumbled on his bad leg. The surgeon caught him and led him back to the low table.

"Nurse, take care of this man and see that he doesn't try to get away again."

Nodding methodically, I fought my own urge to disappear from this awkward situation. I knelt down beside the table that Nathan sat on and held out my hand once again. The cold blue eyes stared into mine with a look of determination. Slowly he brought his bloodied hand forward. I dipped the cloth into the basin and began wiping the blood from the skin around the wound. The silence was agonizing as minute after minute passed with no words. Even the cries of the wounded seemed to have gone silent. Cautiously, I spoke up, anything was better than this unbearable silence.

"It was a bad fight, wasn't it?" I said softly, not looking up.

There was a pause, "We won, didn't we." It was a statement, not a question. As I wiped around the shrapnel, I noticed an old scar on the same arm. It was round, like a bullet hole. *Nathan had not been in any engagements before this, had he?* A memory flew into my mind: multiple shots had resounded. *My finger caused one pistol to fire, Nathan must have also shot at Adam, but ... had Adam shot Nathan?*

I asked quietly, "What is the other bullet scar from?"

Nathan flinched, then said, "He was your friend, wasn't he?" I glanced up, a stinging feeling in my heart. Suddenly the eyes began searching mine. "You still believe him, don't you?" he asked sharply. "I'm not a murderer, and I didn't murder your friend."

Suppressing the old illogical resentment in my heart, I shuddered at the memory. I realized he didn't know that I was the one who had shot Adam.

I replied honestly, "Everyone knows the truth. They know you didn't murder the banker. They know Adam was the real criminal."

Nathan stared at me, "And you?" he asked determinedly.

I quickly changed the subject, "I found something that belonged to you several months after you left town. It was a letter," I looked up, "from your mother." Nathan stiffened. Not receiving a reply, I continued, "I'm sorry what happened between you and—"

Nathan abruptly cut me off, "It doesn't matter." Then he stood up and added angrily, "You had no business reading that. That was your problem in the first place; you couldn't leave people to themselves. You had to go investigating everyone else's lives." Nathan was now moving out of the tent.

I felt the anger well up inside me and retorted, "Well, if I wouldn't have been there that day, Adam would have killed you!"

"Yeah," he scoffed, "and I'm sure everyone would have been just fine with that," saying so, he disappeared from the entrance of the tent. I tossed the rag I had been wiping his hand with angrily to the ground and groaned in frustration.

The Time Has Come
Chapter 26

Amy

GREAT WHITE CLOUDS rolled in from the west laden with snow. Already, flurries were beginning to fall slowly. Standing in the waist high grass, I closed my eyes letting the wind rush over my face. *Winter will soon be upon us.* I stared across the field at the distant house. I would not go any closer, not close enough to see the boards that covered the windows and the piles of leaves that hid the walkways. It was in that house that I had grown from a child to a woman. Mother, Father ... Elizabeth ... they would always be there in my mind. They would be waiting for me by the fire, singing songs ... laughing. The fields of tall grass rippled around the farmhouse and the bare trees waved their branches as the snow fell more heavily. The clouds loomed directly overhead. *I cannot stay,* the sudden realization frightened ... and freed me at the same time. *Men are dying and I can no longer sit idly at home and watch the wounded and dead return to be buried. Never again will I hide my face in the safety of Gettysburg while our soldiers die on distant battlefields. My time has come ...*

* * *

Staring up at the ceiling, I listened to the ticking clock. It was the very early hours of the morning. *Just a little longer.* My fingers gripped tightly to the heavy quilt that covered me. I was afraid, afraid of the unknown, afraid of what I was about to become a part of, afraid of dying. But I no longer cared what Elizabeth would think if she knew, what the townspeople would say when they found out I was gone. *It's time to act on what I believe and never, never look back.*

Slowly I rose, slipped a foot out of the warm secure bed onto the hard, cold floor. Reluctantly, my fingers searched for the scissors I had found while raiding Mrs. Denny's sewing basket. Taking a golden lock in my hand, I stared at it a moment, then biting my lip, I began cutting. The long blonde strands fell along with the tears until at last it was over. Quickly, I dressed in the spare clothes I had found in the closet. The breeches were a strange contrast to the heavy petticoats and dresses. Lifting the heavy sack on my shoulder, I pulled out my Bible from the desk drawer and stuffed it in Father's leather sack. Gathering up the hair on the floor, I tossed it into the fire and watched as the flames engulfed the evidence of what I had done. I took one last glance back at the lonesome room. It looked as if no one had ever lived there.

* * *

Heart pounding, I opened the back door and slipped out into the chilly November air. The stars were beginning to disappear from the greying sky, and the first hints of dawn crept over the horizon. I shivered, buttoning the coat up to my neck. I wished I had a scarf, but the only one I owned looked too feminine. Snowflakes were falling calmly from the sky, and I hoped it would be enough to cover my tracks. I moved through the town like a thief, darting from behind each house to the next. The shops and houses were dark and silent, but I would take no chance of being seen. Light shown on the ground in front of me as a door screeched opened. Sarah Phillips came forth wrapped in a thick shawl and descended the stairs to pick up a brown and white spotted cat that was meowing at the landing. I hesitated, then quickly crept up behind her and covered her mouth. A few minutes struggle ensued in which I realized I had greatly underestimated the strength of my young friend.

"Sarah, it's Amy," I hissed in her ear. I released her mouth and spun her around to face me.

"Oh," she breathed relieved. "You scared me half to … What are you doing?" she quickly looked me up and down, her eyes bulging out.

"Sarah, you won't tell. Please, you have to promise me!" I gripped her wrist tightly.

"Tell what, Amy? What are you doing?" her whisper was rising rapidly. "You know how unseemly this is?"

"Shhh! I'm … I'm running away, Sarah! I can't take it anymore. Staying here worrying about Elizabeth … Kelsey." I muttered the last words and Sarah grew confused, "I can't. I'm a burden to the Denny's. I'm no good around here. I'm finished with it. I have to start a new life."

"But you can't leave! What about Kelsey?" There was a long pause. Sarah wouldn't tell if I asked her. I knew she wouldn't. She could be trusted. Ever since we were children she kept secrets well.

"Kelsey has gone missing. An officer came asking if I knew where he was. No one has seen him. He was ordered to report at the recruiting office, but he never showed up. I suppose they don't want many people to know and stir things up, in hopes that he'll return to town. His own parents have been away visiting Mr. McCarthy's aunt. They have no idea."

Sarah's mouth dropped open, "Oh, Amy, I'm sorry."

I shook my head, "No … It's over between us. You mustn't tell anyone about any of it."

"But where will you go? And dressed like that!"

I sighed, "I'm headed for a cavalry recruiting station. I've heard of one not too far from here. I'll be joining sometime tomorrow night, I hope. Sarah, I'm very good with horses, you know that … I can do this."

"Amy! This is ridiculous! You can't go through with it! You're going to dress like a man for months? Hide your identity?"

Slowly, but stubbornly I nodded, "Sarah, I have to. There's nothing here for me anymore. I know there are soldiers dying. I've seen them come home," I choked remembering the coffins disappearing under the fresh dug earth. "I have a right to fight for my country just as much as any of them; to give my life if necessary." I broke out in a sweat despite the cold, as I spoke these words and felt the weight of them crushing down upon me.

"No, Amy! Those are fighting *men*! You're just a girl! A *girl*, Amy, you can't do it better than they can!"

Tears formed in my eyes as I felt growing emotion. I grasped Sarah by the shoulders. "It's not if I can do it better than they, Sarah, it's what I can do, *myself*, what I can give. And if I can give it all and help just a little, and if my life will save others, then God's will be done. But I *will not* sit by hoping this war will end soon and that our boys will come home. It's just not in my blood." I met Sarah's eyes and saw the tears slipping down her cheeks. Seeing the determination in my eyes, she said, "All right, Amy, I will not be the one to stand in your way. You have the courage that most of us can only dream of having. Go and do all you can."

We embraced. Wiping away tears, I asked, "Will you write to Elizabeth on my behalf so she doesn't worry about me? She mustn't know I'm gone."

Sarah nodded, "I will."

"Please look after the school … and drop by my house … just to make sure everything is well."

"Of course, Amy!" Sarah embraced me one last time, and I quickly turned away and disappeared into the darkness.

* * *

A sort of blizzard had whipped up within two hours, and I struggled to stay on the road. The houses along the path were invisible behind the screen of falling snow. I had spent the whole day wandering along the road in this blizzard and still there was no sign of the cavalry unit I wished to join up with. My hands were numb and ached terribly as they froze in the thick pockets of my coat. I began to feel desperate to find the camp. If I didn't, I might collapse in the snow somewhere, buried until the spring thaw! I decided that after a day alone, the cavalry regiment would be a welcome sight instead of a frightening one.

"Halt!"

I jumped, my heart pounding. Glancing around, I saw no one. Then slowly a heavily cloaked figure emerged from the storm, bayonet pointed directly at me.

"What are you doing out in this weather, boy?" he called. The voice was high like an adolescent not yet changed to a man's voice.

"I need to speak with an officer," I nervously spat the words out.

"An officer, huh," there was a pause and I guessed he was scrutinizing me. "All right, I'll take you to an officer." The bayonet twitched to the side motioning me to fall in step with him.

"Hey there, Fredricks! Keep an eye on my post," he shouted to a figure that stood on the edge, disappearing into the blizzard. "I'm taking this here fella to the house." I reached up to pull on my leather sack; it felt hard and cold.

"Officers are quartering at the house. Mrs. McPhee's our hostess." He snorted, "Wish she had a big enough house to accommodate the entire regiment. You a runaway?"

I glanced over, but could hardly see the face beside me. It was all covered up with a hat and scarf. "Don't really have much to run away from," I answered.

"Uh … You're a might young to be on your own already," he mumbled from inside the scarf. I could have said the same about him judging from his half-grown voice, but I kept to myself. We passed rows of white tents popping out of the snow, nearly drowning. Bits of hay peeked out from under the canvasses, trembling in the harsh winds. There were no lanterns, no fires, but I saw a small light inside one of the tents, perhaps a candle. The guard hit the side of the canvass with the butt of his gun.

"Lights out in there!" Instantly the tent became dark as the light was snuffed out. I shivered wondering how warm a tent could be in this weather.

"Most of the boys here never been south of the Pennsylvania border; never seen a Reb before. I was in a skirmish awhile back before I transferred to the cavalry. Thought riding would be better than walking."

"Is it?" I became curious.

"Got its ups and downs … you'll decide for yourself once you get in with the common privates. Officers have it better. Naturally."

Out of the night rose a two-story log cabin. A warm light glowed from its glass-paned windows. Snow sat on the roof like frosting on a gingerbread house, and smoke trailed up into the night air.

"Well, here's the officers' snug quarters. Reckon you don't know too much about how things run around here," he eyed me. "Wait by the door until I send you in. What's your name, boy?"

"Michael, Michael Jones,"

"Well, Michael, the Colonel don't take no nonsense from anybody, so stay sharp."

A lump caught in my throat as the guard approached the cabin and spoke to the men standing beside the door. One of them nodded and said something. The door was opened and a burst of light poured out. It enveloped me into its warm embrace as I stepped dreamily into the house. For a moment, I became aware of nothing but my numb limbs thawing and aching all over as the cold left my body. The light was bright, almost blinding, compared to the winter storm that roared outside. The guard had disappeared and I stood as directed near the door. The smell of fresh biscuits, pine needles, burning oak and coffee overwhelmed me and I felt weary down to the very bone. My trek from Gettysburg had taken longer than expected due to the blizzard.

Slowly, I became aware of a murmur coming from what I assumed was the parlor. Suddenly a short, grey-haired woman, apron tied around her waist, scurried past with a plate of biscuits, the aroma trailing behind. I glanced around at the cozy looking home. There were sturdy logs piled up in a corner, a heavy rug under my feet and calico curtains hung in the windows. It seemed so peaceful and homelike that I could almost forget my reason for intruding. I imagined I was visiting an old friend. Drowsiness surrounded me and my knees began to buckle.

"Follow me, boy," a voice roused me. I quickly stepped from my cozy corner and followed the guard into the parlor. A group of officers were gathered, some sitting in hard wooden chairs at a rectangular table, while others stood near a fire that glowed and cracked in the hearth. They talked quietly amongst themselves as if someone were sleeping in the rooms beyond. A few glanced up at me, but I tried not to pay too much attention. We approached a wooden door and the guard opened it and stood back. My heart pounded. Now was the moment for which I had been waiting.

The door creaked shut behind me and I nervously glanced back at it. I couldn't make out any definite objects in the poorly lit room. Shadows seemed to lurk in every direction. A single light flickered from one corner. A desk and chair sat before the fireplace unoccupied with papers scattered all over. My eyes adjusted and I saw a silhouette in the window. A tall thinly built figure stood in the window with hands clasped behind his back. Finally, he turned.

"You're the young man that my guards found wandering near camp?" The words sounded indifferent.

Staring at the still shadowy figure, I felt myself growing suddenly smaller. I bit my tongue to awaken it, "Yes, Sir."

"Where are you from?" The voice was deep, full and confident.

"Gettysburg," I choked the word out.

"Are you headed somewhere?"

"Here, Sir ... I," I hesitated, "I came to join you ... your regiment." There was silence and all seemed to be frozen still. Then the silhouette disappeared and made its way around an object in the room and came closer, stopping just a few paces away. The dim fire light fell upon black boots, the blue uniform, trimmed with yellow cavalry stripes down the pant leg, a red sash and the bars on the shoulders. However, it revealed not the face which was still veiled in the darkness of the room.

"How old are you?"

"Eighteen, Sir," I thought it better to remain as young as possible, since being a woman would make me appear hardly over fifteen. There was no response and I could feel his eyes scrutinizing me. He walked a slow half circle around me and I involuntarily held my breath. It seemed ages before he stepped away and faced the fire, thoughtfully gazing at it.

He then turned and said, "I've been needing an aide; do you think you can handle the job?" I swallowed hard. *An aide to the colonel? It would be a safer job, wouldn't it?*

Quickly I decided, "I can, Sir."

He examined me once more, "We'll see." The words sounded daunting. "A two-week trial. Major Sanders will train you," opening the door, he spoke to the guard at the entrance. The man quickly left on some errand. The colonel opened it wide and stepped back. "Mrs. McPhee will show you to a bed. You'll report to this room at five o'clock tomorrow morning."

The grey-haired old woman was standing a little in front of the door. I stepped toward her, though my legs felt like they had been rooted to the floor and they began to shake.

"What is your name?" The colonel asked again from the dim room.

"Michael, Sir. Michael Jones."

"Very well. Tomorrow morning then, Corporal Jones."

I was led down a short hall into a room. Mrs. McPhee held a candle in her hand and set it on the mantle of the fireplace. She then went to a closet to pull out a large quilt.

"I think this will do. There, set your bag over there and settle down on this bed." Her gnarled fingers unfolded the quilt and she laughed a little, "You'll be gettin' up early I expect, so I'll set a cup of tea there on the table. I imagine the colonel will want you in uniform. Hmmm … Don't know why you young boys are so eager to join in this fightin'. But then everyone has their reasons. I just hope yours' is enough to get you through what's ahead." She paused, "Now would you listen to me going on so?" She began mumbling almost completely to herself as she made the bed.

Exhausted, I soon found myself lying on my side in a dark room covered in a warm quilt. It was almost like being home. As I closed my eyes, I tried to imagine Elizabeth in the room beside mine, but the low murmur of voices outside my door made it impossible to forget my whereabouts. Hearing the wind howling around the cabin, I remembered the boys outside in the winter storm. But I was too tired to feel guilty for the warm bed and thick quilt that surrounded me. I was drifting off. *What time is it? Sometime around midnight.* A door squeaked open and shut … muffled voices … a question.

"We'll see how he does," said the familiar commanding voice. More voices, discussions, and a dark veil fell over me in a luxurious sleep.

A New Start
Chapter 27

Elizabeth

THE DAY DRAGGED slowly past. I sat huddled in my own tent in the women's encampment. We were situated about a hundred yards behind the soldiers' winter shelters that had been erected to wait out the coming season.

These past few weeks I had been busy mending woolen jackets and knitting socks in preparation for the cold. I had met a few of the wives and a young woman, for whose acquaintance I felt very grateful. I lay down the last woolen sock in the pile I had been working on all day. Pulling back the tent flap, I saw that dusk had crept up while I had been occupied. With the darkness came the renewed sense of loneliness I felt every night since arriving. For several nights after the Battle of Belmont, I had been considering going back to Gettysburg, but then a deeper feeling pervaded. *What would I go back to? An empty house. Gossiping Women. Patronizing people. A sympathetic sister and brother-in-law. No, I can't go back. There is so much more to this world than all that. So much I can do ...* I glanced around the quiet encampment. The soft, distant sound of a fiddle reached my ears. *So, I can't go back ... and I can't just sit in the tent hiding any longer.* I forced myself to stand and follow the soft notes toward a campfire situated in between the men and women's encampment.

A large group sat around the fire humming low, sweet notes along with the instrument. Scanning the faces, I spotted the young woman who I had met during the days I had spent here. Ellen Parker was a couple years younger than me and from what I could tell, she despised the "proper lady-like ways." When we first met, she promptly told me she would much rather be fighting in the war with her brother than all this fussing about sewing and cooking. Feeling a bit awkward about approaching the group, I slipped onto the log beside her, nudging her with my elbow. They were just ending the last verse of "It Is Well". The girl smiled at me as she started the next song, singing along with her brother, Will, who sat across the fire pit. The song they sang was new to me, as it seemed to be for most of the others as well. But as I listened, the words seemed to bring peace to the atmosphere. Will's tenor voice blended beautifully with his sister's soprano and seemed to linger in the still night air.

> *Sweet hour of prayer, Sweet hour of prayer,*
> *That calls me from a world of care,*
> *And bids me at my Father's throne,*
> *Make all my wants and wishes known:*
> *In seasons of distress and grief,*
> *My soul has often found relief,*
> *And oft escaped the tempter's snare,*
> *By thy return, sweet hour of prayer*

After they had finished, we all sat quietly, meditating on the words. Leaning my head back, I gazed up at the bright stars. After another long silence, a woman's voice broke the tranquil moment.

"Well! Now we might as well sing something jolly!" She smiled at those seated around the fire, then slapped her husband's arm. "Well, Samuel? Think of something jolly to sing!"

The surgeon raised his eyes from the fire and said rather gloomily, "Oh, Margret, leave the people in peace." I suppressed a smile as Ellen leaned over and whispered, "Wouldn't that be quite a shock when Doctor Samuel Alton thinks of something jolly," she giggled.

"Ah! Miss Ellen! I see you have found something jolly to sing about? Well then, let's hear it!" Mrs. Alton reclaimed her seat beside her husband. I couldn't help but notice the man rolling his eyes, as he leaned his head in his hands and stared gloomily back into the flames.

Ellen began:

> *Stand up, stand up for Jesus,*
> *Ye soldiers of the cross;*
> *Lift high His royal banner,*
> *It must not suffer loss!*

We all joined in for the chorus:

> *From victory unto victory,*
> *His army shall He lead,*
> *Till every foe is vanquished,*
> *And Christ is Lord indeed!*

I examined the group as we continued and noticed the quiet soldier I had met the first day. He had continued to help me over the last few weeks with the meals. Most of the words we exchanged were on my part. Nevertheless, Daniel, as he was called, was beginning to slowly join in the conversations. Seated beside him was John, who had arrived in camp a while after me. It was comforting to have one connection from my hometown, someone I had grown up with. Also, near the fire was Paul Hanson, the talkative soldier I had met the first morning of my stay in camp. Beside him was Mark, a middle-aged, quiet man. Dark curly hair topped a face of silent contentment as he listened to the others singing around the fire. Several other men and their wives sat around, enjoying the time they could spend together. A feeling of relief came over me as I realized Nathan Tyler was not in the group. I had spent the last few weeks trying to avoid him and I'm sure he was doing the same.

* * *

December 1861

"All right, Ladies," Doctor Alton began in his slow, deep voice. "The commanding officers have suggested that today the surgeons train their nurses in the proper procedures. And we will continue to do this on a daily basis. I know it's the dead of winter and all of you would rather be sitting warm and comfortable in your tents," then he said under his breath, "or at least I would," then continued, "But, we have our orders and so ... here we are."

Mrs. Alton gave a short laugh, "Oh Samuel! What a hoot you are!"

I suppressed a smile along with the other ladies. It was good to feel the urge to laugh again. It seemed too long since I had felt that way, and even though at times I felt lonely for my sister and Gettysburg, I think I was finally starting to feel at home here, among these kind people. Doctor Alton was slowly raising his melancholy eyes toward his wife, with not the least inclination of a smile. He sighed and continued, "First I'm going to go find us a victim to practice on. You ladies wait here."

Plodding out from us, he left the large tent canvas. At the Battle of Belmont, all had been chaos; no one knew exactly where to help, but all had assisted as best we could, wherever we found the need. Now that it was winter, and the war would be held off until spring, we could focus on preparing ourselves for the next battle.

Besides myself, Mrs. Alton and Ellen, there were two ladies assigned to help Doctor Alton. One was the wife of another man in the camp, Mrs. Dickerson. Mrs. Dickerson was a very thin, serious lady. Her hair was wound into a tight bun at the back of her neck and she wore a pair of spectacles down on the tip of her nose. She was very reserved and always seemed to have one eyebrow raised in contempt. The other was a Mrs. Higgins, a nervous woman, who, once she started talking, just continued jabbering on quietly to herself. She was a small woman of about thirty-five years. She had left her five children with relatives to follow her husband into battle. It seemed, however, she did not enjoy this part of it, if any. Leaning over to her, I asked, "Mrs. Higgins, are you eager to learn how to properly administer the procedures for the wounded?"

The woman determinedly shook her head, "Oh Miss Matthews, I don't think I'll be able to do it, really I don't. Once, when I saw blood, I nearly fainted!" Just then Doctor Alton returned with his 'victim'.

"Hello Ladies! The name's David," the young man nodded to each of us. "Doc here says I'm to be your patient to practice on. Oh!" Abruptly he groaned and grasped at his leg. "Oh! It's my leg!" He stumbled around and landed himself squarely on the operating table. Popping back up in a sitting position, he removed his hat and bowed playfully as we laughed and clapped for his demonstration. Only Mrs. Dickerson did not seem in the least bit amused. She gazed at the young man over her spectacles and lifted her eyebrow even higher.

"That's quite enough," Doctor Alton said in his quiet manner as he pushed the young man back into a lying position.

"Oh, David! What a hoot you are! Just like my Samuel!" Mrs. Alton cackled out loud. David raised himself from his position with his brows furrowed. He pointed at Dr. Alton and mouthed, "*Him?*" Doctor Alton came over and pushed him back down, the whole time David giving us a playful confused look at the comment of Dr. Alton's being a 'hoot'. Ellen giggled beside me. Seeing it was time to start work, I nudged Ellen and nodded toward Doctor Alton, who stood before us holding clean cloths and surgical utensils.

He began in a monotone voice, "This man was shot in the leg and the bullet is wedged in the bone." David gave a loud cry at the words. Doctor Alton rolled his eyes and mumbled, "I should have gotten us a better patient." I turned and laid a hand on my mouth, pretending to cough as I couldn't retain the laughter. "All right, Ladies, let's examine the patient." We all gathered around the table where the young man lay.

"You know, I don't believe I've ever had so much female attention in all my life!" David joked. Doctor Alton indifferently laid a sheet over the patient's face. He proceeded in telling us the proper way to remove a bullet and cover a wound. He explained how to determine whether or not the leg should be amputated. I carefully wrapped the cloth around David's leg.

"How's that?" I asked the surgeon, proudly displaying my work. Doctor Alton came over, felt around the wrappings and then glumly shook his head.

"No, no, this will never do," then he sighed and showed me the proper way to do it. I smiled at his melancholy behavior and re-wrapped it as he had shown me.

An Important Task
Chapter 28

Amy

A DOOR SQUEAKED. *Elizabeth is starting breakfast. No, she's gone.* My eyes opened to a dark room. A strange, soothing herbal scent filled the room. Sitting up I found a warm cup of tea had been placed on the nightstand. *Mrs. McPhee.* As I lifted the heavy blanket, a rush of cold air swept in about me and I gulped down the soothing warm drink quickly. The sensation cleared my foggy thoughts. *It must be nearly five o'clock in the morning.* Quickly, I rose and found a wool uniform draped across a chair. *Would it fit?* Propping a chair up against the door, I changed as fast as possible. To my satisfaction and relief, the jacket turned out to be slightly bulky, but not large enough to be returned for another. *It will do.* I used father's old comb to brush out my cropped hair and tried to make it look similar to the way the boys in town had worn theirs. I did my best, but pulled my cap on tight to my forehead and slid into the black leather boots.

Pushing open the door, I found the house to be vacant. Light glowed from the kitchen; Mrs. McPhee was up cooking for her "guests." In the parlor, there was not a trace of the company of officers who had been present the night before, save the ashes in the corner tray. The colonel's door was slightly ajar and I gently tapped it after taking a deep breath.

"Enter," was the short reply. I pushed it open and saw a fire was started. I could see now a bed that sat in the corner, a large armchair placed upon a thick rug, and at the desk sat a blond-haired man of about thirty.

His head was bent as he intently searched through the papers that were scattered about the desk. I approached timidly and he glanced up; soft green eyes met mine. The man rose suddenly, "Corporal Michael Jones, I believe," he hesitated. "I'm second in command of this regiment, Major Robert Sanders."

"Good morning, Sir." *So, it wasn't the colonel I had spoken with last night.* I felt relieved. I had been more nervous at the colonel's questioning than when I had taken my teaching exam. I had been dreading our next meeting.

To my surprise a slight smile played on the major's lips, "I'll be training you as the colonel's aide ... and giving you some basic instructions, since you joined us so recently."

Training with Major Sanders was nothing like what I imagined. He patiently walked me through very basic protocol: when to salute, how to salute, how to introduce an officer before allowing him to enter the colonel's presence for a conference, and where to stand. By mid-day I had a proper salute and a firm grasp of military protocol. The major was a gentle and patient teacher and I greatly appreciated his understanding of my lack of military formalities. *I could not have asked for an easier position.*

"All right, Corporal Jones, I believe we will resume at one o'clock," he said drawing out a pocket watch to check the time. "I think it's important you become acquainted with the camp before we continue. I shall be your guide."

Be seen? Outside? Around the camp? The darkness last night had hidden me from curious onlookers. I saluted and turned sharply to leave the room. Mrs. McPhee was hurrying about again preparing the table. It was snowing more gently now and despite my fears, I longed to get a breath of fresh air. Officers began to crowd into the room and I squeezed my way unnoticed past the swarm, which was an easy task, since they seemed to be occupied with each other. Most talked boisterously among themselves as they entered. To my surprise, I found many of them looked little over twenty, with the exception of a few gentlemen who appeared to be in their late thirties. I managed to squeeze out the door just as a young captain entered. He glanced down as I hurried past pulling on the heavy winter coat that had been issued to me.

Standing on the front porch, I gazed out at the sea of tents extending itself into the field to the right of the cabin. White canvases sat snug in the thick blanket of snow, smoke rising from between the tents. Long lines of picketed horses tossed and munched hay. I had never seen so many horses in one place, hundreds of them, mainly bays and chestnuts with a few greys and blacks. They were all well-built Morgan horses, I guessed. Turning away again, I saw men huddled in heavy winter overcoats sitting around the fires, clasping steaming cups in their gloved hands. The smell of coffee, hay and some delicious gruel filled the air. I wandered off the porch and watched the snow falling all around me. It was nearing Christmas and my thoughts wandered to the days at home sitting around the hearth while Father read the birth of Christ, mother knitted, and Elizabeth and I sat huddled together drinking warm tea. The smell of mother's gingerbread cookies baking in the oven filled the house with a comforting aroma.

A strange dog came up beside me and sniffed my boots. His tail wagged cheerfully and he gazed up at me with gentle eyes. I crouched down to pet him.

"Hey there," I murmured. The dog seemed to smile and turned a circle happily, then bolted away. I watched him go. Then suddenly, I became aware of someone watching me. Turning my gaze quickly, I saw a black stallion standing like a statue in the snow just ten feet away. On his back sat a man in a heavy overcoat, a saber attached to his side, and a plume in his hat.

"The uniform fits you well, Corporal Jones." The voice I recognized, but the face, which I hadn't seen before, was younger than I would have guessed. Dark eyes shadowed by thick brows watched me closely from under the brimmed hat. A neatly trimmed mustache and goatee decorated the handsome but solemn face. I felt pinned down under the haughty gaze, yet slowly rose to my feet.

"Thank you, Sir," was all I managed to say. Then suddenly remembering my training, I saluted as best I could. The colonel raised his hand to return it, but his face was unimpressed. The stallion turned with hardly a jerk of the reins and walked toward the house. I followed awkwardly. With a twist in my gut, I wished it had been the major I was to serve.

* * *

Evening had come at last and found me in the colonel's room leaning over a map of troop positions along with a list of the various corps, divisions, brigades and regiments. I found the military education fascinating, and therefore, devoured all such documents, maps and anything the major was able to find. He commended me on my studious nature and quick mind. However, the colonel seemed unimpressed. Sanders sat beside me explaining where the headquarters of generals could be found and so forth.

"You see, Corporal, every so often the colonel may send you to deliver a message. However, we're not on the front lines, and therefore, communication has not been so vital." He began rolling up the map, "Once we've caught up with the infantry, there will be more of that to be sure."

"Major, if I may," I hesitated, looking up at him, "what exactly is my … role?" Major Sanders looked pensive as he paused like a father trying to find a way of explaining something to one of lesser knowledge.

"Well, corporal, an aide's number one duty is to the colonel." He folded his arms, "You are his personal assistant. Sometimes acting as a secretary, yet in some ways you are the closest trusted officer, a confidential assistant." He smiled over at me and I slowly began to better understand my role, a personal assistant … to the colonel. I could see being an assistant, but a confidant … Somehow the colonel didn't strike me as a man who needed reassurance.

Sanders leaned back with a deep sigh, "Corporal, I believe you have one of the most responsible and … complex jobs in this regiment." A slight smile came over him as he glanced at me. Just then Colonel Anderson appeared in the doorway. We rose to our feet.

"As you were." He removed his hat and overcoat, placing them on a hook in the wall and made his way to the window. Sanders began stacking papers and I distractedly continued my work. The colonel stood like a statue beside the window, hands clasped behind his back, shoulders back and feet apart, staring out at no apparent object. The clock ticked louder and louder in the corner and the scratching of my pen sounded irritatingly loud. A strange tension had entered the room that caused even the silence to be distracting. I had a hard time keeping on task. A quarter of an hour later, Sanders removed himself from the room and I was left alone with the colonel, finishing a small stack of papers Sanders had left me to study.

The clock continued its loud ticking and the fire snapped and popped behind me. Suddenly the colonel moved from the window and seemed to wander about the room pacing from one end to the other. This distracted me more than anything and my brow furrowed as I tried to concentrate on the list before me.

"How long have you lived in Gettysburg, Corporal?" The sudden question caught me off guard.

"All my life, Sir."

"Since 1845?"

Quickly estimating, I answered, "No, Sir, 1843."

Nodding, he said nothing more and I continued my studying. The pacing footsteps neared and a hand reached over my shoulder and stole away an unopened envelope. He lingered there a moment, then went to the fire and sat in a thick armchair. The night ticked away and neither of us stirred. Finally, when I had finished, I glanced up at the clock surprised it had only been three quarters of an hour. I rose to my feet and turned to bid the colonel goodnight. He held the opened letter in his hand, leaning back in the chair with one leg crossed over the other. He stared at me as if he had been watching me from behind the entire time.

"Sit for a moment, Corporal." His hand twitched in the direction of the chair across from him. Hesitantly, I approached and eased myself into the comfortable chair. The colonel watched me all the while with an unchanging expression. Sitting directly across from him, I could hardly look him in the eye. After an extremely awkward moment, he spoke.

"You're very young, Corporal, but that means nothing to me. As long as you can hold your own, you will stay, but time has yet to tell what war will make of you. Our life is hard and can be deadly." He folded the letter and placed it on a nearby table, "Major Sanders has no doubt given you rubbish about his idea of what an aide's duties are. I know his thoughts on the subject well enough. But I'll have you know, I'm not inclined to share my thoughts or concerns with staff officers as some may be in the habit of doing. I am capable of handling matters on my own and avoid seeking advice from any, save my second in command. All other duties the major has assigned to you, will be carried out as explained. Your orders will come directly from myself as a result of your position in this regiment." He paused to light a cigar, which fumes soon filled the air like an intoxicating fog. "If you hold out these next weeks you may come to some use. But I have never seen a soldier worth speaking of that was trained in so short a time." A long sigh of smoke was let out into the small room. After a pause, he said, "You may take your leave now, Corporal."

Feeling a little weak, I rose from my chair and saluted. The bed I sank into felt more luxurious than it had felt the night before, and I massaged my tense shoulders as I lay staring at the ceiling. The day had been one of the longest I could remember, yet I lay awake for some moments musing over the colonel's words. Then in the solitude of my room, I vowed I would prove my worth as a soldier.

Christmas Pudding
Chapter 29

Elizabeth

December 25, 1861

OPENING MY EYES, I glanced down at the entrance to my tent. Out of the crack in the canvas, I could see thick clumps of snowflakes falling slowly to the earth. Groaning, I turned onto my side. I was still trying to get used to sleeping on the ground. The first few nights I had not even been able to sleep. Now it was just a matter of getting used to the cold and frozen ground. Reluctantly, I sat up on the blankets.

"It's Christmas!" I whispered to myself excitedly as the realization dawned on me. Dressing in one of the few cotton gowns I had brought with me, I fastened the buttons and twisted my hair into a bun. Lacing up my boots, I gathered a few parcels and stepped out into the snowy morning. Breathing in the cold air, I smiled at the new and special day ahead. The sky was overcast at the moment, but the gently falling snow created a beautiful scene around the winter encampment. In the distance, I saw a group of soldiers on horses slowly riding along the rows of tents in my direction. I stopped in astonishment. There weren't many officers riding in this area lately. As they approached, I noticed the man in the front. He was thickly set, with a scruffy beard and a cigar stuck between his teeth. His uniform was not elegant in appearance, but it was the bars on his shoulders that caught my attention. I stood frozen in amazement. The horseman stopped in front of me. The officer tipped his hat.

"Good morning, Miss."

I stuttered at first, then controlled my voice, "Good morning, Mr. General ... Sir." I curtsied, feeling the blood rise in my cheeks.

"We are very grateful to have young women volunteering for the cause. I thank you." The horses stamped and snorted, their breath visible in the cold air. The staff surrounding General Grant sat patiently watching our conversation. Trying to think of the words, I answered him.

"I am proud to be of service, General."

General Grant smiled at me, "Merry Christmas, Miss."

"Merry Christmas, General." The soldiers began to move off. Suddenly I thought of the packages I held. "General! Sir!" I hurried after them. The horses stopped once more. Reaching up toward him, I held out one of the parcels.

"Please accept this gift. It isn't much, just something I made," I said, offering it to him. A small spark lit the general's eyes as he took the package from my hand.

"Thank you, young lady, I'm very grateful," he replied sincerely. Then, handing it to one of his staff members, said, "Mr. Rawlins, would you hold onto that for me?"

"Certainly, Sir," Rawlins replied, then tipping his hat to me, said, "Allow me to thank you, Ma'am, for your kindness to the general." I nodded and watched as the horses rode off. *I wish Amy was here. She would have been so excited to have met the general!* The loneliness returned unexpectedly. *She's probably enjoying her first Christmas with Kelsey. I wish I could see her again. It's only been about two months, but it feels longer.* I sighed. Last night I had written her a letter and gave it to someone who would eventually get it to a steamboat going up the Ohio River. As I passed one of the tents, Daniel appeared from inside the tent flap.

"Merry Christmas, Daniel!" I eagerly held out one of my packages and added sincerely, "I just wanted to thank you for everything you've taught me and helped me with."

A small smile came over the worn face, "Oh no, thank you. You're the one who's helped me with a lot of things. Well now. What's this?" he began unwrapping the package. Pulling out a knitted scarf and gloves, he stopped in obvious amazement.

I excitedly added, "I found soft material in the storage tent the other day. Feel it, Daniel!" I eagerly pulled the scarf toward him. Glancing down at his dirty hands, he wiped them on the side of his pants before gently touching the soft cloth.

Slowly raising his head, he said softly, "Why … thank you, my girl. It's … it's been a long time since I've gotten—" he broke off, then simply said, "Thank you." I watched him, realizing he was the first man to call me 'my girl' since Father. It brought back so many memories. Smiling sadly, I hurried off to disperse the rest of my gifts.

A light glowed from inside the colonel's headquarters. I approached the guard standing outside the tent flap. My heartbeat quickened in awkward anticipation. Feeling rather silly, I wondered if I should just turn around and give my gift to someone else. However, knowing all the time and care he put into his position, I felt it was a nice gesture to show appreciation for the colonel.

"I'd like to speak to the colonel please," I choked out the words. The guard raised an eyebrow in question. "I just have a Christmas gift for him, Sir." The guard seemed to relax a bit, then ducked into the tent. A few minutes later, the tent flap lifted. I fully expected to see the young guard again. Instead the colonel himself appeared! Colonel Brandt was a tall man in his mid-thirties, with dark hair and eyes.

"Good Morning, Miss," his voice was serious, but tinted with kindness. In his intimidating presence, I involuntarily took a step back. My fingers instantly rubbed above my eyebrow awkwardly and my eyes dropped to the ground. I fumbled for one of the packages in my hand.

"I … I just wanted to give you a gift … for Christmas, Sir." Nervous that he might get the wrong impression, I waved my arm across the encampment, "On behalf of your regiment, Sir." I quickly peeked up at him long enough to catch the twinkle in the dark brown eyes as he accepted the parcel.

"Well, thank you, Miss," he handed it to the aide who had just walked up beside him.

"And your name is?"

"Elizabeth Matthews, Sir. I am from a little town of no consequence in Pennsylvania." The colonel nodded and an inquisitive look came over his face.

"A long distance for a young lady to come to help the Union cause. But, we thank you for your willingness to assist. God knows we shall need nurses in the coming battles. Miss," he tipped his hat and turned to go. I curtsied in return, thankful that he did not pry into my reasons for coming this far.

* * *

Skimming the top of the thick pudding, I raised the ladle to my mouth. The sweetness on my tongue was a rare treat. A hand reached into the pot; a finger swept up some of the dessert. I smacked it down with my spoon.

"David Miller!" I scolded playfully. David smiled sheepishly as he licked his fingers greedily. "You'll have your share later!" I smiled, shaking my head. As soon as I knew I had the ingredients I needed, I had put together Pennsylvania pudding for the men in our regiment. It was to be a Christmas surprise. Soon, the pot was surrounded by young soldiers eager for a taste. Ted Logan, a blonde-headed young man with a swagger, crossed his arms and stood staring into the thick liquid.

"You sure you know what you're doing?" he asked skeptically.

I looked at him, "This is *Pennsylvania* pudding. Of course I do." A playful mummer rose from the men.

Ted stared deeper into the pot, then scolded, "There's not enough raisins!"

A voice came through the crowd, "Raisins aren't really a commodity around here, Private Logan," the men parted as Colonel Brandt passed through them and came to inspect what the commotion was about. It seemed he was a very serious man, but I could tell that there was a playful side to this soldier; yet the men respected him greatly.

"What do we have here?" he asked.

"Just a treat for Christmas, Sir," I said shyly, curtsying.

Colonel Brandt smiled at me, then glanced around at the men. "Spread the word, we'll all meet in the center of camp, at our regimental flag tonight. There will be a devotion by our chaplain and then we can celebrate this special day." The men cheered and the younger ones threw their hats up.

The flames shot high into the night sky, lighting up the regimental flag. I stepped carefully as I carried the chilled pot of pudding toward the large group surrounding the fire.

"Elizabeth! Can I help you with that?" Turning, I saw Sarah Phillip's brother, John, from my own hometown.

"Thank you, John," I answered gratefully, letting him hold one of the handles. "Have you heard from your sister at all?" I asked. The boy smiled and answered in the affirmative.

"Have you?" he asked me.

My heart sank, "No," then I added, "But I just sent her a letter a while ago, she may not have gotten it yet. She's probably very busy in any case. She was recently married to Kelsey, you know."

The men whooped when they saw the pudding come into the center of the circle. I straightened up, my back aching from the kettle. Stepping back, I watched in satisfaction as the men attacked the pot, helping themselves to the treat. The others, those more patient and mature, sat back on the logs that had been placed about the fire. The chaplain stood staring wide-eyed at the group. I couldn't help but notice the look of holy indignation at the greediness of the men in front of him. A soft laugh escaped my lips at the sight and I found a seat next to Captain Clark and Daniel. Once the swarm had settled down into their places, the chaplain stepped forward and said somewhat severely, but in his usual soft voice, "... he is as greedy as the grave, and like death is never satisfied ..."

A silence came over the group. I noticed Ted nudging Will with his elbow in amusement. "Excuse me while I retrieve my Bible and hymn book from the tent," as the chaplain moved away, a few of the men burst into stifled laughter. David stood up and began walking around the circle, hands on hips, imitating Chaplain Allen's look of disgust. Captain Clark, sat silently enjoying his dessert. Captain Clark enjoyed bantering with the men and teasing them when the time was right, but was mature and attentive to detail. As David moved past Captain Clark in his imitation of the chaplain, he suddenly spun around and took hold of the dish in the captain's hands.

"Sinful man!" He shouted, "Thou shouldst be ashamed of thyself!" The men around the fire roared with laughter as the captain and David fought over the plate of pudding. Losing his grip, David stumbled backward, but the plate of pudding had flipped squarely into the captain's face. A general outcry rang through the group, followed by another roar of laughter. The captain peacefully set down his plate beside him, and slowly took a handkerchief out of his pocket to wipe at his red beard. When the laughter had quieted down, he said, "Thank you, Private Miller," still dabbing at his pudding-covered face, "that was very amusing." Nevertheless, a slight smile remained on the captain's face.

Just then the chaplain returned. He eyed the group suspiciously and then began to turn the pages of his hymn book. The chaplain led the group through "Silent Night", "The First Noel" and "Away in a Manger." Clearing his throat after the last song, he flipped through the pages of his Bible. As I listened to the beginning chapters of the gospel of Luke, I looked around the circle and found the ladies I worked with as well as some of the soldiers I had grown fond of. I felt an endearing sense of family, and I knew I wasn't alone anymore. I listened more intently to the chaplain's voice. He had moved to a different passage as he threw in his comments.

As I stared up from the flames, I noticed a figure moving toward the group. He stopped where the light could only show dimly on his face. It was Nathan. The uneasiness returned. Whenever I saw him, the events of the past, the feelings, and the emotions surrounding all that had happened with Adam Carter rushed in. *Why do I still feel like he is a criminal when I know he is not?* It seemed the original prejudice and suspicious feelings I had of him just wouldn't dissipate. *He's just so quiet and separated from everyone. It makes him seem suspicious*

I focused once again on the chaplain's words as he went off in another direction, "Judge not, that ye be not judged. For with what judgment ye judge, ye shall be judged: and with what measure ye mete, it shall be measured to you again ..." As he spoke the words, I felt someone staring at me. Looking up from the fire, my gaze locked on the shadowed face across the circle. Catching Nathan's penetrating stare, I quickly dropped my eyes back on the ground in front of me.

A Bit of Kindness
Chapter 30

Amy

THE SWEET AROMA of sausage, pancakes and syrup seeped under my door and filled my small room. I breathed in deeply while dressing for the day. *Christmas day!* I leaned against the window sill to admire the fresh blanket of snow. *How beautiful! I wonder if any of those poor, cold souls out there will be able to rejoice in such weather.* The temperatures had dropped all through the night and I could see frost on the window pane. My heart longed for the festive traditions I would have been sharing with Elizabeth had it not been for this war. She would be setting a very similar breakfast on the table, and calling up the stairs for me. Then that night we would make the trek through the snow to the McCarthy's for a candlelight supper. Though some would not be present, we carried their memory very close to our hearts as we celebrated. After we were all thoroughly satisfied with the bountiful feast, eggnog and Irish fruit cake were passed around, and we'd sit by the fire and listen in respectful silence to the story of the birth of Christ.

Sighing, I tore myself away from the beautiful scene. Doubting that such a man as Colonel Anderson cared at all about the traditions of Christmas, I descended the stairs into the hall that led to the parlor. Four officers were gathered in the room. To my great shock and horror, all bundled in winter clothes, standing directly across from me, were Mrs. Clemens, Mrs. O'Conner, Mrs. Denny and Sarah Phillips. What they had come for, I could not even imagine. My gut twisted. As Major Sanders noticed me, he raised a hand.

"Corporal Jones, will you inform the colonel that these good ladies have come by wagon from Gettysburg and wish to speak with him."

I nearly choked before I could speak a word, "Right away, Sir." Sanders nodded and glanced back at me curiously. I hurriedly knocked on the colonel's door and entered, welcoming any escape. The room was dimly lit, but the colonel was sitting on the edge of the bed having just awakened. The bed, however, was still made from the day before and showed hardly a sign of use. He eyed me while buttoning his shirt, looking rather cross. A bit mortified at having intruded upon the colonel's privacy at such an unseemly time, I hesitated.

"I'm sorry, Sir. Major Sanders asked me to inform you that some ladies from a nearby town have asked to see you in the parlor." I timidly interjected, eyes locked on the corner of the ceiling.

He rose without the slightest change of expression and motioned to me, "If you will assist me, Corporal." I took the bright red sash and began wrapping it snugly around the colonel's waist. His hand reached down and corrected the folds in the cloth.

What can I say to defend my case? How can I deny the charges the ladies are about to lay at my door? Oh, Sarah, my trusted friend, why have you done this?

Taking the heavy coat from its peg and sliding it over his shoulders, I smoothed down the blue cloth quickly as I had seen mother do to Father's Sunday coat. I stepped back a few paces while the colonel finished with the many buttons. He turned finally and motioned toward the door. I stayed a few paces behind as we entered the parlor, carrying the colonel's hat in the crook of my arm. The officers stood at attention and the ladies instantly turned their curious gaze upon the colonel, who waited patiently for Sander's introduction, as he scrutinized each lady from head to toe.

"Colonel Anderson, this is Mrs. Clemens, Mrs. O'Connor, Mrs. Denny and Miss Phillips. They've brought a few clothing items and some baked goods for the men," Sanders watched the colonel intently, waiting for his reaction. There was a long pause, in which I guessed Mrs. Denny was awestruck at the colonel's commanding presence. She dared not open her mouth. I almost smiled to myself as I stole a glance at her silent face.

After a few moments, the colonel motioned to some chairs. "Will you sit, ladies?" The women sat as if on command and the colonel approached them, but remained standing. He seemed to be contemplating their offer, "I believe you misunderstand the status of our regiment. Our men are not a charity case such as the Rebel army. We are equipped with a bountiful resource of goods. The men are well fed and clothed and lack for nothing, I can assure you. Your charity may be taken to a more pitiful case. It would be a waste here." The ladies remained motionless and I read the disappointment in their eyes. They had worked so hard. They deemed their gifts so valuable to the men. My heart softened, and I felt compassion for them. "I'm afraid your charity is misplaced … generous, but misplaced."

"A bit of kindness, Sir, cannot be unwelcome by the men," Sarah had spoken up in her gentle voice, interrupting the colonel. "In my opinion, it would not be a slight to the men, but a humble offer of our admiration. Out of the great fullness of our hearts, we offer what little we may to help in the preservation of our country. And after all, if I may, Sir … it is Christmas." The colonel studied her as she gazed up at him determinedly. Her eyes moved past him and for a split second, she met my gaze. "What harm can it do to give what little we have to offer in a show of our gratitude?"

Proudly, I stood by and watched my friend courageously argue her point. There was a pause in which everyone seemed to hold their breath. The colonel's eyes narrowed and for a moment I thought he would become very ungracious at having been interrupted.

"You have a persuasive tongue, Miss Phillips, and I will allow you to do as you please." He turned to the other silent women, who had been struck by temporary muteness, "but I'm afraid I must warn you. A soldier's camp is no place for ladies. Therefore, if you are certain you wish to continue as planned, Major Sanders will accompany you."

Sarah was the first to rise and she smiled shyly, now blushing at her outspokenness. "Thank you, Colonel, you are very gracious." She curtsied, and the colonel bowed slightly as the ladies filed out, retrieving their baskets as they went. Sarah shot a glance over her shoulder at me.

"Major, if you would escort the ladies through the camp," Anderson said watching the ladies depart. Sanders saluted and motioned me to follow.

Reluctantly, I did so, pulling on the heavy winter coat. Closing the door behind me, I was met by the merry voice of a harmonica, laughter and the smell of coffee beans. Sanders had assigned another guard to the parade of ladies, who had fallen into step beside Mrs. Denny.

Chattering away, she made her way through the camp of curious soldiers, always the center of attention. My own dear friend, Sarah, lagged behind, generously handing out delicious cookies with a shy "Merry Christmas," in her sweet quiet way. Some soldiers accepted them politely and exchanged a few kind words. Others hung back in reserve, and I heard a few uncouth whistles from a rowdy looking bunch.

The three older women moved quickly on ahead, shivering with cold and Sanders followed behind them. I paused to wait for Sarah, who to my surprise was making conversation with a few of the younger soldiers. These young men were very attentive and well mannered. I turned and slowly began walking away, sure that she would soon be following. Glancing over my shoulder, I saw her trying to catch up with me through the snow, and I slowed my pace. Perhaps we could get a few words in private. She may have news from John or possibly … Elizabeth.

There was a sudden commotion behind me and as I turned I saw Sarah in the midst of a rather rough looking group. Her bonnet had fallen and in an attempt to retrieve it, she had been run into, nearly falling over. One soldier caught her around the waist just in time and commenced in teasing her about the fallen object in a rather ungentlemanly manner. I had to do something! My heart suddenly froze in fear at the thought of having to approach such a group of soldiers.

"Please," Sarah begged, trying to get away from them. The men continued to laugh and jest at her expense, one even kicked the bonnet just out of her reach. Suddenly a captain rode up in the midst of the assembly.

"What's going on here?" he demanded angrily. His eyes lighted upon the girl.

"Just having a bit of fun, Sir," the soldier complained.

The captain assessed the situation, "Well, it does not appear to amuse the lady or me, Private, so move along. All of you!" Grumbling, the gathering dispersed and the captain swung down from the horse, removing the cap from his blond head.

"Thank you, Sir, I'm a bit embarrassed at my dilemma," Sarah took a step toward her hat.

"Please allow me, Miss." The captain retrieved the bonnet and dusted the snow away, "I'm afraid our men have not made your visit very pleasant. Please accept my apologies."

"There's nothing for *you* to apologize for, Sir," Sarah continued dusting off the bonnet timidly, not wanting to meet the captain's eyes.

The young man smiled, "Excuse me, I'm Captain Robert Sanders."

"Sarah Phillips," she looked up, her pale cheeks brightening. The captain suddenly noticed me standing by and his smile faded at the sight of me, "Corporal. Are you responsible for this young lady's wellbeing?"

"I ... um," I stuttered for a moment, "Yes, Sir."

"I suggest you take better care of your charge then and act the part of a gentleman." He approached suddenly, "I should report you at once for your neglect. Whose command are you under?"

"Mine." The captain spun around to see Colonel Anderson seated on his black stallion. The captain didn't respond for some time.

"Sir, I ..."

"Enough said, Captain," The colonel moved up beside me and sternly instructed, "Return to Major Sanders immediately." Then with a spiteful and quieter tone, he put in, "It appears I was wrong to entrust to you such a simple task." The stallion spun around and as I plodded off with a heavy heart, I heard the colonel say, "Captain, will you see to it that this young lady is returned safely to her friends?"

Just up ahead, I saw the major patiently standing by as the ladies handed out their goods. He leaned on his sword gazing about and caught sight of me approaching. I felt my face flush at the thought of my humiliation as Sanders watched me.

Just as his mouth opened to speak, the young captain saluted, "Lovely day to be out for a stroll, Major Sanders." He glanced over to watch as Sarah rejoined the ladies.

"Was it not just yesterday you said you despised the winter weather in any form. Or perhaps you've discovered the day is improved by the company which you keep," the major's eye sparkled. The captain, seeing what his superior was driving at, instantly changed his tune.

"I have no time to keep company, Sir. I'm kept occupied by my present duties, which are far more critical under the present condition of our country than my own personal social life." The captain's cheery mood turned to business.

"Even in war there is time for personal matters, Captain. As long as they don't interfere with your work." Major Sanders stepped forward to begin trailing the ladies again and I fell in step behind him, keeping enough distance to remain unnoticed.

"I find it is best to set aside personal matters in such circumstances as these, Sir, or one should lose his focus on the goals set before him. Is it not true?" The captain glanced over to Major Sanders, whose eyes were fixed on his charges.

"Though this is true, I worry that you over work yourself, nephew. You are a good soldier, one of the best we have."

"Your compliments are too generous, Sir. I'm only doing my duty." Major Sanders laid a hand on the young captain's shoulder. I saw the young man give his uncle an endearing look.

"I should get back. I have a meeting with the colonel," He flipped the reins over his horse's head.

"Another assignment?" The major paused to watch him mount.

A smile spread across the young man's face, "Yes, Sir. Can't stay in one place for too long."

Drawing near, Sanders laid a hand on his nephew's leg, "Take care."

"Always, Sir."

"And think of what I told you," he glanced over his shoulder at the crowd that was gathering about the women. The captain smiled and whipped the gelding about. "Godspeed, Captain," Sanders returned the salute as the young soldier rode off.

A Respectable Man
Chapter 31

Elizabeth

"MISS MATTHEWS! PLEASE bring the ladle from the storage tent!" I reached into a wooden crate and pulled out the long spoon. Even though I was supposed to cook for the men in my regiment, many times I found Daniel in the midst of preparation for some of the meals. Approaching the man with the ladle, I decided I would try to talk my troubles over with him. We had spent many days together preparing and serving meals for the men, he had become almost like a father to me.

"Daniel," I began, still feeling awkward about calling him that. But when I had asked him his name he had simply told me to call him by his first name. The man glanced down at me as he stirred the stew.

"Something on your mind?" Daniel prodded, seeing that I wanted to talk. I sat down on the stump beside the kettle and looked up at the kindly face.

"Have you ever been angry at someone for something … well, something that wasn't even their fault?" I stopped, confused at my own words, yet hoping that they made sense to him. Daniel suddenly slowed his stirring and stared off into the distance.

His countenance changed, and after a long moment, he said in a low voice, "Yes."

Watching him, I sensed that this question had brought up a painful subject. Anxiously, I tried to think of a way to explain my irrational anger toward Nathan for past events and the tension I felt whenever he was around. Daniel spoke up abruptly, interrupting my thoughts.

"I've learned that anger is not a good thing to hold in your heart. It slowly destroys you … and those around you." He knelt down and poked a hot coal with a stick. "Like a pile of coals, it smolders and you can't tell but it will slowly destroy anything near it." I nodded at the truth of the words. I tried to imagine how I would feel if I had no anger toward Nathan, but something was still there … some tension, some distance. I didn't feel comfortable trusting him. It seemed Mrs. Denny's remarks, and all that had happened before the truth came out, were still lingering.

"You see, there's this young man in camp. We met back in Pennsylvania. Some events happened. He was accused of murder and now I just feel tense and awkward around him. He was proven innocent, but I just feel like I could never treat him like a respectable young man." Daniel watched me for a moment, then continued his stirring.

"What, may I ask, is your definition of a 'respectable young man'?"

"Well, a respectable young man is friendly, sensitive, presents himself in a proper manner …" my voice faded as I watched a small smile spread across Daniel's face, "What is it?" I asked slowly.

He stopped his stirring, dropped the ladle, and leaned on the posts which upheld the kettle. Looking across the encampment he said, "Miss Matthews, I don't know, but I think respect should be something that a man deserves, something he earns, by his actions. Qualities that will not change with situation or circumstance: things like deeply-rooted character, courage, perseverance and selflessness." I stared at the crackling fire, surprised at myself for not remembering these things. I had been taught all this, but it seemed as time wore on, my ideas had changed. Perhaps I had let my standards of what a man ought to be, slip away and be replaced by lesser notions.

I sighed deeply, "Daniel, I'm sure you were once a fine young man to be around."

The man's face turned with a look of pain. After several moments his voice came, soft and somewhat choked, "No. No, Miss Matthews, I was not a respectable man at all. I was …" he sighed, "quite the opposite."

A deep look of regret and sorrow overcame his countenance and I was sorry I had mentioned something to cause him pain.

Quickly I added, "But you are now."

He turned back to me with a small smile, but shook his head humbly. Tapping my chin gently with his rough finger, he said, "I only hope to be."

* * *

February 17, 1862

Another victory for the Union cause! I smiled when the news reached my ears. General Grant had landed the army on either side of the Tennessee River. We had bombarded and won Fort Henry on February 6th. Fort Donelson was some 12 miles from Fort Henry and guarded the Cumberland River approach to Nashville. Our troops had some trouble with the winter weather, yet General Ulysses S. Grant had continued the march toward the fort. On February 14th, Union General Foote's ironclads moved up the river and began their bombardment of this fort. The noise from both sides had shook the earth beneath us. I had watched the puffs of smoke and fire, and the incessant pound of cannon fire rang in my ears. After days of fighting, our troops were about to begin another attack on the fort, when white flags were seen flying above the ramparts. General Grant met with the general of the fort, General Buckner, an old West Point classmate of Grant's. Buckner soon found out that Grant would not accept any terms except "unconditional surrender." General Grant had won another victory for the Union cause and had opened up the way to Tennessee. For this victory, our own brigadier general was promoted to major general. After this battle, he also received a sort of nickname. As his initials were U.S.G. for Ulysses Simpson Grant ... so they called him "Unconditional Surrender" Grant.

* * *

We had suffered over 2,000 casualties, and those wounded still needed to be tended. Campfires lit the night sky. I watched the warm flames, thankfully. During the attack on Fort Donelson we were not allowed to light fires for fear the light would notify the enemy of our position. Temperatures had dropped far below freezing point, causing much suffering among us. I moved carefully around the forms of men stretched out on the snow and ice, their moans and screams carried on throughout the long night. My heart ached with each cry and my stomach was still not very strong when I saw the bloody results from the fight. At times, it was hard to differentiate between the dead and the sleeping.

Light snowflakes fell silently around me as I made my rounds through the wounded. It had been a long, cold night, and the darkness was finally beginning to gray. At a distance, I noticed Ellen knelt down beside a soldier. Ellen had been growing weak and, despite her hearty attitude, she had a delicate nature. I had worried about her these past few weeks as she seemed to weaken with the cold and travel. As I drew closer, something stopped me in my tracks. Ellen's head was bent so far forward as to lay on the shoulder of the soldier she had been tending. He lay stiff and motionless. I choked on my breath as a dreadful feeling passed through my heart. My mouth moved to form words, to call out to my friend, but nothing came. Eventually, I was able to move my feet, which felt like iron, and approach the two stone-like figures. I stood behind the kneeling girl, then falling to my knees beside her, I took her in my arms. She fell back limply into me. Her face was pale and cold. Snowflakes lay on her long eyelashes and covered her cheeks.

"Ellen …" I choked, "Oh … no … please … Ellen, dear." I pulled her to me and, bending my head on hers, my tears covered her young face.

* * *

A pale pink hue began to break through the darkness. I rubbed my neck and twisted my head. My eyes were heavy from lack of sleep, and my body numb with cold. I felt sick from the night of blood and death. Finding Ellen dead in my arms upon awakening sent a flow of tears once more. Morning had dawned and those few soldiers who had been left to help with the wounded began the horrible procedure of lifting them into the wagons. The awful screams of immense pain cut through the air. My heart cried out with each of them. After they had the wagons loaded and were beginning to move out, I sat in the same place, still holding the girl. Footsteps slowly approached, snow crunching. I was aware of Captain Clark nearby, who had been one of the soldiers chosen to stay behind. Squatting down beside me, he rubbed his beard and stared at the ground searching for words. I stared blankly ahead, caressing the young girl's cold cheek with my finger. In that moment, I didn't want to go anywhere, do anything more. The whole army could leave us here in the snow for all that I cared. The captain laid a rough hand on my shoulder and shook it gently.

"Come, let me take the girl."

My grip tightened around her, and a sudden terror struck me. "No!" I yelled, more harshly than I meant.

A moment passed, "Elizabeth, you have to let her go," he said softly.

"No! You can't take her too! I won't let you!" I tore my shoulder from under his hand and moved away from him, pulling the limp body with me. "Leave us alone! It's no use! It'll go on forever. More will die!" My voice suddenly shook, losing its determination. My hands went numb, losing my grip on the girl, I burst into tears as she dropped into the snow.

Captain Clark ran up, gripped my shoulder, and turned my face toward him, "She's not here anymore, Elizabeth," his voice was firm. Then he added gently, "You can let go." I wiped at the tears that streamed down my face. He gave my shoulder a tight squeeze, then lifted the girl in his arms and carried her away.

The Englishman
Chapter 32

Amy

BUSTING OUT THE door from the colonel's room, I nearly ran smack into a gentleman standing just outside.

"Excuse me, Sir," I apologized flustered.

"No harm done, lad," the man gave a charming smile to match the thick British accent. I stood dumbfounded for a moment until Major Sanders, who was standing beside the young gentleman, spoke up.

"Corporal Jones, this is Peter Kingston. He's come from England, crossing the ocean like many others to observe how we are putting down the rebellion in the South. Only Mr. Kingston here is a reporter." I nodded, still slightly confused at the idea of a foreigner being so interested in our country as to come all the way across the ocean, putting himself in danger, simply to observe … a war. I stood frozen until I remembered my manners.

"It's a pleasure, Sir."

The reporter seemed to look me up and down suspiciously, all the while making me extremely uncomfortable.

"The pleasure's mine, Corporal."

"Please notify Colonel Anderson, Corporal," Major Sanders stated, motioning to the door.

"Of course," reentering the room, I announced that he had company. He didn't appear overly enthused. After the introduction, I was sent to ask Mrs. McPhee for some coffee and tea. I felt extremely rude, bossing the poor elderly woman around, so I stayed to lift the heavy kettle and pour the water for her. She thanked me over and over again for the small service and insisted I go attend to the colonel or I may get myself in trouble. Eventually, I heeded her advice.

"Thank you very much, Colonel. I'm much obliged," the Englishman was saying, as I entered the room. Colonel Anderson motioned them to the chairs near the fire and then glanced over at me.

"Mrs. McPhee is preparing the drinks, Sir," I stated.

He nodded and sat opposite his guest. Major Sanders looked a bit concerned at me, as I stood awkwardly, ignorant of what was expected of me. I knew it would be totally improper for me to sit causally down with the colonel and his guest, but I felt he expected me to stay in the room nonetheless. I looked to Major Sanders for some kind of a clue. His eyes directed me to a pile of papers on the colonel's desk. I found some letters addressed to a superior commander, and I placed them in envelopes, working as I listened to the conversation.

"I think you'll find our regiment one of the most well equipped. I keep a close eye on supplies for my men as well as our mounts. Our supply wagons are always close at hand. President Lincoln personally saw to the cares and needs of our regiment."

"Indeed," the English reporter looked impressed.

Anderson leaned back, "I hope the winter will not be too boring for you."

"I'm certain I'll find something interesting to write about, Colonel. I hope to send at least one pamphlet a month on the exciting news of the war back to England. This is a great opportunity for me, Sir, to be with your regiment. I always do my best to get up close and personal for my readers. The world has cast its eye on this young country, eager to see the outcome of this war."

Anderson nodded and offered the reporter a cigar, but he waved a hand.

"We're honored to have you, Sir. I think you made a wise choice to follow our cavalry regiment." Across from him, the young man's eyes sparkled with certainty. "You'll never find such well-trained and disciplined soldiers, as well as excellent horses, in either army." Anderson blew a stream of smoke into the cloudy air.

"Quite a boast, Colonel. Indeed, I'm eager to see your men perform."

"You won't be disappointed, Sir. At my request, we've been fitted with the fastest, well-trained horses. No doubt the rebel army will be using their work horses and dandy prancers. We've quite an advantage on our foe," the colonel stated proudly and tapped his cigar.

The Englishman's eyes narrowed, "And how, may I ask, did you come by so many fine war horses as you asked for?"

The colonel smiled slyly, "It never hurts to have a father whose position places him conveniently close to the president."

The reporter sat back a little surprised and gave a slight laugh, "I should say not, but surely with such a well-equipped regiment comes more responsibility." There was a pause and I glanced up again, Anderson seemed to be thoroughly enjoying his boast, but I noticed Major Sanders looked rather uncomfortable. The reporter waited eagerly for an answer.

"I must confess, our regiment is not an ordinary one, Sir, but I can say no more on the subject. The time will come when you will see and understand." My curiosity sparked at this comment, but then Mrs. McPhee entered the room and began pouring out cups of coffee and tea. I took a gulp of the tea, thankful for the warmth of the liquid. Smiling sweetly as I thanked her, she left the room, shutting the door gently behind her.

The night grew long as the colonel inquired as to Mr. Kingston's situation in life. It was nothing overly interesting, a lonely bachelor with a passion for his work. He had always dreamed of being a reporter and traveling to different lands. He had been particularly interested in visiting our fair land and was very grateful for the opportunity, although he wished it had been under better circumstances. I found myself nearly nodding off to sleep until Major Sanders coughed and gave me a look. Finally, they rose and the colonel bade me show Mr. Kingston to a room that Mrs. McPhee had prepared for him.

"Oh, I don't want to impose on the lady of the house. I would be just as comfortable sleeping in a tent," he offered most sincerely.

I was surprised, but Colonel Anderson raised a hand, "I wouldn't dream of it, Sir. Mrs. McPhee said it would not be a problem."

"If you're most certain."

"I am. Corporal, show the gentleman to his room."

* * *

"Excuse me." Startled, I turned around quickly to face the reporter. He held a hand to the door frame and seemed to be looking for something. It had been a week, and I still could not warm up to this English reporter, who had intruded into my safety zone. There was just something about him. I felt as if he was watching my every move and all the while he was disgustingly polite and far too charming, which added to my irritation.

"Sorry, Sir, the colonel is out making his rounds," I said rather offishly. I went back to my work, turning my back on him.

"Actually, Corporal, I was just searching for a good pencil, mine broke you see." I heard him clear his throat, and then the door clicked shut behind me. Glancing at the desk, I quickly found a sharp pencil and held it out to him. The reporter didn't take it from me, instead he looked down at me.

"Have I offended you in some way?" The question caught me off guard.

"Of course not, Sir," again I shoved the pencil toward him feeling nervous. He gave it a short glance.

"Come now, Jones, let's not play this strange game anymore. Why can't we be friends? I've been here a week and you've been avoiding me, ridiculously well, I must say. I'm not sure why? I get the faintest feeling you rather despise me."

Glancing down at the floor, I shifted. I could not stand to look him in the eyes for very long. He seemed to look straight through me.

"No, indeed, Sir. I don't mind your being here." I slammed the drawer shut a bit harder than I meant to. He raised an eyebrow and I felt my face turn red.

"Well, then, we can be friends?" There was a softness in his voice that my feminine heart could not refuse. I turned to face him. A humble look was etched on his face. Slowly nodding, I handed him the pencil and he grinned charmingly. "Thank you, Jones."

"Your welcome, Sir."

"And from now on it's Peter."

I couldn't help but smile, "Very well, Peter." He winked and left the room. Somehow, I felt as if the pencil was not the thing he had come in for to begin with.

Finding Purpose
Chapter 33

Elizabeth

WE RECEIVED NEWS of a battle in Mill Springs, Kentucky. The Union had pushed the Confederates, under General Johnston, south, giving the boys in blue control of Kentucky and much of Tennessee. We were now marching toward a place known as Pittsburg Landing, which was twenty miles away from Corinth, a crucial Southern railroad link and city for the transportation of men and supplies. This was to be the target. However, General Halleck sent orders for Grant to wait on the attack until Buell's army of the Ohio arrived from Nashville.

The wind swept around the folds of my skirt and flipped dust up into my face. Shading my eyes, I glanced behind me as the long line of blue stretched beyond the rise in the dirt road. Dust rose from beneath the tramping feet. When I finally saw Will again, it had been extremely difficult to give him the news of the death of his young sister. He had felt it was his responsibility to keep her safe, and it tore him to the core to know that she was lost to him. He had taken to watching over me as though I was his sister, in an effort to fill the gap left in his heart. Coughing, I slowly made my way over to the edge of the road, in an attempt to avoid the thick dust. A hawk called out, swooping downward, eyeing the formation of Union soldiers far below. I quickly edged off the road and into the grass. Spring was truly here. I breathed in the fresh air deeply.

"Mmm, some fresh cornbread would be good right about now," a voice from the line of soldiers said, smiling. I knew the comment was directed toward me.

Faking a frustrated look, I stated, "And how do you expect cornbread when everything is packed away in the wagons?"

The soldier chuckled, "Well, instead of being lazy and strolling along, you should be in the wagon preparing the dough!"

Rolling my eyes playfully, I laughed quietly as the bantering continued with added voices. Even quiet Mark chimed in, though most of the men didn't notice.

"If we don't get some soon, I might have to holler at ya." Turning away, he watched the ground shyly and smiled to himself, pleased at his own joke. Just then the line began to slow down and eventually came to a halt. Orders came back through the lines to make camp. We had reached our destination, Pittsburg Landing, in Hardin County, Tennessee. It was situated near the Tennessee River.

After several hours of setting up tents and seeing that the scanty evening meal was being served, I eagerly raced toward the banks of the river. Anxiously, I moved to the water's edge, hoping I would have some time to enjoy the scene before the soldiers decided to invade the peaceful moment. Bending down, I fingered the water. It was still cold from the past winter. I sat back against the tender, green grass and cracked open a book I had managed to bring with me. After a few minutes, a group of soldiers, laughing and talking, made their way down toward the riverbank. They stared in my direction. I shifted uneasily, then concentrated on the words.

A small splash of water hit my face from a stone thrown. Starting, I heard laughter coming from the group of soldiers down the riverbank. I bit my lip, and tried to ignore their teasing.

"Good afternoon, Miss Matthews!"

I spun around and recognized John Phillips. He came with another small group, which included Will Parker, Ted Logan, David Miller, and Nathan Tyler. Breathing a sigh of relief, I suddenly felt safe with these men between me and the other group down the river. John and Will plopped themselves down on the grass beside me and began chatting about the strange taste in the meal this afternoon. Ted and David, who had torn off their boots, paused a moment. Then remembering my presence, they only rolled up their pants legs and waded out into the river. They soon began flinging water at each other playfully. I noticed Nathan sat a little way from Will and was staring solemnly across the river to the opposite shore. Ted, cupped his hands and threw some cold water toward David. David retaliated by kicking up the water toward his opponent. In doing so, he lost his balance and fell backwards fully into the cold river. Those on shore cried out in laughter. Will tossed small stones at the soaking David, yelling contemptuously at his clumsiness. David was sputtering and shaking the water from himself. Combing back his dark, sopping hair from his forehead, he suddenly burst into a big grin.

"Take that!" He came at those who had laughed, splashing water furiously. Laughing, I instinctively shielded myself with the book. David picked up a glob of mud from the banks and tossed it wildly. His aim hit Nathan right on the forehead. The group continued laughing, but the smile instantly disappeared from my face. I grimaced waiting for the reaction. I was surprised at the small grin that spread across Nathan's face as he wiped at the mud that decorated his brow.

"Thanks a lot, David," he said sarcastically. Before I knew what was happening Nathan had scooped up some of the mud near him and hit David square in the chest. An all-out mud battle had started and the men from down the riverbank rushed to join in the fun. Smiling to myself, I quietly moved away from the chaos. This was their battle.

* * *

Days dragged past slowly as we awaited the arrival of Buell's troops. Morale was soon low and the soldiers were tormented by boredom, sickness, bland meals, and the daytime heat. Then, in early April, rain came down heavily, soaking the roads, the countryside and everyone in it. I so wanted to somehow cheer the soldiers up, but even the little I had to prepare for meals started to turn my stomach as I made it. However, I made due with what I had. A positive attitude in the midst of such odds was not always easy, but if it helped those around me, it was worth it. Ever since Ellen had passed, it only reaffirmed in my mind how fragile life is. As I spoke with the friends I had made, watched them smile and heard them laugh as they interacted with each other, I felt a sudden fear that they too might be gone soon. For one day Ellen was here, so full of life, and the next day she was gone. As my mind wandered through the memories of Ellen and the soldiers who had passed on, I had moments of regret, wishing I would have told them how much I appreciated their friendships, how I admired their leadership and bravery, and just how much they meant to me. I decided, from that moment forward, to treat people as if I would never see them again, and not to be afraid to tell or even demonstrate to someone that I cared about them. For if I didn't, there was a chance that they would be gone the next day, and they would never know just how much they had been appreciated. Looking up into the deep blue sky flecked with clouds, I also determined to live everyday like it was my last.

* * *

April 6, 1862

I remembered a sudden flash of cannon fire and the terrifying sound of muskets breaking into our monotonous routine of camp life. The ground shook, and the canvases of our tents were torn and some caught fire. There had been some skirmishes the days before. We had known the Confederates were out there, but in what strength, we did not know. We hadn't foreseen such a battle coming. The high commanders had ordered the men not to start a fight. Yet, some of the subordinate officers had tried bringing to their attention that there were already skirmishes taking place, but they would not listen. The Confederates' strength had taken us by surprise and now all was disorder and ruin.

Mangled and distorted bodies covered the fields. Musket fire rattled through the air continuously. Occasionally, the boom of cannon added to the intense clamor. Scrambling around, I searched through the dead bodies behind the lines for extra gunpowder and bullets. Chills covered my body, despite the warm temperature, as I saw the faces of young men, their eyes staring blankly back into mine. Try as I might, I could not escape the visions of these men and boys with their families, working on farms, laughing and talking with their loved ones … Now who would tell these families that their son, brother, father, husband would no longer return to them: that they would no longer see their smiling face, or hear their joyful call as they walked over the threshold. What a terrible thing is war …

I hurried back to the line of soldiers. My hands shook as I tried to remember the steps Captain Clark had taught me. During the slow, long days, I had asked the men to teach me some useful techniques or procedures. Among other skills, I learned how to load their rifles. The Captain's calm voice rang in my ears, "Reloading a rifle is done in nine steps." I reached into the bag of cartridges and pulled one out. Clamping it between my teeth, I tore off the paper. Carefully, but hurriedly, I poured the powder into the barrel and charged the cartridge. Grasping at the cold metal, I pulled the ramrod out and then shoved it down inside the barrel. "Return the ramrod, then half-cock the hammer," he had directed slowly, an amused smile on his face as I had fumbled clumsily with the rifle. He had chuckled the first time I had asked him to teach me, but then realizing I was serious, he became quite a good teacher. Gazing toward the line of gray ahead, my vision was blurred by the smoke and clamor. I quickly removed the old cap and replaced it with a new one. "Nine, shoulder arms," Captain Clark had ordered softly. I handed the loaded rifle to one of the soldiers and began the process over again.

"Fire at will!" Colonel Brandt commanded. He stood, calm and confident, in the face of heavy fire. Nothing seemed to phase the colonel. He moved behind the men, ordering and encouraging them as he moved down the long line of blue. The continual rattle of musket fire reverberated the air which was thick with smoke and fog. The Confederates began another fierce attack on our line.

"Miss Matthews, return to the rear. Help with the wounded. They're coming too close for you to continue on here," Colonel Brandt was suddenly kneeling down beside me with concern in his voice. Just then a bullet whizzed through the air. A sudden burning stung my hand. Instinctively, I dropped the gun I had been holding and reached toward the pain. Colonel Brandt caught me by the shoulders and moved me quickly away from the musket fire. Sitting me down on the ground, he tore at his shirt and wrapped the piece of cloth tightly around my hand. The bullet had grazed my flesh, but thankfully it had not lodged itself there. Biting my lip, I could not help the groan that was escaping.

"Miss Matthews, you must get away from here. Keep going until you're away from the battle lines. Hurry!" He yelled. I watched him in a daze as he pulled his sword out of its sheath. An eerie sound pierced the air, it was the rebel yell. The strong colonel ran back toward his men, waving his sword and calling to them. Bravely, the colonel summoned the men to him and led a charge into the face of the enemy. The rattle of heavy gun fire began again; boys in blue dropped all around. Many of these troops, on Grant's front lines, had never before seen a full-scale battle like this one. Courageously, Colonel Brandt inspired the wavering, inexperienced troops by his words and actions. The men re-grouped and in one last desperate attempt to hold the line, the colonel called for a bayonet charge. The flash of steel and clang of metal rang through the thick air as the men prepared for the assault. The bugler sounded the order, and in a haze, I watched as the regiment followed their colonel into the claws of death. Time seemed to move slowly. The figures before my eyes swayed in and out of focus. I struggled to pull myself up, remembering the colonel's words. But, before I could obey Colonel Brandt's order to leave the battle front, I realized the front line was moving back toward me. The eerie sound steadily grew louder and the thunder of many feet came with it. Our lines turned and began running toward me in a panic. Many of them were shot down before my eyes. Gray overtook blue. I was suddenly pulled up by a rough hand and turning my face upward, I stared into enemy eyes.

Southward Bound
Chapter 34

Amy

"I MUST SEE the colonel at once!" Captain Sanders reached for the door. Placing myself in his path once more, I felt my temper rising.

"Captain, I cannot permit you to enter the colonel's apartment just yet, Sir. If you will only wait just a moment, you will receive an audience with him." The Captain glared at me a moment then angrily tore his hat off.

I thought he would wait, but suddenly, leaning closer, he whispered harshly, "You don't understand what's at stake here, Corporal. I demand you—"

"I'm under the colonel's direct command, Captain," I shot back, shaking in my boots but angry enough to stand my ground. "And as such, I will take no such demands from you." I turned to enter the room and slammed the door in the Captain's arrogant face. I wished I could make him wait half an hour, but the message sounded very important.

Crossing the dim room, I found that the colonel was still deep in sleep. His back was toward me and a blanket lay over him. His white shirt was unbuttoned at the throat and his usually neat hair was ruffled like a young schoolboy.

"Colonel," I whispered and waited a few seconds, "Colonel." I laid a hand on his shoulder and he instantly jumped and gazed up at me.

"What is it?" his voice was soft.

"Captain Sanders has returned and says he has some urgent news, Sir."

He stared a moment. I stepped back waiting. He leaned onto one elbow and paused sighing, "My coat, Corporal."

"Sir!" The Captain, relieved at the site of his commander, jumped to a salute as I opened the door.

"Corporal, you're dismissed. See to it that no one interrupts us. No one." Saluting, I left the room reluctantly and stood just outside the door. Not a sound came from within.

"Corporal Jones?" I glanced up at Major Sanders. His kind eyes gazed down at me a little worried. At his side stood the elusive Peter Kingston, who held a mug of tea in his hand.

I answered, "Captain Sanders is delivering some urgent news to the colonel, Sir. He asked not to be disturbed." Peter Kingston raised an eyebrow.

"He's back? So soon …" The major looked down and rubbed his chin roughly. Suddenly the door swung open and the pale captain emerged.

"Uncle! I mean, um Major Sanders." He saluted quickly, "Colonel Anderson requests your presence at once, Sir." The captain stepped aside to let Major Sanders into the room. I glanced over at the young captain, who tugged on his hat and disappeared out the front door. Peter Kingston was strangely silent. He rubbed his neatly trimmed mustache and shifted an eye toward me. I was sure he would pepper me with questions, but to my surprise he simply raised his cup to his lips and swallowed. Five minutes ticked by before Anderson and Sanders appeared in the door with faces that looked made of stone. A scowl, I would have never suspected, was etched into Major Sander's usually kind face and his hand was on his sword hilt. I straightened, and Kingston stepped out of the way. A group of officers that had entered the parlor in silent anticipation now followed Major Sanders out the door. Mrs. McPhee stood wiping her flour covered hands as she watched the door slam shut.

"Corporal," the colonel stated, "have a guard ready my horse. Pack everything. We're moving out."

* * *

The tents were disappearing and the clutter that lay about was gathered up and packed away. The sound of orders echoed through the valley. The bugle was sounding loud and clear. Horses were saddled, supply wagons loaded, and soon the colors were brought into formation. The colonel waited with the major as the men lined up. I scanned the rows of faces. Many of the eyes that met mine as we passed reminded me of John, Henry and so many of the other young men, who had disappeared from our town, leaving it so empty. No doubt the families and friends of these young men were missing them very dearly. They were only boys, many perhaps only eighteen, some even younger. Some straight out of West Point, had come to fight a man's war, answering the call of their president.

I pulled up just a little behind the major, near the color bearer. Suddenly, I caught sight of Sarah near a small grove of trees. How solemn and fearful she looked now wrapped in a shawl. The welcome spring breeze blew her brown curls. She raised a hand. I wanted to rush to her and say goodbye one last time. Tears welled in my eyes. *But what was she doing here again?*

Suddenly a horse and rider cantered toward her. I thought some officer had come to remove her. Then I noticed the blond hair as the cap was swept gallantly off. He stayed mounted and I could see a few words were exchanged. A slender pale hand was raised and pressed against the soldier's lips and released before he cantered away again with a last glance backward. My eyes met Sanders' as he had observed the same romantic scene. He smiled and turned away. War and love, what a startling idea, that such things could co-exist. Suddenly my heart ached like it was being squeezed from the inside. I could feel his hand in mine, and his strong arm around my waist guiding me. Music playing, lights flickering, I could see the dark brown eyes full of quiet confidence, gentle love ... then he was gone. I shook myself out of the daydream.

"Corporal," Sanders motioned me to my position. The red and white stripes, and the brilliant white stars set in the deep blue snapped and fluttered in the wind. The flag bearer, a young boy, all bundled up in an oversized blue uniform, stared straight ahead at the line that was forming before us. Then the bugle fell silent waiting for the next order.

Colonel Anderson spurred the black stallion forward, "Gentlemen! Today we have received a disturbing report that some Union families' lone farms near the Virginia and West Virginia border have been burned to the ground, livestock slaughtered and women taken captive by some unknown Rebel forces. We don't know the size of this force, but the general has asked us to find this group that dares to destroy our peaceful homes. We will not allow the Rebels to threaten our very homes, families and country. We will take the battle to them! I have full confidence that you are more than well equipped with the knowledge and training you've received to destroy this rebellion! You were especially hand-picked for this regiment. Now is the time! Trust in your ability and perform your task. Let us hasten with all speed to the task ahead of us to destroy the foe. Thirty-fifth Pennsylvania Calvary, forward to victory!" A loud cheer arose, and officers began shouting orders as a bugle sounded. Fresh spring grass and mud kicked up from beneath the hooves of a thousand horses as we cantered south toward the border of Pennsylvania, to the enemy … away from Gettysburg.

The Gates of Hell
Chapter 35

Elizabeth

SOLDIERS IN GRAY lined the planks of the railroad cars as they prodded the prisoners up the ramps and into the dingy rail cars. Still in shock from the scenes of what I felt had to be one of the bloodiest battles in our history, I followed Will in line as we waited to fill the train cars. Crowding in among the Union prisoners, I pushed my way to a corner, feeling awkward in the midst of all the men. *I'm sure they don't usually take women as prisoners* ... Uncomfortable, I scrunched down in the corner of the wooden car, grasping at my injured hand. In shock, I realized that I hadn't noticed the pain again until now. Will sat down beside me. John sat beside him and Nathan stood silently staring out the opened doorway. Although I didn't want them to suffer captivity, I was so thankful to have these familiar young men with me. Once the car was full, the Confederate soldiers pulled down the plank and together shoved the big door closed. My eyes adjusted to the dim car. It was crowded and already the smells of battle and sweat filled the enclosed space.

Holding my throbbing hand and burying my head in my arms, I waited until the whistle of the steam engine sounded and the cars lurched and chugged in an effort to get the long train moving. Soon, between the cracks in the boards, I could see the trees and landscape flying quickly past. My insides tightened. *Where would they take us?* Before long, the exhaustion of the fight overcame me, and the scenes and anxieties drifted from my mind.

I was in Gettysburg. Wind blew through the rustling tree tops, as I walked underneath the blue sky. Slipping my hand into the woman's beside me, I looked up at her lovingly. Mother smiled down at me as we walked along the dirt road on the outskirts of the town. Ahead, Father chased Amy, picking her up and twirling her around. The young girl giggled, throwing her small arms around the tall man's neck. Then came winter days. A fire crackled in the hearth as Mother made homemade bread and drizzled honey over it. Sitting on Father's lap, we snuggled close, listening to him read stories ... of the boy who defeated a giant with only a sling and stone; the girl who became the Queen of Persia and saved her people; the Savior, Jesus, who gave His life for us ...

Lurching, my head snapped forward. Catching my breath, I looked up. The burning sensation returned to my hand. I squeezed it with my other, tightening the cloth Colonel Brandt had wrapped it with. Complete silence reigned over the soldiers. All that could be heard was the creaking of the wooden boxcar and the straining of the metal wheels along the tracks. Glancing around, I noticed most of the prisoners slept, sitting in the positions they had first taken. Beside me, Will leaned his head back in a deep sleep, as did John. But beside them, I noticed Nathan, still standing, leaning one arm against the wall of the rail car above his head, gazing out into the passing countryside. Realizing we were the only two awake, I felt the sudden awkwardness returning. Staring straight ahead, I closed my eyes, hoping to appear asleep.

"Why did you come?" Nathan's voice caught me off guard. Flinching, I opened my eyes and looked up at him. I knew he was referring to my leaving Gettysburg. He stood in the same position as before, staring intently out the cracks between the boards.

Searching for words, I started slowly, "I ... I just wanted to get away ... I guess." Nathan's eyes darted over the dark countryside, it was night now.

After a long quiet moment, he asked in a low voice, "From what?"

Feeling a bit like my privacy was being invaded, I answered back with a question, "Why did you come?" There again was the predictable silence which always seemed to elapse before Nathan spoke.

He turned and looked at me, "Do you really think I would have stayed after what happened?"

"The constable found the evidence. They knew you were innocent. He found the money in Adam's room."

Nathan shook his head and stared off again, "It doesn't matter." A quiet moment pervaded. "Even if everyone knows the truth, the doubt has already been placed in their minds. Once someone shames your name, it's hard to come back from that," I could hear the deep hurt in his voice, then he said quietly. "They'd never trust me." I shifted uneasily, realizing Nathan had just described the very feelings I had been wrestling with ever since I met him.

"The townspeople would probably be more forgiving than you give them credit for," I offered.

Again, Nathan shook his head, then asked bluntly, "Would you have trusted me if I had stayed?" Not receiving a reply, he added, "I didn't think so."

The anger and ache in his tone pierced me. For the first time, I began to get a glimpse of what he must have suffered from the townspeople's rejection and suspicion of him ... and I realized that I had also been a cause of that pain. The note from Nathan's mother flashed before my mind. Suddenly I grasped just how much rejection he must have lived through.

"I'm sorry," I heard my own voice whisper. Nathan's head turned quickly. Looking up, it was hard to discern in the dingy train car, if the cold blue eyes truly did soften.

* * *

In the midst of a cold, rainy morning, the train finally came to a halt. My insides twisted as I faced the unknown possibilities of living in a prison camp. The creaking door slid roughly open, and even though the sun was nowhere in sight, I still had to shade my eyes from the sudden change in lighting. A Confederate soldier's voice pierced the air.

"All right, up and out!" There was the noise of shuffling as the prisoners struggled to get to their feet after being cramped for more than a full day in the train car. Not willing to move, I sat silently watching the others as they slowly moved in procession out of the train. Nathan, Will and John began to move away. Turning back, Will offered his hand to me.

"Come on. It'll be all right," his forced smile assured me. Nodding, I took his hand and got to my feet. Nathan and John stood waiting for their turn to move down the ramp as I joined them. The rain pattered down on the wooden roof above as I stepped out into the gentle downpour. The two young men looked back at us as we walked down the ramp before we came to another halt. I read the concern in John's eyes as he looked at me, then around at all the prisoners. Turning away, he whispered something to Nathan who stood beside him. Nathan glanced back at me, then answered John in the same quiet tone. Looking up at Will, I noticed his young face was still smudged and stained with the dirt and soot of battle. He intently watched the line of Confederate soldiers as they prodded our troops down a muddy path with their rifles. After a few minutes of walking, we came to several four-story buildings that were connected to make one large prison. A burly, rough man stood waiting outside the prison as we came to a halt. He spat tobacco before shouting in a gruff voice.

"Welcome to Richmond, Virginia. This is to be a home to you dirty Yanks," he laughed as he motioned toward the buildings. I felt myself waver as a sick feeling overtook me. Will's hand steadied me as he gently pushed me in front of him toward the gates. Suddenly feeling the rough man's eyes on me, I jerked my gaze toward the ground as we began to pass through the gates.

"Wait a minute!" A thick hand wrapped around my arm and pulled me from the line. "What have we here? A pretty little lady prisoner, eh?" I struggled to free my wrist from his grip, but there was no point. His thick hand pressed in hard like steel. I could almost feel the bruises forming from his grip, and my injured hand throbbed all the more from his grasp. Those ahead heard the noise and turned around.

"Is that necessary, Reb?" John yelled, trying to get back to me through the passing prisoners.

The rough man twisted my arm and asked, "So, what kind of treason have you committed, pretty lady?" Pain from my injured hand intensified, shooting through my body. I cried out, as I attempted to free my arm from his iron grip. A commotion started as more prisoners turned to see what was happening and the Confederate soldiers yelled at them to move on. Will had almost pushed his way up behind me, when someone ripped the tightening grip off my arm. It was Nathan. I stumbled backward, clutching at the emerging bruises.

Will caught me, "Are you all right?"

I nodded, "We'd better get back in line." My heart pounding rapidly, a shout caught my attention.

"What do you think you're doing dirty scum?" The big man had shoved Nathan off. "You think you can touch an officer and get away with it?" He swung a quick punch on the jaw, knocking Nathan into the muddy pathway. The prisoners slowed and swerved to keep from stepping on him as they moved on, being prodded by their captors. Some stopped and stared. Nathan pulled himself from the muck, slowly wiping at his bleeding lip. The smeared mud on his face covered the flush of anger, but could not hide it from his eyes.

The officer wouldn't let up, "You think you can do anything, don't you?" Approaching Nathan, he reached with his left hand and jerked at his collar. Snarling, he whispered, "You're mine now filthy Yank." Suddenly, with his right hand, he threw a punch at Nathan's stomach, knocking the wind out of him. The young man's body froze up as he fell to the ground, his mouth opening in an attempt to gasp for air.

This action threw both the prisoners and the Confederate guards into an uproar. Suddenly, boys in blue turned on their captors and others took the opportunity to flee in the midst of the fight, the Confederates chasing them. Will was struggling amongst his comrades in an effort to reach the officer and Nathan. Wild with terror at the scene before me, I stood frozen in the midst of the chaos. A gunshot cracked. The fighting quieted, as the noise echoed against the surrounding buildings. A middle-aged officer approached through the rain. The beastly man, who had begun the whole commotion, straightened himself up and went to meet the officer. Giving a smart salute he said, "Sorry, Sir, just dealing with some unruly prisoners." The officer looked around at the men before him. He twirled his gun expertly and shoved it back in the holster. Nathan had made it to his feet, just getting his breath back. The officer moved past his subordinate and watched for a few more moments, observing the weary, battle-worn prisoners. An almost compassionate look was on his face.

After a few moments, he said softly but sternly, "That's enough, Sergeant. Take the prisoners into the camp and be done with it."

"Sorry, Sir, it won't happen again." The soldier leered at Nathan from the corner of his eye as he spoke.

"See that it doesn't," the officer answered quietly and moved away.

We entered a dark corridor. Doors leading into large cells lined the aisle. I flinched as I looked into one of the cells. There were men, some looked as though they had just come from the army: healthy, strong and vigorous … but some … could I call them men? No, these were almost skeletons with skin clinging to them and tufts of hair on their heads. Gasping unconsciously, I turned my head away, but the other side of the hall held more of the same ghastly figures. I felt a hand touch my arm. It was John. The tenderness mixed with determination in his eyes comforted me. I glanced to my other side and found Will, also walking close by. His face was set in stony silence. Turning halfway, I searched the rows of prisoners following after us, my eyes eventually rested on the muddy and bleeding face of Nathan. My heart ached at the sight, as I realized I was the cause of his disgrace. I shook my head at the thought. *Why would he do that?* Looking back once again, I caught his eyes. They stared back calmly.

* * *

We were moved into one of the large prison cells on the ground floor. The soldier holding the door was the same ruffian that had caused all the commotion outside the camp. As I reached the threshold, he stuck an arm out, blocking my entrance.

"Since you're so fond of helping your boys in blue," he snarled, "You'll be taking care of the prisoners. Come to the door every morning and you'll be given what you need."

Seeing the arm removed from my path, I stepped into the prison. A sudden panic struck me. *Would we ever come out again?* Gazing around at the gruesome figures in the room, I wondered if we too would end up in the same condition. *Would it not be better to die quickly, than to be a living corpse?* I found an empty corner and rushed to it. Sinking onto the ground, I buried my face in my knees to remove the images around me from my mind.

"I can't do it," I murmured, imagining myself approaching the poor creatures to tend to them. The sight of their grotesque figures made me shrink within myself, but my heart reached out to them nonetheless. After several minutes, I controlled myself enough to raise my head and stare calmly forward.

Will approached. Crouching down, he watched me several moments before saying softly, "You'll make it. You're stronger than you think."

Squad Disappearance
Chapter 36

Amy

NIGHT GREW THICK and an owl hooted in the distant pine trees. I shivered from the cold night. My hands and feet had long since gone numb. My tall, chestnut gelding nickered and lifted his ear toward the silent wood. I saw nothing and nudged him along. At first the excitement had kept me going. It was a beautiful new country we rode through, but as it stretched for miles the monotonous march overcame me. My tired muscles ached, and my empty stomach growled. I longed to lay down on a soft bed and feel the warmth of the fire on my face. I glanced up ahead to the darkening woods and wondered when Colonel Anderson would signal a stop. We plodded through another field. Aragon once more pointed his ears to the right and sniffed the air. *Perhaps it's deer...* I thought, and I relaxed myself in the hard saddle. The signal came for us to halt and I slid off Aragon.

"See to the men, Major Sanders," Anderson stated and waved a hand toward the column.

"Yes, Sir," Sanders turned away with a swift glance back at me. The colonel glared down upon me from his high position.

"Well, Corporal," he dismounted gracefully. "Prepare to set up camp."

"Yes, Sir."

Suddenly Peter was beside me and Anderson noticed him, "Ah, Mr. Kingston, I hope you don't mind, but you will have to share a tent with Corporal Jones."

"Not at all." The reporter stated dismounting. My heart froze, mortified at the idea of sharing a tent … *quick, think of some excuse!*

"Sir, if I may. Let Mr. Kingston have the tent. I shouldn't mind staying outside under the stars."

Anderson glanced back at me, "You'll most likely catch some sickness and then I shall be out of an aide. Not a word about it." I watched his back as he moved down the column of weary travelers.

"Very kind of you, Corporal," Peter said unstrapping his bag, "but we need as much body heat in one place as we can get during the night."

* * *

Huddled in the tent, I tried to close my eyes and rest. *After such a day, I ought to be asleep by now.* The night was strangely silent, and I saw not a light from under the canvas. The tent flaps admitted my tent mate as he crawled in. With a rolled blanket under his arm, he flopped onto the straw covered ground.

"Well, these are the best beds in town I suppose," he chuckled, trying to be lighthearted about the conditions. Smashing myself up against the tent side, I pretended to fall asleep. Peter produced a small book from his satchel and began scratching away. Curious, I watched him a moment, one eye open. He leaned up on one elbow, jotting down words on a piece of paper as if his life depended upon it. His thin hand gripped the pen tightly, and his bright blue eyes were intent on the words. I closed my eyes drifting off to sleep.

* * *

I twisted in the wool blanket and felt a pain in my side. Flipping around, I saw it was still dark outside, yet I was able to determine that Peter Kingston was gone. Propping myself onto one elbow, I glanced about. I felt a pounding in my head. *The hard ground and cold night air must be the problem. I* laid back and rubbed my forehead. I heard the sound of footsteps outside my tent and the flap drew back.

"Tea, my friend?" Peter held out a steaming mug. I took it gratefully. He climbed inside, holding his own cup steady.

I cupped my hands around the mug, "How long have you been up?"

"Only long enough to make a cup of decent tea," he winked. I smiled, feeling very lucky that I had such a gentlemanly tent mate. He, again, scribbled in the book he carried and quickly tucked it away. I emptied the mug and laid on my back, my head pounding. I sighed.

"You all right?"

Rubbing my temple, I said, "I will be in a minute."

As the day progressed the pain didn't leave me, and I even felt dizzy and lightheaded. The last rays of sunlight lingered above the pine forest. It was a gorgeous land we travelled through. How lovely was this land, with its calm fields and forests that God had created with just a word. The colors of the sunset shown through the tall trees that blanketed the earth. I glanced back at the reporter riding just behind me. He was writing as he held the reins in one hand. He licked the tip of his pen and scribbled some more. Pulling at the gelding, I waited until he caught up. Colonel Anderson didn't seem to mind if I disappeared for a while. Peter was hopelessly absorbed in his notepad. The beginnings of a map and some notes covered half the page, but on the other side was written a poem.

"Do you ever take a break?" I asked.

He glanced up and smiled, then poked the pencil back into his breast pocket. Looking ahead and noticing that Colonel Anderson and Major Sanders were engaged in conversation he began,

"Spring blossoms hang in the trees, in the air, in the breeze

The farmer takes up his plow his seed

As his lady watches from the window,

she balances a child on one hip

a broom in hand, content to watch her sturdy man.

The fields are bright with new green life,

the trees closing in surround them.

No neighbor in sight, no enemy's hand,

They work in silence, a peaceful land."

He snapped the book shut. I breathed in the fresh air and glanced away from the scene I'd heard described. Then I saw ahead on the horizon a black cloud of smoke. It seemed everyone caught sight of it, for the column slowed a little and Colonel Anderson raised a hand. I rode up alongside him leaving Peter behind.

"Get Captain Sanders up here now, Corporal."

Whipping my horse about, I spurred him to a canter down the line until I found the Captain halted next to his company. Before I could say a word, he was headed for the front of the column and I followed him.

"Is this one of the places, Captain?" Anderson pointed a gloved finger toward the smoke that rose ahead.

"They've come farther," Captain Sanders spoke as if to himself.

Anderson glanced at Major Sanders, "Send out a squad, Major."

A quarter of an hour later, Anderson pulled out a golden pocket watch, then anxiously looked up. The sun had passed on, leaving us in the growing darkness.

"Forward," Anderson calmly placed the watch back and gave the command. As we passed into the darkness of the forest, the horses seemed to become restless, and I gripped the reins tightly.

"Easy, boy," I tried to calm the flighty gelding.

Suddenly, through the branches of fir trees peeked the glimmer of a red glowing light. Slowly the branches moved away and opened upon a small farm. The wood was still smoldering. Animals were scattered across the yard meandering about. A cow stood near the house staring blankly at us. The squad that had been sent out was nowhere in sight. A chill ran down my back. It was as if they had vanished without a mark or sign, not even a sound. Millions of hoof prints covered the wet ground producing a muddy slush.

"Colonel Anderson!" A shout came from farther back. Following Colonel Anderson we spotted Captain Sanders crouching on the ground. His finger traced a dark hoof print in the mud. The captain, looking confused, gazed up at the colonel, "These prints, are … black, Sir!"

He Will Yet Deliver Us
Chapter 37

Elizabeth

EVERY DAY, FOR two months, I awakened to the horrors and smells of disease, sickness and death. Every day I would stand at the entrance of the camp and wait for the Confederate guards to bring me the prisoners' daily rations. I did what I could with the meager portions, wandering between the rows of famished creatures, rendering what little I had to give. I was grateful for all the medical training I had received from Doctor Alton during my time in the regiment, so that I could help the prisoners during their suffering. Sometimes it was not even just food that they craved, so much as the touch of a hand or a word spoken in friendship.

My sense of smell began to grow accustomed to the stench of death, but my eyes could never forget the terrible scenes and images that were before them each day. For not all the men were pitiable creatures. Some were ruthless and malicious. Troublesome times bring out what is truly inside a person. Either a man will grow stronger and persevere through the trial and come out better for it, or he will let the trial control him and bring out the evil within himself. I was grateful to have men like Will, John and Nathan there with me, for indeed, some men became like animals, hating and abusing even those who suffered alongside them.

Will tended to my wounded hand more than I did, and it healed as best it could considering the circumstances. I felt ashamed to think about my own small pain when so much horror surrounded me. My heart ached as I watched men, who I did not even know, die in a most miserable fashion. But my heart bled at the end of two months when Will, the one to whom we all looked to for encouragement, became very ill.

I moved quickly to his side one morning, reassuring myself that today he would be better. *Surely, he would always be here to comfort the rest of us.* We needed his strong spirit. I knelt down beside him as he lay near the wall of the prison.

"Will?" I whispered, "Will, how are you feeling?" The young man's eyes blinked as he looked up at me. His brow was sweaty as I touched it. "You're burning with fever, Will," I choked. Rushing over to the wooden bucket and dipping a rag in it, I laid it on his forehead. His face twisted in spasms of agony. The last crimson streak of the departing sun speckled the opposite wall through the cracks. Realizing with anxiety that this may be his last day, I unconsciously began to wring my hands as he tossed fitfully in the straw. My heart ached as I looked up at the rotting ceiling. *Please, please, if he is to leave us ... don't let his pain last for long ...* My mind flew back through all the memories, all the kindness this gentle young man had shown me.

"Oh please, please let this pass quickly ..." I pleaded quietly. A murmur from the form beside me caused me to open my stinging eyes. The endearing face stared somberly into mine. Then a veil of concern fell over the tired visage and he struggled to raise himself. I touched his arm gently, "No, you mustn't. Lie down and rest." I summoned all the strength left in me and added quietly, "You know, Will, it may not be long before you are at peace in—," the knot in my throat choked the rest of my sentence. I tried to continue, "And you will then see Ellen once—" Clasping my hand to my mouth, the sobs became uncontrollable. The cold hand clutched at mine. I looked once more into the young face.

"No ... no Elizabeth ..." the weak voice whispered softly. Then the eyes directed themselves from me and gazed through a small crack in the wall. It seemed he was in a far off land. Then the voice began again; gentle at first, but grew stronger as it went on. "... we were burdened excessively, beyond our strength, so that we despaired even of life; indeed, we had the sentence of death within ourselves so that we would not trust in ourselves, but in God who raises the dead; who delivered us from so great a peril of death, and will deliver us, He on whom we have set our hope. And He will yet deliver us …"

A tear rolled down my cheek, "Second Corinthians …" I murmured.

* * *

It had been a week since Will had passed away. Holding up yet another young man's head, I slowly tipped the canteen, letting the water pour between his cracked lips. The dark prison walls loomed above, casting a shadow across his pale face. I straightened up looking across the group of men, some huddled in makeshift tents, some sleeping flat on the muddy ground. The sunken cheekbones and hollowed eyes pierced my heart. The young man before me twisted in his misery and called out delirious with fever. Looking into his face, I saw that he was just a boy, not a man. The weariness of war and lack of nutrients had brought on the appearance of age quickly.

"Water … Mother, I need water. Please … please make your lemonade. You always did make the pain go away, Mother …" I laid a hand on the sweating brow.

Through the tightness in my throat I managed, "Shhh … it'll be all right." The thin arm reached up and I grasped the hand, bringing it to my cheek.

"Please … I need to go home … they need me there …" he suddenly drew a sharp breath, then whispered, "they need me …" A deep, long sigh followed.

I dropped to my knees beside him, "No … oh … please no." Feeling the hand relax, I let it fall in mine to the soft ground. Shaking my head frantically, I fought the cry of distress that surged within me. Standing up, I flew over to the gate of the compound. A Confederate guard stood there. Grasping the iron bars between my hands, I cried out to him, "Don't leave them in here any longer! Please! Let us out! They'll all die!"

Vaguely, I felt strong hands grip my shoulders and turn me away from the gate. "They'll all die!" I repeated, more quietly. Feeling myself being set down on a wooden crate, I laid my face in my hands. Several minutes passed. Regaining control of my senses, I slowly looked up. Nathan sat pensively watching me. Already I could see the beginning effects of the prison camp on his young face. We sat in silence for a while.

"His family ... they may never know ..." I choked. Nathan stared off toward the walls of the prison. "I can't do this anymore," I paused and sucked in my breath, "I just can't stand to see people, living human beings, suffering like this. Skin so thin you can almost see through it," I raised a hand to my forehead and leaned into it. "Some of them don't even look like people anymore." I wiped at the tears that gently passed down my cheeks.

There was another long silence, then I heard Nathan say under his breath, "We'll get out."

The Cottage
Chapter 38

Amy

IT WAS A dark windy day. The forest pine branches hissed in the breeze and surrounded us. It had been a month since the company disappeared and after a thorough search there had been no sign of them. Everyone was always nervous and on edge, even the horses seemed to be uneasy. They shied at every little noise and searched the forest with wide eyes. Anderson insisted we follow an old hidden trail to the south that he believed the Confederates were using on their journey back to the heart of Virginia. A young boy, who we saw just up the road plowing a field, had informed the colonel of the trail saying he'd seen horsemen on it two nights before.

"They moved so swift and noiselessly I wouldn't have seen 'em except my horse spooked and I happen to catch sight of 'em. So dark I couldn't see if they was Yankee or Reb! Like ghosts they was."

Bang! A shot rang out and echoed through the forest. Everyone turned and Anderson swung his stallion around and was instantly upon the nervous young recruit.

"You'll bring the whole Reb army on us! Keep a calm hand on that rifle son or hand it over!"

"Sir, I … I'm sorry, Sir," the boy stuttered. I could see the fear in his eyes. He was a young one, not even able to shave yet.

"Watch these jumpy ones, Sergeant." Anderson ordered, then rode on. My heart pounded louder and louder in my ears as the forest grew dark and thick.

Squinting, I leaned forward, "There's something up there, Sir."

Sanders glanced ahead, "An old shack. Perhaps we should camp here for the night, Sir?"

The young boy, who was our guide, glanced at the colonel, "These woods is pretty thick, Colonel. I'd wait 'til ya get out into the field, if ya ask me."

"Well, I didn't, so we're camping here," Anderson growled, a bit agitated. Major Sanders rode down the line to give the orders. The regiment was halted, and the colonel and I rode up to the shack. It was a ghostly building, but I dismounted and followed the colonel inside.

We stood facing the back of a musty, dirty room. Cobwebs, thick with dust, clung to the corners and windows. *What I'd give for a broom and a rag right now.* Reaching up I swept away some cobwebs from the door frame.

"We'll stay here for the night."

"Yes, Sir," my heart sunk. *I would prefer sleeping in the middle of a swamp than in this ghostly shack in the middle of a haunted forest.* Quickly, I left the shack to bring in the saddle bags and wool blankets. A gust of wind suddenly raced through the trees. The men were already settling down, tying their horses and currying their matted coats, while the beasts munched contentedly in their feed sacks. Our young guide waited on his pony as he stared up at the trees, looking a bit nervous. He gripped his reins and rubbed a hand down the neck of his pony. As he did so, his eyes lighted on me, but as nervous as he seemed, there was no fear in those young eyes. Throwing down the supplies inside the shack, I set about making it comfortable. Not a single fire was lit on orders of the colonel. The men ate slabs of dry salted pork and left-over corn cakes. Some mixed cold coffee and drank it. After arranging the room, I stood near the window, having scarfed down the poor meal. The food sat like a rock in my stomach and I wished I hadn't eaten. I felt far too nervous to digest a single bit of it. The wind whistled violently in the thick pines and swept through the camp. The men tried their best to keep the tents down. Colonel Anderson had come up beside me to survey the camp.

"Do you think they are close, Sir?" I asked, glancing up at him in the dim dusky light.

"I believe so, Corporal … It's too quiet. The wind in the trees is the only noise you'll hear tonight. Rebs have scared every other creature. I'm sure we'll hear from them soon."

A chill ran down my back and sinking down onto my blanket, I left the colonel standing alone at the window. After giving orders to double the guard, he crossed the room unbuttoning the heavy jacket and saber belt. My eyelids were heavy with sleep and I fell into a half conscience daze. Hearing Sanders enter the room, I saw his vague figure standing above the colonel, who was leaning back against the wall. Their voices mingled in a melodious tone that lulled me to sleep. Suddenly, I was back home again. Father and Mr. McCarthy were talking, their voices creating a monotonous murmur …

"He's exhausted, poor boy. Fell asleep sitting up against the wall."

There was a pause, then a gentle voice, "He's a good lad." Footsteps approached, and I was gently lowered. "Rest easy, Michael."

* * *

Blinking, I stared up into the dark. *Still night.* I listened, waiting for the hooting of an owl. I waited … and waited … *Something's not right.* I sat up. The wind was blowing and all was quiet, too quiet. Slowly, I crept from my bed and peeked around the door frame. The camp was still. Then suddenly, I caught sight of a lone figure … a dark shadow. The figure was creeping among the sleeping soldiers. My heart froze in fear and every fiber of my being shrunk in terror. They were here! Numb all over, I watched the shadow retreat back into the forest. Hands quivering, I drew my pistol and crawled to where Anderson lay.

"Sir," I shook his shoulder, and he was instantly awake.

"Corporal! What is it?"

My mouth went dry, "They're here in the camp!"

His eyes grew wide and he stared at me in disbelief.

"I saw a figure dressed in all black among the men. He retreated to the forest."

Anderson was reaching for his pistol, "Major Sanders." He motioned to me and I woke the Major quickly and informed him. Together we moved to the door and stared into the night. Nothing moved among the camp or forest.

"What would they want, sneaking about our camp? Check with the guards and see if they've heard or seen anything suspicious," Anderson sounded irritated. Major Sanders woke a captain nearby and together they scurried off. "Where did you see this figure, Corporal?" Anderson demanded.

"About right there, Sir." I said, pointing a finger to the center of a group of sleeping soldiers.

"Impossible," Anderson hissed, "I doubled the guard. No one could have gotten past." Waiting for Sanders and the captain to return, I became discouraged and began doubting I had ever seen the lone figure. I almost wished they would come again just so Anderson would believe me. Suddenly Sanders was running toward us. The young captain was at his heels. His face was as pale as a ghost.

"They're gone!" he shouted, waking the soldiers sleeping nearby. "The guards, Sir! They've disappeared!" Sanders halted directly in front of us. "This note was pinned under a bayonet where a guard had been posted." Anderson snatched the note away and read it under his breath.

Colonel Jason Anderson,

    My compliments, Sir. Your supply wagons serve an excellent dinner. Many thanks to you for your generous contribution of ammunitions this very night. The confederacy is in your debt.

Till we meet again.
Yours respectfully.

"So, they're simply robbing us blind in the middle of the night then," Anderson crumpled the paper in his fist. "Get the boy back here. We should move out." I threw the saddle onto the colonel's stallion, glad to be leaving.

"Colonel!" Sanders appeared after searching for the boy, "He's gone, Sir! The guide, he's gone!" Not a word came from the colonel's lips, but I knew inwardly he was boiling with anger. We could not leave these woods in the dead of night with no guide.

"Stupid boy …" He fumed, "Get the men up and fires blazing!" He ordered and turned away muttering, "Thieving wolves don't come near a flame."

* * *

The next morning, Colonel Anderson had sent Sanders and I out on a short mission to a nearby town where we had found out a superior officer was encamped. After reporting the news of the recent events, we headed back to camp.

"I could surely eat something, Sir." I grumbled. Sanders glanced over at me and smiled. "Perhaps we'll come upon a kindly farmer with a good cook for a wife. Aye? Would that suit you?"

"Yes, Sir!" I grinned and pressed on with the hope of something fresh for a change.

Unexpectedly, a small cottage rose before us. It had no farmyard, only a small vegetable garden in the back and a smoking chimney. There was a soft sobbing sound coming from the opposite side, and Sanders gave the signal for me to follow. Turning the corner, we came upon a woman kneeling on the ground besides the corpse of a young boy. The scene was horrible. I jumped from my saddle without a thought and rushed forward.

"Ma'am!" I cried, "What happened? Who did this?" I fell down next to her and her tear-stained face turned toward me.

"Get back!" She shrieked. "Ya wasn't here to help when they came! Ya would leave us to the enemy and not lift a finger! Where are ya soldiers when we need ya! Ya let the lot of them tear us ta bits! I hate ya! All of ya!" She fell upon the lifeless body again sobbing more loudly. Sanders stood over me. He reached down placing a hand on the woman's shoulder and she scrambled away suddenly terrified.

"Don't touch me!" She sobbed again wailing uncontrollably. "No man here to protect us! They came like ghosts in the night, killin' and destroyin' and takin' what isn't theirs. They killed me boy! Killed him when he tried to defend me, just up and shot him like he was a dog!" She screamed. "He

wouldn't let 'em lay a hand on his mum! So, they just up and shot him ....
said us Irish wasn't fit for nothin' anyhow." She wiped the tears with the
back of her hand and turned a despairing face to us. "Took advantage of
me, he did. Their leader, the devil they follow!" She covered her face with
her hands and I could see her whole body shaking. "Just kill me. Please, I
don't want to live in this world no more. I don't." Her pleading cries for
death were more than I could bear. Brushing the red hair from the young
boy's ivory face, I kissed the cold forehead, my tears spilling onto his brow.
I heard Sanders move to where the woman was curled up into a ball on the
ground sobbing like a child. He placed a hand on her shoulder, which she
tried to shrug off.

"Easy," he whispered and slowly scooped up her slight body. She
seemed to fall into unconsciousness. "The boy, Michael."

The boy was thin and fragile like his mother and I easily lifted him
from the red stained grass where he lay.

"We'll take them to the nearest town," Sanders said once he was up on
his horse again.

"Yes, Sir." As we rode from the house, I glanced back, sick at heart.
Then I saw a flash of something black in the woods.

The ride back to camp was silent and long. Some kind townsfolk took
the lady in, and the church said they would attend to her son's funeral. As I
gently lowered the body down to their waiting hands, I felt as though I were
giving up my own kin. Sanders had not said a word as we rode and a
strange look of anger had set upon his face. He kept a steady pace and I
hurried to keep up. I was weary to the bone when we finally rode into the
encampment. The fires were being lit and the men talked as coffee brewed.

Sanders motioned me to my tent, "I'll let the colonel know we've
returned." Watching Sanders disappear into the colonel's tent, I climbed
into my own and fell onto the blanket laid out.

"You look weary, my friend," Peter's soft voice spoke. When I didn't
move I heard him lean closer.

"Michael? What happened?" We stared at each other after I recounted
the tale. "When did this happen?"

"Last night," I answered, ripping up a piece of straw.

"Do you know about where the cottage was located?"

The question was so direct, it caught me off guard, "Well, just north of here." I stopped.

He fell onto his back and stared up at the canvas. I studied him a good moment. His face, though troubled, showed an expression of deep thought. He seemed to be working on something. I couldn't make this strange young reporter out. He was charming, friendly and open. Yet sometimes I got a vague sense of something secretive about him that I didn't like. After deciding I would keep watch over my friend, I rolled over.

* * *

"Finally," I watched as the boots disappeared into the night. I began sifting through Peter's sack. A couple of empty books, notebooks, a sketch pad and even some notes on our movements. *What could he be doing in the middle of such a dark night?* I lay back down since there was nothing else I could search through. Rolling onto my side, I gazed out into the darkness. Crickets were chirping calmly in the tall grassy fields while a cool breeze blew in from the west. I was reminded of a night not long ago with Kelsey. *Oh Kelsey ...* I sighed and wiped the tears that rolled down my face. Then through cloudy eyes I saw a black form standing just inside the tree line. I focused and leaned further. A black horse and rider stood perfectly still facing the camp like a ghostly guard. Suddenly he whipped about and disappeared into the forest. I wondered what had made him disappear.

Footsteps neared the tent. The flap was removed. Peter Kingston climbed back into his bed. I dared not move, but listened to the sound of his breathing.

A Lighter Shade of Darkness
Chapter 39

Elizabeth

A HAND CLAMPED over my mouth. Gasping, I awoke. In the darkness above me, I heard a voice whisper, "Come with me."

We exited out of the small makeshift tent I had constructed for myself in a far corner of the prison camp. Every night since we had been captured, either Will, John or Nathan had sat awake just ten feet from my tent. They did not realize that I knew they were there all along. I thanked God for their protection.

The cool night air blew through the windows and cracks in the wall. The ever present stench of death and disease hung thick as the darkness itself. I wrapped my ragged shawl around my shoulders. Not knowing what was happening, I stepped quickly, trying to keep up with Nathan's long, but silent strides. We moved across the filthy ground to the other side of the cell's boundary. Soon a figure joined us. It was John. Nathan nodded to him and a small smile came over John's weary face. Some of the prisoners had erected a storage tent on the other side of the big open cell. Approaching the canvas, I noticed a couple men outside the tent. Without a word being said they opened the canvas and motioned for us to go in. My eyes adjusted to the darkness. I found that a few other prisoners were already inside, sitting on crates and boxes. Nathan directed me to sit down as well. We sat quietly in the storage tent. Every few minutes a man or two would come in and join us. No one said a word. My curiosity rose with each person that entered the tent. *What is happening?* Soon the men who stood watch outside the structure moved inside. The prisoners parted, allowing the men to move to the back of the tent.

Carefully they shoved a crate aside, revealing a large, black hole. I stared in amazement as the realization began to dawn on me. One by one the prisoners disappeared into the ground. A wave of apprehension suddenly came upon me. Nathan signaled for me to go next. Suppressing the sudden fear, I obeyed and sat down at the edge of the pit. My feet dangling into empty space, it seemed as if there was no bottom to the hole I was descending into. Glancing back up, I saw Nathan nod in assurance. Letting go, I dropped into the darkness. Feeling around blindly, my hands touched a wall and floor of cold earth. Pressing myself against it, I waited hearing noises above me, indicating the men who followed. Soon I felt a hand touch my shoulder. Knowing it was Nathan, I followed the sound as he began to move through the crawl space. John followed close behind. Going through the utter blackness, I felt as if I was moving into a void perpetually. Soon a lighter shade of darkness could be seen above.

Climbing out into the night, I looked back and saw the dim outline of the prison building. A vague sense of freedom came over me. The prisoners ahead waved a silent good-bye to their prison mates and moved into the sparse woods beyond the town. John came up beside me.

"We're free," he sighed in relief. Laying a hand on his shoulder, I smiled at him. Nathan joined us.

"We have to move quickly … away from the town," he scanned the surrounding area. Suddenly a light flashed near the prison building. Several lanterns and torches became visible. A loud voice echoed through the quiet night.

"There they are! Get 'em boys!" The pounding of hooves came rushing over the short distance that separated us from the prison camp. Shots rang out. The prisoners around us scattered.

"Go! Go!" Nathan's voice yelled to us. Turning frantically, I dashed toward the woods ahead. John and Nathan followed. More gun shots echoed in the still air. A sickening thud resounded on the ground beside me. Stopping, I spun around and gazed at the form on the ground.

"John!" My breath caught in my throat. Nathan fell on the ground beside him, checking the boy. After a moment, he jumped up.

"It's no use. He's dead."

I stared numbly at his still figure. Images of our life back in Gettysburg flew quickly before my mind. Young children playing in the quiet town. Mothers calling us in for supper. Hands gripped my shoulders.

"Listen to me! We have to go, now!" Nathan's voice rang vaguely in my ears. I again realized how fragile life is. One moment he was there, alive, talking and smiling ... the next moment gone, still and silent. The urgency in Nathan's voice soon pulled me out of the sudden trance.

"Listen, run to the woods, I'm going the other way ... they'll chase me not you," he said hurriedly as he watched the horsemen coming in our direction.

"But ... you can't—," I stuttered nervously.

Nathan stared hard into my eyes, "I will come back." Not knowing what to say, I glanced around frantically. "Elizabeth," he grasped my shoulders, "I will come back." The pounding of hooves and shouting voices drew nearer. With one last look, Nathan shoved me in the direction of the woods. Obeying his command, I raced toward the tree line. My heart pulsed rapidly. Entering the trees, I was hidden in the dense brush. Hearing the noises turn in another direction, I knew they were following Nathan. Slowly stepping forward, I emerged from the shadow of the woods. In the distance, from the torch light, I discerned two men jumping off their horses.

"No," I breathed. A sickening feeling overwhelmed me as Nathan was captured. Turning around, I fled farther into the darkening countryside.

Beware the Night
Chapter 40

Amy

THE MARYLAND COUNTRYSIDE we moved into was beautiful, with its farmhouses tucked away in the rolling hills. *How much of this I would have missed if I had stayed home. Breathtaking! Simply breath-taking!* A bright red sun sat on the hill tops, clinging to the evergreen branches as it shot its last rays diffidently across the sky. Birds chirped happily in the branches as they sang their last song of the day. At the end of the road ahead sat a small town between two hills. I could hear soft music playing in the distance. As we cantered closer, I saw blue uniforms in the streets. Wagons were parked along the side of the road and soldiers roamed about flirting with the local girls. Very few officers were about and as we entered the town, the ladies took their eyes off the infantry men to gaze in awe at the handsome young horsemen that rode confidently with shining boots and glittering sabers. I heard a few awe-struck gasps and many fans quickened their fluttering. Colonel Anderson, staring stoically ahead while pretending not to notice their admiration, seemed to have grown a good couple of inches. The foot soldiers glanced up, hardly a welcoming look in their eyes. They had marched far and long. The dirt of the country roads covered their boots and pants legs. A saber was drawn by an officer. He raised his hand halting the line as we reached the courthouse.

An array of officers stood on the porches and balconies. Ladies gathered about offering drinks. Anderson glanced around for the commanding officer and then dismounted. I slid off my gelding for the first time in hours. My legs felt weak. My sword caught at my side. I readjusted it and followed after Colonel Anderson and Major Sanders.

The infantry officers examined us as we climbed the stairs with spiteful eyes. I drew in closer to the colonel as he planted himself squarely on the porch, pulling off his gloves and returning their gaze. The officer in the way of the door stepped back and saluted. Anderson led us through the open door and into a large entryway of the courthouse.

"Sir," an aide approached and saluted.

"Where's your colonel?"

"Upstairs on the balcony, Sir," he said, motioning. "Shall I inform him of your arrival?"

"Yes, at once, Corporal," Anderson glanced about. The young man disappeared up a flight of stairs. As we came upon the balcony, I couldn't help but gaze in wonder at the view. The air was fresher and the sky brighter. Fields, hills and mountains reached far, directing my eye to where the sky met blue mountain peaks.

"Colonel Anderson." The plump colonel seated upon a large chair plucked the cigar from between his teeth. He rose and saluted in one giant motion. His officers looked us over. Sanders stepped aside and motioned me to do the same.

"Sir," Anderson took the hand offered.

"How's your outfit?" The officer motioned him to a seat, which he took gracefully.

"Very well, we've been keeping busy."

Laughter from the streets caught my attention, and I glanced down upon a vial scene of two men with a lady in front of the local saloon. I turned my eyes away. Further down the street a young man stood with his cap in hand as he held the reins of his steed. A young lady with dark hair stared shyly down at him from her porch. He offered up a flower which was taken by a pale slender hand.

"Gentlemen," an elderly lady, who stood in the doorway, addressed the colonels. "The ladies of our town would like to hold a ball to commemorate your arrival."

"That is very generous of you, Madam," Anderson rose. "The men will be grateful I'm sure." Sanders glanced over at me and raised an eyebrow playfully. My stomach turned. *I could not be in a ball! I couldn't lead! How awkward to be a man!*

"Colonel, Sir, perhaps it would be best if I secured a place for you to pass the night." I nervously offered, as we marched down the sidewalk to where the men were making ready to spend the night.

Anderson glanced over his shoulder at me. "Don't be concerned, Corporal. You needn't waste your time. We'll find a place right now."

Staring down at the boards, I tried to find an excuse to stay behind. Sanders shot a smile my way. His eyes twinkled with laughter. He must have thought I was too shy to go to a ball. As I looked around, I caught sight of Peter Kingston staring at me. He had a similar look in his eyes. Although playful, it was different in some way. His look was seemingly amused as if he entertained a different idea. With that, I dared not utter another word. We entered into a post office where a man stood at the counter. The loud clicking of spurs and the tromping of boots caught his attention and he glanced up.

"What can I do for you, gentlemen?" he looked a bit frightened and his hand quivered as he placed the letters on the countertop. The building was neatly kept. Anderson took his time looking about, thinking nothing of the good man's valuable time. The man waited eagerly and a young lady stepped up beside him, an apron tied about her waist. Her curly brown hair bounced on her thin shoulders as she stopped suddenly, surprised. I noticed Anderson locked his eyes upon her pretty face as she blushed and glanced down.

"My daughter, Katherine." The postmaster took her hand.

"How do you do, Miss," the colonel swept his hat off. She curtsied, timidly. "Sir, if we may beg room and board in your house tonight?" Anderson addressed the postman though he kept his eyes otherwise occupied.

The man glanced about, "Yes! Certainly, Sir. We've not much, but we offer all we have." He nodded, "That is, if you don't mind, we have another gentleman staying as well. He came a day ago."

"Not a problem, Sir. We thank you for your kindness. We are in your debt," Sanders bowed.

The man smiled and glanced over at his daughter, "Kate, prepare some rooms for these gentlemen." To us he said, "We live just across the road." The girl weaved through the officers and out the door.

Anderson turned back to the father, "Thank you, Sir." Bowing, he replaced his hat before we departed. The streets were now crowded with soldiers and civilians, who consisted mostly of women. It seemed as if a festival had come to town. Excitement filled the air as the sky dimmed. The ball was to take place across town in a large assembly building. We rode through the narrow streets like a parade. The regiment was to put up camp in a big open field. Horses were cared for, fed and watered. Tents were raised and fires lit. I was instructed to take a report of the companies. The officers gave a hasty report, eager to be off to the festivities.

After the report, Colonel Anderson rode up with the rest of the staff in glamourous array, and I mounted up. The moon rose to full height as we reached the ball and we were greeted by the infantry colonel and staff. Music and laughter filled the air. The ball room was bright with the glowing chandeliers and candles in the windows. A bountiful feast had been prepared.

"Welcome, Sirs," a short stocky gentleman bowed with a big grin on his face. "I am the Mayor of this lovely town and have the pleasure of welcoming you tonight. I hope you enjoy yourselves."

"Thank you, Sir," Anderson stated and shifted his eye to the crowd. "I'm sure we shall."

Major Sanders smiled and bowed to the man, who was promptly brushed aside by Anderson, who seemed to be on the hunt. Standing close beside Sanders, I watched as the elaborate ball ensued. The hoop skirts rustled across the floor to the music. I glanced about searching for Peter Kingston, but saw him nowhere. *I wonder where he disappeared to ...* After a while, I decided to go for a stroll to avoid an encounter that might lead to a dance. The cool night air filled my lungs and I gazed up at the stars that sang in the clear night sky. It was a quiet night with hardly a cricket chirping. Even the horses and dogs kept silent watch. I rubbed the muzzle of my gelding tied near the other staff horses and strolled into the garden.

Suddenly, I heard a voice. I glanced around a bush and saw Colonel Anderson and the postmaster's daughter. She seemed distressed.

"Pity, a lady such as you is wasted on a small country town." Stepping closer, he caught the soft brown hair gently and she turned to face him. I saw fear in her eyes as she stepped back. "You know I come from the capital city. You'd make quite a stir there."

"Colonel, you flatter me, but I wouldn't dream of leaving all I've ever known. I've grown up here. This land is a part of me. Besides that, I must take care of my father." She glanced over his shoulder to the building and then back to him.

He smiled, "There's nothing here for you, my dear. It's not the exciting city of Washington. I could give you all your heart desires. You'd see places you never dreamed of ... balls, operas." He kissed her hand and she quickly drew back.

"Sir, I'm sorry. I must get back to the ball. I promised I'd help." She took a step toward the ballroom, but he caught her arm and she whipped around.

"Kathrine, don't leave just yet." He smiled and motioned toward a bench, "Sit, or have you no time for a lonely soldier?"

"Really, I must go." She tried to pull away, "Sir, release me at once." A cruel smile spread across his face.

"Oh, Kathrine, but I have more immediate plans for you and I." My heart was pounding furiously. *I must do something! But what?*

"You heard the lady, Colonel." Suddenly, Peter Kingston was standing just ten feet away. The girl gasped and glanced hopefully over to where he stood. The Englishman took a few steps closer. I saw his hand resting on his belt.

Anderson looked annoyed, "What say do you have here?" Peter suddenly pushed back his coat to reveal a pistol.

"I'd say I have about six good reasons."

Suddenly, a loud cry came from the camp. Horses screeched and shots were fired. A chill went down my back. The enemy! Sprinting into the street, I squinted into the night. The camp was pitch black and the noise rose to horrifying chaos.

"Colonel!" I shouted at the top of my lungs and suddenly Anderson was beside me as well as Major Sanders. We stared in terror.

Finally, Anderson shouted, "Get the infantry out here! We're under attack!" We mounted our horses and galloped after Anderson down the slope to where the invaders had begun their deadly surprise attack. As we approached, I could see dark forms riding toward us in a long sweeping line. The thunder of the attackers drowned out the screams and shouts of our men running like animals about to be slaughtered. The Rebel cry turned my blood cold. My horse rose on his hind legs striking out as I clung to his back.

"We cannot hold against them, Colonel!" Sanders shouted, "Pull back into the town, Sir! We must!" A bullet whizzed past my ear and I ducked in terror.

Anderson whipped his horse about angrily, "Ya!" He kicked his spurs into the big stallion.

Up on the crowded slope, a loud blast met us as we reached the top and the fleeing men fell to the ground, struggling to get back on their feet. The cannon was reloaded and the orders shouted. My gelding whipped about fearfully, tossing me to the hard ground. I scrambled to my feet, trying to calm the terrified beast, while I could hardly keep my own wits. Soon the ground shook with cannon blasts and the sky lit up with flashes of bright orange light, making a terrible glow over us all. Clinging to the side of the gelding, I could not bring myself to put a foot in the stirrup. My knees were buckling beneath me.

"Get on your horse, Corporal!" Anderson shouted at me. I just stared up at him, wide-eyed, with hands clenching the saddle.

Anderson leaned over, "I said get on the horse. Are you a cavalryman or a coward?" The colonel then placed himself between two of the cannon stations.

"Easy, boy," I choked and climbed upon the tall horse. The infantry colonel was suddenly beside us.

"Drive them back, Captain!" He shouted at the cannoneer in charge.

"Where are your troops, Colonel?" Anderson asked more calmly. The colonel glanced back toward the town.

"They are assembling, Colonel. We will stop them here." Anderson nodded and rose up in his stirrups. The officers were now taking hold of the fleeing troops and forming some sort of defense. I could see deeper into the valley where the horses had been tied. A great volley was taking place. Our men would not give up their horses.

"Get down there to where the horses are picketed!" Anderson shouted at one lieutenant, who had most of his company assembled. The frightened young man saluted with a shaking hand and shouted to his men. They disappeared into the valley. As the sky lit up periodically, I could make out the form of the oncoming enemy. Their line was broken, and the black wave that had been sweeping in full speed through the valley was now at half speed. Our men had time to get organized and fight back. Suddenly, the infantry advanced from behind us and resisted any further advance by the enemy. They drove them back. It was a bloody tangled mess.

Out of nowhere came a man staggering up the hill. His face swathed in blood as he screamed in agony. Someone ran out and grabbed him, dragging him behind the lines. As I stared after them, I realized for the first time I was trembling uncontrollably. The enemy retreated and there was a strange silence. Even the wounded seemed to hold their pain filled screams in anticipation. A few officers shouted orders to their men, preparing for another attack.

Anderson squinted into the black night. He leaned forward and then kicked the stallion, trotting down the slope a little way. My hands were clenched around the reins and I could scarcely move them. I broke into a sweat.

"Do you see anything, Corporal?" Anderson called out.

Squinting, I blinked into the still night, "No, Sir, nothing."

"I can't hear ... Sanders. Are they reforming?" Anderson called back to us.

"No, Sir, I can't hear a thing. It's silent as a grave out there."

Anderson looked frustrated for a moment. "I don't understand. It was too sudden." Sanders shook his head and glanced down unable to answer.

"Colonel!" The infantry commander was beside us breathing heavily. I stared at the large form slumped on the elegant steed. "They must have thought they tangled with the whole Union army."

Anderson shook his head, "No. They're up to something, Colonel. They're too cunning for that."

The colonel glanced about, "But they're gone."

"I know. I don't like it one bit. Get someone down in the valley to check on the horses, Major Sanders!"

"Yes, Sir!" Sanders shouted. A gunshot went off and the horses shrieked.

"Don't shoot, you fools! Union!" The shout came from the valley. Sanders sat silent beside me as if waiting for something.

"They're out there waiting! We must form up and quickly!"

"Colonel, get your men in that valley!" Anderson shouted to the heavy man, who trotted away shouting orders in a lazy fashion. Soon the infantry set up defenses in the desolate camp. I waited patiently, glad to sit in silence as Sanders and Anderson consulted with the infantry colonel. I heard not a sound; not a horse nickered, no wounded cried out in pain. As I stared into the night, I saw the shadows move in the forest. I knew the enemy had not left us.

The Valley of the Shadow
Chapter 41

Elizabeth

COLD, WET MOSS rubbed against my cheek. Rolling over, I suddenly sat up. *Where am I?* The tall trees loomed and spun around me, silhouetted against a moon lit sky. An owl hooted warily and a distant howling added to the eerie feel of the night. I scooted up against a tree and leaned my head back on the damp bark. Reaching up, I pushed the moist hair from my forehead, but only succeeded in rubbing dirt into it. Mud stained my hands, face and dress. In my mind, I could only envision the horrors I had seen in the prison camp. Each night, I tossed and turned with nightmares ... or memories ... there was little difference. *How long had I been here? How long had I wandered, stumbled and hungered in this endless wilderness?* Within the dense forest it was hard to determine night from day. In the darkness, I groped for warmth and comfort. The trees reached out their dark hands toward me. Sweating, I crawled to my feet.

"Water," I whispered eagerly into the cold night air. Falling against a tree, I felt the ground dropping out from under me. Reaching up to feel the heat coming from my forehead, I came out of my delirium long enough to realize I had a high fever before slipping back into the madness. Suddenly John was there, and Will. I watched them as they smiled and talked together. Farther in the distance a form stood with its back to me. The figure's wrists were tied behind his back and his clothes were torn and dirty.

He suddenly turned his face back to look at me. It was Nathan, his eyes were focused and full of determination.

"Nathan," I breathed. The forms disappeared. A strong hand clamped around my mouth. I pulled at the black glove that encompassed my throat. Helplessly, I struggled with the strong arms that held me. Whipping my head around, I looked into the dark face of a man, one eye was covered with a black patch. The fever, in addition to the strength of the man, was too much for me and after a long struggle, I collapsed limply into his arms.

I awoke, finding myself propped up against another tree. Yet, this time there was not the daunting solitude of the forest, but the intimidating company of many men in black. I shrunk into the tree for protection. I recognized the strong figure that approached me; the man with the eye patch. He lifted me effortlessly to my feet and, without a word, led me by the arm to a little clearing in the dense woods. The full moon shown clearly into this section of the wilderness. I glanced nervously around me at the tall, dark forms that stood just inside the circle of trees. Suddenly they snapped to attention. The man who held my arm gave a smart salute in the direction we were facing. In unnerving anticipation, I stared into the thick darkness of the woods. My eyes slowly adjusted and I could just barely make out the figure of a tall man, slowly moving toward the light. He stopped just short of the moonlight. I could just make out his apparel: tall, black boots, black riding pants, black jacket with a short black cape. His hat was black, even his buttons did not glisten in the night. His saber was just as dark on the handle as was the scabbard.

The man beside me stated, "Sir, this is the woman we found just outside our encampment. Thought you might like to question her, Sir." The man pushed me forward a couple feet. The leader raised his eyes and watched me for several moments. Then suddenly, almost fearfully, he took a small step deeper into the shadows, as if afraid to unveil his face.

"State your name and business here, Ma'am," he commanded sternly, but softly.

Sweating with fever and fear, I swayed on my feet, nearly losing my balance. Clearing my throat, I answered dryly, "I'm lost. Sick. Need water." Wiping at my chapped lips I added, "Please just let me go, I need to get back to ... I just need to get back." The tall figure crossed his arms and looked away.

After a long pause, he questioned quietly, "Back to where?" I looked up, not knowing how to answer him. If I told him the truth, surely he would take me back to the prison camp, or worse ...

I dug around in my delirious mind for a reply, "Home. That's all, Sir. Home." The eyes shot up and lingered, gazing hard into mine. I shrunk under the lengthy stare. After what seemed like a lifetime, the leader turned around to leave.

Then he looked back over his shoulder and ordered, "Keep the woman under guard. Give her some water and food." As he disappeared into the cover of darkness, I felt the earth drop out from under me again. As I fell to the ground, someone caught me and I was led away.

* * *

It was still dark when I opened my eyes. My head pounded. Sliding my hand along the cool grass to feel out my surroundings, I realized I was in a small tent. Sweating, I sat up. Murmuring reached my ears, as two silhouetted figures moved along my tent wall. They carried guns in their arms, and walked a routine path. They were indeed guarding my tent. A sudden apprehension shook me. Stiffening, I scooted to the corner of the tent. In the far corner there was a plate of hardtack and a canteen of water. Feverishly, I attempted to gather my scattering thoughts to form a plan of escape. I did not go through such an escape from the prison camp only to be taken captive again by a band of renegade Rebels.

"Miss," a rough voice approached and called to me. I hesitated, then slowly lifted the tent flap. The man with the eye patch was standing outside holding a bundle in his arm and another canteen in his hand. "The commanding officer ordered these to be given to you: a couple days provisions and water. We are moving out this morning and we cannot take you with us. There is a town not far from here, you should be able to get there within a couple of days. Here, he drew a sort of map for you to follow." He unfolded a torn piece of parchment with markings on it and handed it to me along with the canteen and bundle of food. I took them, confused. *Why would he care what happened to me?*

"Thank your commander for me," I paused taking a step away. "Am I free to go?" The man nodded. I gazed curiously at his completely black attire ... even the canteen he had handed me was black. *Who are these men?* I shuddered as I walked farther and farther from the encampment. *Was it some sort of trick? Would they follow me?* I pulled out the map again and tried to make sense of it, my head still pounding. The fever seemed to come and go, and I prayed I would have the strength to find help and a place to recover. I needed to get back home, but at this point I didn't even know where I was.

The Rise of Doubt
Chapter 42

Amy

PULLING THE CLOTH around my shoulders, I climbed from the empty tent. Glancing about, I quickly surveyed the entire camp to be sure there was not a guard nearby. A fog had wrapped itself around the forest and hills as the cool night prevailed. Heart pounding, I traced the steps in the muddy earth that led away from the camp. My hands hit the rough bark as I plastered myself up against it. Still no sign of the pickets. Rain drizzled down almost in a mist so that I could hardly see but thirty feet in front of me. The footprints appeared before me. *What was this Englishman up to?* Deeper and deeper into the forest they led, until the glow from the fire disappeared behind me and the world was ominously black.

The darkness soon enveloped me and the forest that surrounded me was again strangely silent. The path was fading. I worried that I would not find my way back to camp. *If I do return, will I be able to sneak back in before the bugle sounds? If Peter Kingston can do it, so can I.* The prints grew closer together and suddenly took a sharp turn to the right. Glancing up, I noticed a cracked limb and on it a plaid torn cloth ripped upon the sharp edge.

After traveling some distance, there appeared a small town before me. The footprints led to a hotel that sat just on the outskirts. The little town was made up of a saloon, a mercantile, a blacksmith shop, the hotel and just a few homes. It was dark and hardly a light glowed in the windows. Feeling very exposed, I crossed the open streets to the little hotel, but stopped short when I noticed the footprints suddenly disappeared into the alleyway and into the saloon. Swallowing hard, I forced the door open and the smell of smoke and hard whiskey welcomed me.

I coughed and rubbed my hands together, glad to be out of the weather though I would have rather been in a different setting. Two men stood near the counter, bundled up as if they had been out for a long ride in the dark. One of them turned a shifty eye toward me and elbowed the other. The five men gathered around a poker table paid me no mind, and I saw one of them had fallen asleep with his head on the table near an empty bottle. I moved into a dark corner surveying the room for Peter. Something sharp and steely cold touched my throat and I froze in fear as a gruff voice whispered in my ear.

"One sound from you and you're a dead man, Corporal. Get down that hall and don't even think about escaping." Without turning, I did as I had been told and passed through the hallway until the knife at my back jabbed me again. A gloved hand tapped a rhythm on the door. *If Peter knows these men he'll make certain they don't hurt me ... won't he?* The door creaked on its hinges and we entered a dusty, dingy apartment. Before I knew what had happened I found myself on the floor.

"Sir, I found this one following." The gruff voice spoke as the door squeaked shut. Shaking all over, I glanced up into the dim room. A single candle sat on a table, the worn curtains were drawn and the smell of tobacco smoke surrounded me.

"What's your name, boy?" the voice that came from the shadows was full and commanding with a deep southern drawl that sent a chill down my back and I knew these were not men to be reckoned with. A dark shadow seemed to rise from the corner and the figure of a tall man shrouded in black from head to toe stood before me. I choked. Here before me stood our most wanted enemy, the leader of the phantom regiment! The spurs clinked on the wooden floor as he neared and suddenly knelt down before me. The face I knew, though it had changed now with a patch across one eye. The rough beginnings of a beard disguised it further. It all came rushing back to me at once ... the strange soldier with Kelsey at the McCarthy's house, the road in Gettysburg with John, the Inn. It was Lieutenant Morgan. I turned my eyes away. *Did he recognize me?*

"Your name, boy."

"Michael Jones ... Sir." I started drawing back, afraid he would recognize me, then I would be a helpless woman in the hands of Rebel beasts. I remembered Mrs. Denny saying once. *"Yes, who knows what brutalities those Rebels inflict on their prisoners! I shudder to think of a young girl in the hands of those criminals!"*

I shivered in the cold dark room. What kind of a man was this Seth Morgan, one hardened by the destruction of war, tormented by the lives he had butchered? Now I could see, there was no doubt that he was the one in charge of such hateful acts.

"Why did you come here?" He rose above me.

I clamored to my feet, "I ... I was just ..."

The man turned his back on me for a moment then began in a menacing tone, "I know why you're here. You've placed us in a very difficult position, Corporal. Your curiosity has gotten the better of you this time. Now tell me who you really are?"

"Sir, he's *just a boy*." The voice of Peter Kingston came from the shadows, yet he remained hidden from sight.

My interrogator glanced over his shoulder at him. "He's old enough to bear the consequences of his actions. After all he joined the fight." His voice trailed off as he stared at me.

"Do with me what you must, Sir." I felt courage rise deep from within me. "I've seen what you've left behind, the homes you've burned to the ground, the lives you've torn to pieces. You hide, waiting for darkness to do the wicked deeds you have no courage to do in the day. You have no heart and no honor. If this is a sample of what you Confederates so boldly call your right and a defense of your home, then I hate all of you! May God punish you for your unmerciful deeds!" Lieutenant Morgan whipped out his sword and raised it to my throat. I winced, but stood fast as I waited for the blow that would end my life.

"You know nothing! Your colonel is a more treacherous monster than you can imagine! Ask him what happened to that boy on that Irish woman's farm." He leaned in closer so that his face was three inches from mine as he spoke in a whisper, "Ask him what happened to the Irish lady. He's a vile beast. I should have killed him when I had his life under my sword five months ago. I was a fool to spare such a miserable wretch." He dropped the sword from my throat and turned his back to me in one swift motion. My head was spinning. His words troubled me. My heart shuddered within me. I felt suddenly overwhelmed.

"You, Corporal Michael Jones, are not what you make yourself out to be." Stunned, I felt my heart stop. "But ... I think we will have a use for you, Corporal." Fear gripped me as all my worst nightmares stared at me with menacing eyes. *Lord, prepare me now if I must fight ...*

The black form turned suddenly, "I will let you go." The voice was calm and collected. "But you must place this in the hand of your colonel when you return." An envelope appeared before me. "Say nothing of what you've seen here or you'll find us less merciful. And don't think I won't know of your every move, Corporal." Barely able to reach out a hand, I nodded and took it. The envelope shook in my grasp. There was a slight smile on the lieutenant's face, "Perhaps you'll prove a valuable piece in our little game after all."

* * *

A soft breeze blew through the tent flap. The paper fluttered in the colonel's hand as he read. Major Sanders, who stood at his side, kept his eyes on the guard directly in front of him. *He's disappointed in me. Can I blame him? No, you're so stupid, Amy. Leaving camp in the middle of the night. Acting like some war hero ...*

Colonel Anderson lowered the letter. His brow furrowed. He flashed his eyes at me. "How do I know you're not working for them?" His eyes narrowed and he fingered the letter. "Why did you leave in the middle of the night, Corporal?"

"Sir, I noticed my tent mate, Peter Kingston, had disappeared many nights prior and I was suspicious of him, Sir."

"Why didn't you report to me?"

Swallowing hard, I tried to think, "I suppose I was afraid, Sir. Afraid to be wrong."

Anderson paced, "So you decided you needed more evidence and that you would go after it on your own, even at the risk of your own life. Do you know the consequences for deserters around here, Corporal? Do you?"

"Yes, Sir," I kept my eyes on the tent behind Colonel Anderson.

"You're an idiot, Jones. I should have you shot for pure stupidity. Get him out of my sight." Anderson motioned the guards away.

As I turned to leave, I ventured a glance at Sanders. His eyes were full of disappointment like a father over a disobedient son, yet in them I read some hope. He would speak to the Colonel on my behalf. The guard placed a hand on my shoulder and shoved me out. It seemed like an hour before the tent flap was removed and Major Sanders came forth. He turned to look at me, his face still solemn as he mounted his gray mare.

"Release him," Anderson's voice commanded the guards. He stood just outside his tent, arms folded. I rose to my feet.

"Sir, I ..." I stuttered, "Thank you, Sir."

"I don't have time for disciplinary actions now, Corporal. The enemy is escaping my grasp even as we speak. But there will be plenty of time for that once we've destroyed him." My heart sunk. "You should be thanking Major Sanders, you know. He spared you, not I. Seems to think you're worth keeping alive."

* * *

The long road stretched out before us through the open fields as we traveled in broad daylight. For days we rode, cantering over the countryside. I did not know what that letter had contained to make us ride in this manner, but I felt this was not the way to catch our enemy, cunning and clever as he was. I was reminded of the British army traveling in loud long columns while the Indians in the trees waited for the enemy to come into sight. The dust rose from the horses' hooves causing an enormous cloud in the valley we traveled through. Night fell and we camped near a riverbed. It was well past midnight when I crawled out of my tent. I stood on the shore. Sleep did not come easily these nights.

A soft breeze whispered across the river. Frogs croaked and crickets sang all around. The animals never sang when the enemy was nearby. We were safe at least for tonight. I sank onto a log and closed my eyes wearily. It was weighing on me: the traveling, the loneliness, the memories and the nagging questions. *What are you trying to prove? What is this really about, Amy?* I began to question my reasons for coming. I'd made my heroic speech to Sarah. Of course, it had sounded so splendid and honorable. *Was that really the reason?* I did want to help, I knew I did. But deep down inside I knew that was not the only reason. I was trying to prove I didn't need Kelsey, that I was strong enough on my own. The black pit of failure seemed to open its mouth before me. I'd fallen in so many times. I felt as though I was fighting to keep my head above the surface. Now I had let Colonel Anderson and Major Sanders down. I felt like a useless soldier.

Suddenly, I was aware of someone watching me. My eyes popped open and I scanned the tree line. Nothing. Surely, the pickets would know of something. Then there it was in the shadows. Just fifty yards away stood a dark figure of a horse and rider. I squinted. *Could it be?* It did not move, not even a snort from the horse. Then, it disappeared. I ducked behind the log. The crickets that had grown silent suddenly sang once more. I breathed heavily. *They're gone, but why?* Here we were camped on the edge of a river, like sitting ducks waiting to be killed, yet he did not attack.

Morning rose with a pink sky and calm breeze. I rubbed the crick in my neck and sat up against the log. The bugle sounded and the tents were soon packed away. A hand touched my shoulder and I glanced up at Major Sanders.

"We've got to get moving," he said solemnly and turned to go.

"Major Sanders!" Stopping dead in his tracks, he waited without turning around. "Thank you." The words were soft, but they reached him. I could see his shoulders relax.

He turned an eye upon me, "Your welcome, Michael." Watching him go, I felt the tension leave me. He understood.

I rose and prepared for the day that lay ahead of us. The sun rose high in the blue sky. As we rode southward, I spotted the figure of a woman on the horizon. *How strange! There was no town around for miles and not a house in sight.*

"Sir!" I called ahead. Pushing up between the colonel and Major Sanders, I pointed, "Sir, there's a woman on the horizon." Anderson squinted.

"Good eye, Corporal." Sanders stated, as Anderson raised a hand to the column, "Could it be a trap?"

"Let us approach alone," Anderson kicked the stallion into a canter. The staff followed. As we drew near, she stumbled, nearly falling over. We halted a few paces away.

"My lady!" Major Sanders called, "Do you need assistance?"

"Sir, please," as she lifted her head, my heart stopped and my blood drained. Elizabeth! Her face and clothes were spattered with mud. Her dress was torn and stained. Her body was sunken and frail, the bared parts of her arms were boney and white. She looked as if she had risen from a grave. Sanders had dismounted and ran toward her. As he reached for her, she collapsed in his arms. Lifting her easily, he carried her to where we stood.

"Looks as if she's come from a prisoner of war camp." He laid his hand on her forehead, "She has a fever." My stomach twisted. I wanted to reach out and touch her face and fall upon her weeping. "Must have gotten captured during a battle. They sometimes take the nurses to help in prison camps. Miserable beasts! It appears she has rations and water with her somehow though." He touched the bundle of food and a stained black canteen. "She needs rest and nourishment. She may yet make it."

"Perhaps … But we'll leave her at the nearest town. The enemy is too near. Sanders, you and Jones take her to a church in the dark. Alone. We don't need to be seen marching into a Confederate town," Anderson stated.

* * *

Touching the dirt-stained face, I released the tears that I'd been holding back. Major Sanders was outside speaking with the pastor in low tones.

"Elizabeth," I whispered. "We're leaving you here with these good people. I can't stay. You'll get well though. I promise I'll return … soon. Soon. Wait for me. Don't you dare leave me! Please, God, let her be all right." I breathed and dropped my head on her shoulder. "Elizabeth, if you can hear me, listen to this. I promise you here and now, I will return home. You had better be there when I get there because … because I need you … you're all I have left." I kissed her forehead, "I'll be home soon."

Turning a Blind Eye
Chapter 43

Elizabeth

July 1862

MY EYES FLUTTERED at the sudden ray of light streaming through an open window. I pulled the quilt over my head. Consciousness slowly returned. I remembered darkness. I remembered many men in black, then wandering through the forests and open fields trying to follow a map to find help. Then it was a blur in my mind again. Someone had helped me. Some soldiers had found me. They must've taken me somewhere. *Where am I?* I sat up quickly, too quickly. My head swam and throbbed. Falling back on the pillow, I groaned. Suddenly the door opened and a negro woman stepped inside carrying a tray. Seeing my eyes open, a small smile formed on her lips.

She leaned back toward the doorway and called gently, "Missus! The young lady just woke up!" Through the open doorway I could hear women laughing and talking. The rustling of petticoats drew nearer. A woman a few years older than me poked her head in the door. She was tall and slender, with thick dark curls framing her face and cascading onto her light pink calico gown. She smiled sweetly and greeted me, introducing herself as Mary Edwards.

I sat up on the edge of the bed, my head still throbbing, and tried to seem presentable.

"Pleased to meet you, Mary. It seems I am indebted to you. Thank you for taking me in. I'm not sure what has happened or how long I've been here."

Mary sat down on the bed next to me, "Do not trouble yourself. You have been here for several days, in and out of fever. You had us quite worried for a while. Some Union soldiers brought you to a church some time ago. They said they found you in the countryside. You were very weak." Her face changed, "Savages though they may be at times, at least these Northerners had the sense to bring a sick woman to the church." She turned back to me, "Now, what is your story? Why were you lost and sick wandering out in the countryside?"

I uneasily fingered the lace on the nightgown I wore. This was a very Southern woman according to her own words. *How am I to tell her that I just escaped a prison camp because I was aiding the Union cause? How would she react? For all I know she might turn me in to the Confederates and I would go back to that horrible place again.* Her voice broke through my thoughts, causing me to jump.

"I'm sorry. You're tired. You still haven't fully recovered from your ordeal. Rest, my friend. You don't need to tell me your story yet. Perhaps later we can take a walk through the town and talk then?" I nodded and tried to smile through my fears. She seemed like a very nice person. Trusting her would take some time though.

"Nancy, give …" she stopped, "What is your name?"

"Elizabeth Matthews." *Surely, I can give her my real name.*

"Certainly. Nancy, give Miss Matthews some tea and some soup. She needs to regain her strength. Let me know if you need anything."

"Thank you, Miss Edwards. You are very kind," I answered sincerely.

* * *

The nourishing food and plenty of rest I had been given the past couple weeks had truly done wonders for me. Bodily, I felt back to my full strength, yet in mind I still felt very weak. The months I had spent in the army seeing the horror of bloodshed and death had taken its toll on me. Now, with the hellish memory of the prison camp and the deaths of very close friends, I didn't know how much more I could handle. I wanted to run, run back to Gettysburg, back to all that was good and familiar, away from the memories. Perhaps Gettysburg could somehow erase all I had seen and known, and I could go back to how it was before. It was a sleepy little town, where we lived simple lives on our farms, giving to our neighbors and helping one another in good times and bad. I had been so anxious to leave that place and have adventure, and now all I wanted to do was to go back. It was a place in which my deepest concern was where my next coins would come from in order to make a living. *But how could I go back to that comfortable life knowing Nathan was still in that prison camp? How could I forget?*

"Elizabeth!" I jumped at the sound of my name. Mary stared at me. I could see concern in her eyes as we walked along the dirt road in the center of the small town. We were on our way to the small church on the outskirts of the town. There was to be a picnic after the service, celebrating the Southern victory of a recent battle.

"I'm sorry, Mary. I have a lot on my mind lately. Were you asking me something?" I tried to sound lively and interested.

"Oh, I was just talking about the picnic. I'm so glad you are able to stay here and come to these events," she swung her basket cheerfully. The beautiful sunlit day did hold anticipation of a perfect church picnic. *But how could I enjoy it, knowing what was happening on the battlefields, in the hospitals, in the prison camps? How could I celebrate with these Southerners their victory over the Union cause?*

"Elizabeth, you do worry me!" My thoughts were interrupted once again. We stopped walking as Mary touched my shoulder and turned me toward her, "Are you sure you don't want to talk about what it is that has been bothering you? You haven't spoken much even since you've recovered from your illness. You must've gone through something terrible. I did not know you before, but I'm certain you weren't always so dismal. I don't know, but I feel like underneath all that sadness is someone full of life and joy."

I glanced around at the countryside and the white church in the near distance. Then returned my gaze to my shoes as I pushed the dust around with them. "I'm sorry, Mary. I will try to be more cheerful. I want you to know I'm very grateful to you for your care and concern. I can tell you have a good heart and are a good friend to those in your life. I'm sorry I haven't been a very pleasant guest. I don't mean to be a worry to you."

"Elizabeth, I'm just concerned for you. So, if you want to talk about it, I am willing to listen." She squeezed my shoulder. I smiled gently at her kind face. *If only I could share my story of what I'd been through with her. It would be nice to have someone to talk it out with, to muddle through the confusion. I wish Amy were here right now.*

The pastor's sermon ended and we sang a few hymns in closing. A few Confederate soldiers were present. Either recovering from wounds or visiting for the day if their unit happened to be stationed nearby. At the end of the Sunday Service, we all gathered outside in the back of the church for the picnic. I was determined to not spoil the day for Mary. So painting on a smile, I jumped into the group of women bustling around the food and asked if I could help somehow. They excitedly shoved loaves of bread and butter into my hands. The Southern people did not have much to spare for a picnic, but what little they had saved for a special occasion, they did bring today in celebration. I moved to the far table and laid out the bread, jams and butter. Using a large knife, I sliced through the soft loaf. My mind unwittingly flew back to the prison camp. I wandered throughout the groups of prisoners. Their hollow cheeks and dull eyes looked up at me as I passed out some moldy bread. The smells and sights came rushing back. Death rose around me. I saw Will as he suffered and died lying in that filthy place … Throwing the knife down, I gathered up my skirts and ran out toward a big oak tree on the far side of the field, away from the crowds and their celebration and their delicious foods and smiling faces. Hiding on the other side of the thick tree, I sank down onto the ground in the shade and let the tears run down my face.

"Excuse me, Miss," a deep, warm voice startled me. Wiping quickly at my face and jumping to my feet, I stood near a young, tall soldier in the Confederate gray uniform. Taking a step back, I looked up at him. He stood straight and confident. Sandy hair, with a goatee and a mustache, framed the young captain's handsome face. "I'm sorry I startled you, but I couldn't help but notice you seemed distraught. I confess I was watching you when you suddenly ran off. Is there something I can do to be of assistance to you? Oh, Captain Luke Preston at your service, Miss."

I curtsied and introduced myself, trying to wipe the look of sorrow from my face. "Thank you, Sir. I am well. Just a bit under the weather I suppose."

He smiled quizzically, "You aren't from around here, are you Miss Matthews? From the sound of your voice, you must come from the Northern states."

Breath caught in my throat. Mary never once mentioned noticing the difference in dialects. Perhaps she didn't want to pry. Captain Preston walked closer to the tree and leaned against it, then continued.

"The bullet wound on your hand. How did that happen? Out hunting squirrels, were you?" He cocked an eyebrow and bent his head toward me. My shocked expression must've caused him much amusement, for a smirk crept across his face as I instinctively grasped my scarred hand. Trying to steady my nerves, I brushed past him and hurried back toward the gathering around the churchyard.

"Wait, wait ..." the young captain ran up beside me laughing. "You must forgive my forwardness and questions. I was merely teasing you." I continued walking. "Oh, come now! Surely you're not going to ignore me just because of a little teasing?" He was now walking backwards in front of me as he spoke. Seeing the people around us starting to stare, I stopped in embarrassment over the whole situation.

"Captain," I spoke in a hushed tone. "Please do not make a scene. You are forgiven. Now if you will excuse me, I must help the other ladies."

He slid directly in my path as I tried to move around him. "Miss, since there are no hard feelings between us now, I was wondering if you would allow me to escort you to the dance tonight? It's nothing big, just a small gathering here in town, but it will be quite fun." He grinned at me.

Stunned at his presumptuousness and familiarity, I stood in silence for several moments. Finally, I spoke up determinedly, "I must get back to the other ladies."

"At least say you will consider it."

Inwardly I marveled at the persistence of this man. I sighed and relented, "Fine. I will consider it, Captain."

"That's all I ask," he smiled confidently and moved out of my path.

* * *

"Let me fill you in Elizabeth," Mary ventured excitedly as we hung our bonnets up and were putting the extra food away. "Captain Preston just came back on leave from a long battle. The news of the Confederate victory is all over town as you know from our celebration today. There was much bloodshed. It sounds just terrible, but nonetheless, we won! They're saying it is quite the turning point in the war. For a while many people were believing that the Union would end the war very soon. Apparently, we have a new general, Robert E Lee is his name, and he led our troops to victory. They're calling it the Seven Days Battle. Must have taken that long," she chuckled. Mary excitedly shoved the baskets and pots into the cupboard and pulled me over to the table to sit down. She continued, "Some of the officers, like Preston, have come back to their hometowns to visit. However, I'm sure we shall see some of the wounded come through as well. We might have to help tend to them. How are you with wounds and the sight of blood?" I smiled grimly inside. *If she only knew what I have already seen …*

Trying to sound uncertain, I answered, "I will do my best to help where I'm needed." *After all, these were wounded men. Whether they wore gray or blue did not make a difference … did it? Surely, I was not in the wrong for helping the suffering enemy?*

"So, are you going to go with Preston to the dance?" Mary raised her eyebrows at me as she took up her needlework. My mind swirled with so many of my own questions and struggles, and now Mary's as well. She stopped and looked up from her sewing.

"I'm sorry, Elizabeth, I am just a little excited about the dance, and having you here and getting to know you has been so delightful." She leaned forward and laid her hand on mine. "It's like having a sister," she smiled. "So, are you going to the dance with Preston? I think it would do you good, you seem so distant sometimes. You need to have a good time and relax. Forget about all that you've been through and look to the future." The words rang in my head … forget. *Yes, it would be wonderful if none of this had ever happened.* My weary mind would rest for once. Perhaps I could even sleep through the night again without nightmares and waking up in cold sweats.

I suddenly heard myself say decisively, "Yes, I will go with him."

* * *

The churchyard was beautifully decorated for the dance. The sun was setting low behind the hills in the distance. Many candles decorated the tables that were set up around the yard. Food and punch occupied the rest of the tablespace. Captain Preston called for us at Mary's home and escorted us down the dirt street to the churchyard.

A violinist and guitarist struck up a tune and the gentlemen stepped out to request partners. Captain Preston took my hand and pulled me in. "I believe this first dance is mine," he grinned and swung me out onto the grassy dance floor. The night was beautiful, as stars twinkled in the clear sky. The music went on and on, until several dances later the Mayor of the town called everyone to his attention.

He cleared his throat and straightened his tie, "Ladies and Gentlemen! As you all know, we are in the midst of a great war. With the help of Almighty God, we will win our independence from the tyranny of the government!" The crowd cheered, and the Mayor continued, "We have just won a decisive victory over the Union troops. Some are beginning to refer to it as the Seven Days Battle. Many were killed and wounded, but we thank God for this turning point. Perhaps now we shall see more victories and conquer the enemy!" More cheering erupted. "Thank you to all those in service that are here with us today. Enjoy your time this evening, folks!"

A sharp pang of guilt stung my heart as I clapped along with the others. I shook it off and glanced at Preston. He turned and smiled at me, "Shall we take a little walk in the field? The sky is quite glorious tonight." Without waiting for an answer, he took my hand, and tucking it into his arm, led the way out into darker surroundings. We walked in silence for several moments. Then he spoke up.

"So, are you from the Northern states? I know I suggested it the other day, but you never answered me. What made you come to Virginia?"

My throat constricted. *What do I tell him? Well Captain, I came to Virginia in a train car full of Union prisoners!* My mind grasped around frantically for an answer. Suddenly it came to me, "My father!" I cringed as the words tumbled out almost too loudly and decidedly. Trying to smooth it over, I repeated, "My father was born here in Virginia. He and my mother died three years ago. I wanted to come down and visit his home, to see where he grew up as a boy." I sighed inwardly, relieved and somewhat proud of my quick answer.

Preston looked thoughtful for several moments, "Matthews ... Matthews ... now that you say that, I do believe I heard of a William Matthews dying not too long ago and his plantation is going up for sale and some of the housewares are on auction."

I stopped in my tracks, "William is my grandfather. I never met him. You say he died?"

Preston turned toward me, "I'm sorry, Miss Matthews. I didn't realize you didn't know about his death."

"No, no, it's fine. I just didn't know. We were never close." I gazed up at the starry night, then looked back at the group of dancers illuminated by the candlelight. *Now that I had mentioned the whole idea, perhaps I could find Father's plantation.* A sudden longing for my parents tore at my heart. It would make me feel close to them again, just to see his home and his old belongings.

"Would you allow me to escort you to his plantation? I believe I know where it is. It is not too far from here. We could go, if you like?" Preston's voice brought me out of my thoughts.

"Yes. I would love to go." My mind began to wander through memories again. As it did so, more recent memories from the army attempted to creep in as well. Not meaning to, I suddenly spoke my thoughts aloud. "So much death around us. Even my grandfather now. And the war ... so many young men dying and families torn apart."

Preston caught my hand, interrupting my solemn mood. "Though these times are hard, you can't let it get to you. You can only do what you can do, then just live your life and enjoy what little time you have here. You mustn't feel guilty for enjoying yourself, even while so much death is around you. There is nothing you can do about it." He covered my hand with both of his and looked into my eyes, "And I am certainly enjoying this time here with you, Miss Matthews." After a few moments, he motioned back toward the dancing couples. "Shall we?"

* * *

"You know, Mary. For the first time in a long time, I actually had fun. It was wonderful, laughing, talking and just enjoying a beautiful evening."

Mary smiled slyly at me, "I'm glad you enjoyed yourself. You will come to the ladies' tea at Mrs. Hampton's house tomorrow, won't you?"

"Of course I will!" I smiled enthusiastically. A fresh start was a wonderful feeling. Forgetting what was behind. *Preston is right, I need to just lighten up, relax and enjoy the time I spend here.* However, I also wanted to find out about my father and walk the paths he walked as a boy and wander through the fields and home in which he lived.

* * *

The carriage jolted and rumbled down the rough dirt road. We began to pass by field after field. Every so often a large plantation home broke the monotonous landscape. The day was warm, but a steady rainfall pattered the roof of the carriage. I stared out the window solemnly, caught up in my own thoughts. I had spent the past weeks going to tea parties and other social events. Nearly every day Captain Preston had come by Mary's house and we would go out riding, or walking, or sometimes just sit in the parlor and chat. Reflecting on those days, I realized how nice it was to be oblivious of what was taking place in the world. I felt rejuvenated, relaxed and excited about life again. Sometimes I would hear talk of the war and my mind would start to travel back, but I would quickly cut it off and refocus on the enjoyments of the moment. *Don't feel guilty, even when so much death is around you. You only have one life.* Preston's advice would ring in my head.

The carriage jolted to a stop. Preston opened the door and stepped out, offering me his hand. As I took it, I glanced up. In the distance, down a long dirt lane, stood a large plantation house. I never realized how rich our grandfather must've been. Preston opened an umbrella and held it over

me as we walked down the path. Gardens lined the walkway and vine
arbors created beautiful overpasses. The captain knocked on the large
wooden door. It soon opened. A servant allowed us access into the parlor.
Much of the furniture was covered by large white sheets, adding a ghostly
atmosphere to the already gloomy day. Preston shook the wet umbrella out
the half-opened doorway, before securing it behind us. The servant
removed one of the sheets, beckoning us to sit on the elegant sofa.

As he hurried off to fetch the overseer of the estate, the captain leaned
over and whispered, "You know, you could have a large inheritance coming
to you. Did that ever occur to you?" He smiled and leaned back on the
sofa, motioning to the rest of the room's décor. He was right. My father
had been my grandparents' oldest child and, since he had passed on, the
inheritance would belong to my sister and I. My heart began to beat faster
at the sudden realization. *This means we could live our lives without worrying about
financial issues. We could have all our problems and expenses in Gettysburg taken care
of.* My thoughts raced in excitement. An older man in a suit walked in,
suddenly interrupting my imaginations.

"May I help you? I am in charge of these estates as the owner has
passed away. Is there something I can do for you?" We stood up and
introduced ourselves. He stopped short as I gave him my name. "Matthews,
you say?"

"Yes, Sir. My father was James Matthews, William Matthews' son. This
is where my father was raised as a young boy." I reached into my satchel
and pulled out the small photograph that I always carried with me of my
parents. "He moved to Gettysburg with my mother. That is where my sister
and I were born. My parents died of the cholera epidemic three years ago."

The man stood silently assessing the situation. After a long moment he
stated, "I believe you. I know of James' death, and was very sorry to hear
about it." He mused for a moment before saying, "You look like your
father." I bent my head, smiling sadly. "Your grandfather also had a
photograph of you girls." I looked up, not realizing he cared so much as to
keep an image of us. "Did you come to see what your inheritance was?"

"No, I had no idea my grandfather died until two weeks ago."

"Strange. We sent letters to your home in Pennsylvania in the hopes of
reaching you. I was certain that is what brought you here," he stroked his

beard thoughtfully. I choked. I had told Preston I came down to visit my father's childhood home, but did not know of grandfather's death. Yet this man had sent me letters with news of his death.

"Perhaps they were lost in the mail? The postal service is not the most reliable these days. No, I did not know of grandfather's death, I simply was curious about my father's childhood and came for a visit." I cringed inwardly at my flimsy attempt to cover up. Trying not to look at him, I could still see Preston staring at me from the corner of my eye. Struggling to find words to change the subject, I quickly asked. "Do you mind if I take a walk around the grounds and the house? I would love to see the place where my father grew up."

"Yes, of course. But first I need to settle this business of the estate with you, Miss Matthews. Excuse me," he went into an adjacent room and returned with a folder and papers.

Laying them out on a table nearby, he suddenly sighed. He turned to me, a grim look on his face. "Please sit down again, Miss Matthews. You may not handle this news well."

My brow furrowed. *What could he mean?* Sitting down next to Preston, I braced myself.

"Your father ... when he was young, formed an ... attachment," he coughed, "... to one of the slave girls here. When they were old enough, your father ran away with this slave girl and married her. When your grandfather heard of what happened, he was enraged. He disowned your father and therefore he no longer had a claim on any part of the inheritance. After a year, the slave girl died in childbirth, leaving your father with a son. No one knows what became of the boy, but your father ran off to the north and ... well ... you know the rest of the story. So, in my letters I wrote you informing you of your grandfather's death and I let you know that unfortunately, you had no inheritance because of your father's shameful act ..." His voice drolled on and on. The sound was muffled by my shock and utter disbelief at the words he was speaking. Suddenly he placed a small wooden box in my hands. "This is all I have to give you. I'm sorry that you came so far, only to discover this. We will be holding an auction here at the plantation soon, if you would like to return. Best wishes to you, Miss Matthews. I am sorry I couldn't do more for you. Please feel free to tour the plantation." He spoke a few more words, holding a brief conversation with Preston. I walked to a large window nearby, watching the rain drops trickle down the glass pane, still trying to wrap my mind around what I had just heard. I wandered through the dark hallways and rooms of the large plantation house where my father had spent his childhood. My family had always been pro-abolitionists. We believed God created all men equal. But this … *my father had married a slave? Had Mother even known about his past?* I felt confused, and even betrayed somehow. *And they had a child … a son. I have a half-brother … a mulatto.* The young mulatto man who had broken into our house flew into my mind. *Could it be? But how would he have found us and what did he want?*

When I re-entered the parlor, after my tour of the house, Preston stood alone waiting by the door. Without saying a word to each other, he opened the door and the umbrella and escorted me onto the wet walkway. Turning to him, I asked him if he would mind if I walked the gardens alone for a while. Handing me the umbrella, he left to wait in the carriage. After walking about a mile around the extensive grounds, I found a small enclosure with a bench, surrounded by bushes and trees. Laying down the umbrella, I sat on the bench under the trees and opened the box I had been carrying. There were many parchments and notes written by my father. Some were very old, written when he was just a boy, and some just before he had left to the north. There were journal entries, Bible verses, and even some thoughts jotted out quickly on pieces of parchment. I held one up. It was a paper with outlines of little handprints and footprints, created by my father for his son. His date of birth and name was listed. *Marcus Matthews.* He was five years older than I was. Folding it back up, I uneasily put it at the bottom of the box. I began reading through Father's thoughts and favorite verses. Then one of his writings jumped off the page and hit my mind and heart with a single blow.

"I have learned that you cannot undo the distress of your past. You cannot change what happened, and you must never dwell there in your thoughts. Nevertheless, you must allow God to leverage the trials to strengthen you and build you into the person He created you to be. And you must never forget or

abandon the people who walked through the difficulties with you and helped you become better for it."

All the memories, pain, and guilt that I had been holding at bay came rushing back. I dropped my head into my hands. *What have I been doing? What was I thinking?* The experiences of the war and the prison camp flashed through my mind like a bolt of lightning. The scenes and the faces of those I had become so close to during the months of being in the army passed before my mind. However much I tried to forget or pretend they were not there, it did not matter, they were there. They were still out there, fighting the battles, still dying for a cause. And Nathan ... he was still in the prison camp. He had helped many of us escape. He had sacrificed himself. Yet here I was, pretending to be someone I was not. Attending parties and enjoying myself, turning a blind eye to everything that was real and going on around me. *What a fool I am.* Sobbing in disgust at myself, I cried out to Almighty God to forgive my selfishness and complacency. Looking up into the darkening sky, I made a promise as the rain mixed with tears streamed down my face.

"I will not live for myself anymore. No matter how hard life becomes. Lord, you never once thought of yourself and your own comforts. Neither will I. Use me to be a blessing to those around me. Whether on the battlefront or in my own town."

* * *

"You seem rather distant since we visited your Father's plantation. Of course you're probably upset with the news of your father's unacceptable behavior, not to mention having no inheritance because of it." Preston slowed his black gelding to a walk beside the gentle mare I had been riding. I had gone out for a quiet afternoon, alone in the countryside beyond the town. I needed time by myself to sort through everything I had just learned and to make decisions on what I should do next. I had attempted to avoid Preston for the last couple days, and he seemed to notice. I had wasted much time here. I had tried to forget who I was and what my purpose was here. I had been distracted and lost sight of what life was really about. I wanted more than this silly life of parties and "romance." I wanted to live with a mission in mind. It didn't have to be something grand or something others would see and give applause. In my own quiet way, I wanted to live with the life of Christ reflecting in mine. I had found a verse in the book of John. Jesus said to His Father, "I glorified You on the earth, having accomplished the work which you have given me to do." Just like Him, I wanted to glorify God by accomplishing the work He had given me to do … whatever that may look like.

Reaching down and patting the sleek chestnut neck, I answered Preston, "I'm sorry. I have a lot to think about and make decisions about. Now that I have seen my father's plantation and learned what I could of it, I think I need to go home." *Or to the prison camp … to find out about Nathan …*

"Home? I thought we had an understanding here," the tone of his voice hardened. I knew I had been wrong to let him believe that, and it was my fault. In my own anxiousness to escape my real life I had encouraged his attention. Now that I had taken the time to truly think through everything, I knew this man was caught up in the superficial things of life as well. He was very … self-focused, but I had tried to make excuses for him in my mind, convincing myself otherwise. Yet I was still in the wrong for allowing the relationship to proceed this far. Before I could find the words to best answer him, he continued.

"Miss Matthews, I have been nothing but kind and gentlemanly toward you. And after all your encouragement, I certainly would've thought we had an understanding." Several moments passed and when I gave him no answer, he rode up closer and grabbed the reins of my horse, jerking her to a halt. I looked up, shocked at his sudden harshness. He narrowed his eyes and added, "Even after finding out about your father's unforgivable behavior and, not to mention, your lack of inheritance, I still have come in search of you! Surely no other man will do the same after discovering *these* problems."

Pulling the reins out of his hands, I turned my horse to face him. "Captain Preston, yes, you are correct. I was wrong in my encouragement and I am very sorry for it. I should not have allowed this to progress so quickly. We have only known each other a short time. But, as for my father's 'unforgivable behavior' as you so kindly put it, that is none of your business. And I am sorry for not being a rich heiress, as perhaps you wanted me to be. Let me ask you, why *did* you come in search of me when I have all these 'problems' as you say?"

Preston rolled his eyes and turned his horse in the direction of the town, "Perhaps you were a welcome distraction for me from the horrors of war. However, if you would rather give up this 'friendship' we have, so be it. I can have plenty of other distractions. You however may not be so fortunate." A conceited grin spread over his face as he dug his heels into the horse and cantered back over the fields to the town.

* * *

That night, I told Mary what had happened between myself and the captain. She was very understanding, but sorry that it would not work out. She admitted that she had hoped I would marry and settle down there in the town. She was a good friend and I was sorry knowing that I would have to leave her soon. I felt worse concealing my true story from her, but it was too dangerous to reveal all that I had been through to this Southern girl.

Discovery
Chapter 44

Amy

THE NIGHT WAS dark and silent as a graveyard. Not a sound penetrated the thick fog. Only the muffled flow of the river was audible. The men had tied the horses just inside the tree line and were now filling their canteens at the riverside. No one spoke a word as if afraid to disturb the allure of the eerie night. Some of the younger boys glanced nervously about them as they knelt to drink. There was something about the still foggy night, making everyone uneasy. I shivered and felt a hand touch mine. Embarrassed, I realized how close I was standing to the colonel. He glanced down at me and I awkwardly inched away.

"Should we let the men rest here for the night, Sir?" Sanders, who approached from the river asked in a whisper.

Anderson turned to squint into the hazy forest, "No, we'll press on through the night. We mustn't let him get away."

Sanders kicked at the stirrups uneasily. The colonel watched him closely for a moment. Finally, Sanders remained still and rested his hand on the hilt of his saber.

"Is something wrong, Major?" I could see Sanders searching the tree line anxiously.

"Sir ... I can't shake the feeling. Something's not right." There was a long pause and Sanders tightened his hold on the saber until his knuckles whitened.

"Go on, Major," Anderson spoke calmly.

"We've not seen a sign of him in three days. It doesn't make sense. If they would have circled around, we would have seen the tracks."

"You think they've disappeared again," Anderson was beginning to look frustrated. "We'll not give up Major. We must find him this time. We'll meet him on the battlefield and finish him off."

"We will, Sir," Sanders turned to stare across the dark river. The men were now rising to their feet, taking one last gulp and preparing to ride on. One young, blond boy stood up, corking his canteen and gazed toward the forest. His eyes narrowed and he walked forward and stopped at the edge of the fog. I stared at him and my heart seemed to quicken. Something was wrong. The horses had not made a sound for nearly fifteen minutes. The boy leaned forward as if listening and suddenly I realized everyone was listening … waiting … A single shot resounded in the darkness. Then all was still again. My skin crept in anticipation.

"They're here," Sanders breathed beside me. A black horse broke from the fog directly in front of the boy soldier I had been watching. The rider, wielding his saber, appeared black against the fog. He charged toward the defenseless young soldier and struck him down with a savage blow. Suddenly a host of black riders surged forth out of the mist. The clamor of pebbles spitting out from under the galloping horses created a deafening noise about me. Horses lunged out at full length with riders flat against their backs. Their sabers were drawn.

"Defend yourselves!" Anderson shouted hoarsely. The men were frozen with fear. I fumbled, gripping at my pistol as my eyes locked on a single horse and rider that had just burst through the thick fog. The sleek black stallion charged toward me, nostrils flared, a black saber reached in front of his magnificent head. I drew my pistol and slowly raised it with a heavy hand. It kicked as I fired. The horse winced and shrieked, but kept on coming, blood trickling down his broad chest. He rose up on his hind legs in front of me, and the rider raised his saber to strike. As the sword came down, there was a tremendous clashing of metal. Major Sanders stood between us. He struggled under the weight of the phantom rider's saber above him. Teeth gritting, slowly he began to collapse. I aimed at the overpowering figure above him and pulled the trigger, but nothing happened.

"Bullet, bullets," I tugged at the pouch and searched, darting my eyes up every so often to see Sanders engaged in a saber duel against horse and rider. The black rider wielded his horse skillfully in a circle about the Major. I jumped quickly upon the pouch of a fallen soldier and hurriedly tried to load. The horse nearly ran into Sanders and his sword fell to the ground. The black rider pulled forth his pistol.

"Surrender or die!"

Sanders turned from the fallen saber to his enemy. His eyes blazed as he said, "Never." His hand went to the pistol at his side and a shot rang out. He winced, crumpling to his knees. My hand went limp and the pistol tumbled to my feet. The black saber was raised ready to deliver the final blow. Blindly, I rushed forward and threw myself thoughtlessly across the fallen body as the saber came down. A sharp pain surged through my side. The screams and shots went silent around me and a black veil covered my eyes.

The air would not come ... I choked desperately. I heard a blood curdling scream and a thud. I felt a warm wetness somewhere ... *my hand.* A horse shrieked madly above me and the sounds seemed to fade again. Desperately, I fought to keep awake. *Don't close your eyes; you'll never open them again.* I stood on the edge of an abyss, ready to topple in. I fought. Faintly I heard familiar voices.

"Quick! We need to get him out!"

I was suddenly aware of some movement beside me. They were taking Major Sanders ... they must be. My hand reached out to touch him. *Is he dead?*

"It's not that I can do it any better than them, Sarah. It's what I can do, myself. What I can give. And if I can give it all and help just a little, if my life will save others, then God's will be done ... Forgive me, Elizabeth forgive me ..." Darkness surrounded me as my eyes fluttered opened. My body slid limply onto the ground. The pebbles, the stones, they held me. *I can feel them. I am alive.* A warm wetness soaked my hand. *Where is it? Where? The blood, I can feel it ...* Something white stood out in the darkness. *I've seen it ... yes, the moon.*

* * *

A cold hard bed was under me. An aching pain in my side. I wanted to scream at the top of my lungs, scream for mother, for father or Elizabeth, anyone! Voices echoed all around me. Something soft was under my head, a voice in my ear.

"Won't make it home. You need to get the bullet out now."

"But, Sir."

"Now." I felt a hand on my jacket. *No, stop ... I can't ... you mustn't ...* I tried to shout, but heard nothing. Someone called out and the sound of many feet on the hard ground faded into the night. They were gone, but the softness under my head remained.

"The wound is deep ... I can't operate without ..." The words faded out and I felt a warm hand touch mine.

A soft accented voice whispered in my ear, "Hold on, *Amy* ..."

Hope Dawns on the Horizon
Chapter 45

Elizabeth

THE NIGHTMARES WERE still there. They had never completely left. I had only tried to ignore them, turning my mind to trivial thoughts such as dresses and social gatherings. I had escaped the snare of this frivolous living, which made me grateful, but now the visions of the prison camp returned more often, even during the daytime. What I had seen at the camp and during the battles was too much to bear. I wanted to go home, but the image of Nathan being taken prisoner arose again and again in my mind. *How could I go back to Gettysburg knowing he was still in that horrible prison camp? Was he even alive?* I had to find out for myself. I couldn't endure life without knowing whether he was dead or alive. Not after what we had been through, not after what he had done for me. Before going back to Gettysburg, I had to discover Nathan's condition.

In the morning, I told Mary I was going to visit my grandfather's estate for a few days. The last couple days, I had been cautiously asking around town, in hopes of discovering how far we actually were from the prison camp in which I had been held captive. I learned that it was only a couple days journey at most. I made sure I was far enough away from the town before I turned in the direction of the prison camp. Once I was out of sight and on the lonely roadway, I opened my satchel and withdrew some old garments perfect for my disguise.

* * *

Situating the clothing around me, I shrugged. *It would have to do.* Pulling the shawl nearer around my forehead and chin, I tried to conceal my youthful face. Adjusting the basket of food on one arm and teetering with the cane in the other, I slowly moved along the dirt road toward the prison. I had left the horse in a nearby forest, tied to a sturdy tree. My stomach shrunk and lurched as I drew nearer to the walls that had been all I had known for those dreaded months. I bent my head back to the ground, trying to remain hunched over as I came closer to the entrance. The familiar smells of death and unwashed bodies overwhelmed me as a guard opened the doors to my request of bringing food to the prisoners. I shrank into the shawl around my face and tried to steady my racing heartbeat. As the doors closed behind me, I panicked and it took all within me to move forward. Reminding myself why I was here, I kept telling myself I could easily turn around and the door would open to me. The door would open. There was grass and sky outside. The door would open ... the door *would* open.

"Old woman!" I jerked up at the sound of a harsh voice and realized he was speaking to me. My disguise had really worked. "Bring that food over here!" Remembering how some of the guards would take the food meant for the prisoners for themselves, I clutched the basket closer to me.

"Young man, I would like to give the food to the prisoners myself. If you don't mind." I tried to make my voice raspy, which was not hard with the tension and fear in my throat. The soldier looked disgusted, but pulled his keys out and flung open one of the gates.

"Go ahead. I don't know why you bother. They're all going to die anyways," he muttered as I stepped past him into hell. I jumped and shuddered as the gate clanged behind me. *Turn around, go back and it will open back up. It will open back up. He will open it back up.* I rubbed my hand over my face trying to fight the anguish and panic setting in. *Pass out the food. Look for Nathan.* I methodically began handing out the food to those strong enough to take it from my hand. I was suddenly back with John, Will and Nathan, in this same prison passing out the meager rations, as I had done every day since being captured. There was John, trying to help me. There was Nathan watching calmly, helping in his quiet way. There was Will ... dear sweet

Will, always comforting, always encouraging. The tears began to stream uncontrollably down my cheeks. My mind snapped back to the present. Will and John were both dead … from this very place … and Nathan. I had to find Nathan.

I began asking those who were more alert, "Excuse me, do you know Nathan Tyler? Have you seen him?"

As I passed the food into their hands. Most shrugged and quickly devoured the bread, a look of fear in their eyes. I moved along as quickly as I could, not wanting the guards to suspect I was searching for something. At last, having no food left to give, my heart sank as I moved back toward the gate. I forced myself to hobble and use the cane in my hand. *He had to be here. Surely someone knows him.* Nearly ten feet from the gate, a hand touched my shoulder.

Turning around, a young man whispered, "Ma'am, forgive me. Did you say you were looking for a man named Nathan Tyler?"

My throat constricted, "Yes."

The prisoner glanced around, making sure the guards could not hear and pulled me farther from the gate. "Forgive me, Ma'am. Nathan Tyler was here. He helped many men to escape. A few men at a time would sneak out by a tunnel they had been able to conceal from the guards. Nathan tried to escape once with a group, but was caught and brought back. After that, he led several groups out by a new tunnel but he would always come back to save more. I was just brought here a few weeks ago. But the other prisoners told me his story. I was hoping to be part of the next group to go out, but then the guards found the new tunnel and …" suddenly his eyes widened in realization. "Ma'am, you're not his mother are you? Oh Ma'am, I'm so sorry."

I grasped the boy's shoulder, "What? What is it?"

The soldier's eyes dropped to the ground, "They found the tunnel … they found out Nathan was the one leading all the escapes. They … Ma'am … they …" his eyes slowly raised to meet mine. "They hung him, Ma'am."

Time froze. A cold chill ran over my entire body. Every muscle loosening, the basket fell from my hand. Shaking my head, I stepped back from the young soldier. He spoke to me, reaching out his hand, but I heard nothing come from his lips. All sound was silenced. The world became misty, cold and quiet. Drifting through the gate, I passed through the big doors of the prison and wandered down the dirt roadway.

* * *

Thunder cracked across the sky. Rain pattered continuously on the roof above me. Occasional flashes of lightning lit up the little room with a pinkish glow. I jumped and pulled the covers up around my face. I slowly drifted off into a restless slumber. Before me appeared the image of Nathan's face and the sound of promise in his voice as he assured me that he would come back. Images of soldiers in gray pulling Nathan's arms together in a knot raced before my mind's eye. Then slowly, the gruesome figures of prisoners in their camps revealed themselves to me once again. The horrific scenes of dead prisoners being carried out by their captors haunted my dreams. *Wait ... that face ... one of the dead prisoners who was being carried out ... it was ... no please ... yes, it was ... Nathan!* A lightning bolt brightened the enclosure and a burst of thunder sent me into an upright position. Hands shaking, I tightened my hold on the blanket around me. Rocking back and forth on the small bed, I trembled at the visions which had passed through my mind. *If only they were just the nightmares they seemed to be! If only I had been there sooner. Perhaps I could've done something. Maybe he could've escaped. But no, instead I had been enjoying the comforts of life in a small Southern town, ignoring all the truth around me.* The tears wet my collar and hands. I sobbed in despair, dropping my head into the damp cloth of the blanket. Not only did I cry out for one man, but tears flowed for all those who I had seen suffer and die.

* * *

Sunlight streamed through the window, causing the raindrops which hung in various places to glisten on the glass. Realizing the cramped position I had slept in, I sat up and slowly rubbed my neck. The emotions of the night before came rushing back, bringing sickening darkness into the bright day. Pulling the worn book off the nightstand, I flipped through the pages ...

"Yea, though I walk through the valley of the shadow of death, I will fear no evil: for Thou art with me; Thy rod and Thy staff they comfort me."

* * *

"Ow!" I yelled, throwing down the cloth in frustration. I put pressure on the finger to stop the bleeding. Mary looked up at me in concern, but said nothing. My mind was so distracted lately that I couldn't even sew a straight stitch anymore. *Why was I still here? I had planned on going back to Gettysburg after discovering Nathan's whereabouts. What was I waiting for? Some kind of hope, some kind of answer to my distress? He's dead. Nothing will change that.* I stood up in irritation, throwing the worn dress back on the table. Yanking aside the door, I wandered out into the fields beyond the town. Stomping through the tall grass, I didn't even notice the beautiful wildflowers that scattered themselves throughout the field, or the soft breeze that carried their subtle scent through the air.

The sun was warm upon my face and shone brightly in my eyes. I couldn't go back to the warfare … to the unceasing death and destruction of human life and friendships, at least not yet. Staying here was not going to bring him back to life. Living near the prison camp would not help keep the memory of him alive in my mind. *Why is it so hard to leave?* I knew it was time to go home to my sister and friends. Maybe there I could begin again. The word sounded so sweet. *Home.* Even if I did go back to help with the war effort later, first I needed to go home. Again, the doubt crept in. *Perhaps I should never have gone to the army in the first place. Maybe it was a terrible mistake. I could've saved myself so much heartache.* Shaking off the thought, I reminded myself why I had gone. I wanted to make a difference, to help somehow. Whether I did or not, God only knows, but I had tried and I prayed I *had* helped someone in some way.

* * *

Mary stood in the doorway as I gathered some food, a canteen, a blanket and the box Father had left me and piled the items into a couple of bags.

"You're really leaving then? You're sure you won't stay a while longer with us?" she asked in disappointment. After gathering everything together, I walked over to her and laid my hands on her shoulders.

"I have to go back home, I need to sort some things out. I need to see my sister." Mary looked away, I could see she was fighting back tears. I continued, "You've been a wonderful friend to me, Mary, and I shall never forget you and your kindness. But ... I really must go."

The next morning, I hugged Mary goodbye. I had found a family that was going north with whom I could travel. Mary had offered one of their horses, but I could not accept it. I slipped out before anyone in the town would wake up. I did not want them to ask too many questions, and most of all, I did not want to see Captain Preston by chance. I looked over my shoulder for the last time at the town where I had spent the last several weeks. I felt I had grown from all I had learned and gone through there. Yet, my soul ached with the remembrance of Nathan, Will and John, who had all died just a few miles from there. However, I knew they were truly no longer there, and so ... I began my journey home.

* * *

The late summer sun hung high in the sky as our wagon traveled up Emmitsburg Road. My heartbeat began to quicken as I saw the familiar fields and farms on our way into Gettysburg.

"Excuse me, Sir, would you mind if I got off here?" I asked. A sudden desire to walk down the dusty old road toward home rose within me. How lovely it would be to see the brick farmhouse rise up in the distance as I strolled down the lane. The driver shrugged.

"Your business, Miss ... do as you like." He reigned in the team and I climbed quickly down, thanking him for his trouble. As the wagon rumbled off and the dust settled around me, I lifted my skirts and stepped lightly along the road in eager anticipation. *How wonderful it will be to see Amy! And how surprised she will be when I show up. I wonder how she and Kelsey are doing ... perhaps they will have some exciting news for me.* I grinned inwardly. Soon I could see our old home just down the road. Tears sprung to my eyes as all the memories this place held came to mind. It felt as though I had been gone for many, many years. Looking around to make sure no one was watching, I broke into a run as I drew nearer. It still looked in good shape as Mr. Barnes, and Amy no doubt, had been looking after the place in my absence. The windows were still boarded up and the old swing in the oak tree rocked softly in the breeze. I situated myself between the thick ropes and pushed my feet off the ground, leaning back and gazing up into the green foliage. Breathing in deeply, I soaked in the peaceful atmosphere of the farm and the countryside. Home ... Now that I was here I wasn't sure if I could ever leave again. I knew I wanted to help, but being here, I felt completely held and comforted in the familiarity of this land and town. I reached my hand down and let it sweep across the tops of the flowers that Mother had planted near the swing. Bleeding Hearts they were called. *A very fitting name*, I thought as I studied the delicate pink flowers. At least this place was far away ... far away from the destruction, the death, the bloodshed, the broken hearts and torn friendships. This place, with its charm and beauty was beyond the sickness, beyond the wounds, beyond the reach of swords and bullets and beyond the bleeding hearts of so many torn from their loved ones and all they held dear.

* * *

"Mrs. Denny, what do you mean they are gone?" The words came choking out. The plump woman's eyes grew wide and she pulled me inside and sat me on a cushioned sofa in her parlor.

"My dear girl! Oh dear! What a shambles! What a horrific discovery!" She reached for a muffin and quickly swallowed it, as if that would help the problem. Then she continued, "The marriage never even took place! Kelsey disappeared! And soon after, your sister vanished! No one knows the girl's whereabouts!" She hissed as though afraid of being overheard. My heart pounded in my ears and I gripped the armchair of the sofa. My head swam with confusion at what could've possibly happened.

"No one knows? Mrs. Denny, are you sure no one knows? Surely, she must've said something to someone! How could she leave like that? Where would she go?" I stood up and began pacing the room. *I can't stay here not knowing what has become of Amy! But where to start? How could I possibly find her?*

"Surely you have some horrific stories to tell us yourself, Elizabeth. Being in the thick of war and all! Sit and do tell!" The woman patted the seat beside her as if nothing had happened. *All she wants is some juicy story to share with her friends. Well, she will not get one from me.*

"Thank you, Mrs. Denny, but there are more important things in mind at the moment." I stalked away, letting myself out the door, not waiting for a reply from the nosy neighbor. As I proceeded down the streets, I barely noticed my surroundings. My thoughts were consumed with the news I had just heard. *No wonder Amy never returned my letters. Where was she?*

"Elizabeth!" I was suddenly wrapped in a tight hug. I could not contain the tears of joy mixed with the sorrowful news I bore as I returned the hug of our childhood friend, Sarah Phillips. After a long moment and the exchange of a few words, we cut off the main road and walked into the countryside. The tall grasses waved and bent in the breeze, while the wildflowers dotted the green pastures. We continued walking and I related the adventures of the past few months to her. With a heavy heart, I shared the news of her brother's death as we had escaped the prison camp. Sarah and John had been extremely close growing up and it was not easy to relay such news. I was glad to be someone she could cry with and relive the memories we had of him together. It was nearly dark as we arrived back to my home on Emmitsburg Road. When I asked about Amy, Sarah could not meet my eyes and would not say anything.

"You know something. Sarah! She is my sister ..." I pleaded with her as we stood outside the door.

After a moment, she took my hands in hers, "Amy told me not to tell anyone. But I can't keep this from you!" She turned her head away, tears shining in her eyes. "Elizabeth, your sister disguised herself and ... and enlisted in the army."

I stood in shock for several minutes. The words sunk in slowly. *Why had she done this? Didn't she know what could become of her if she was discovered? Didn't she know the danger of it all besides?* "Is she with Kelsey?" I croaked.

"I don't know Elizabeth. She would not tell me very much at all. However, I do not think they parted on good terms. He left a few weeks before she did. I have no details for you." She sighed heavily, "You don't know how hard it has been to hold this inside ... to only be able to pray for her, not knowing anything of her whereabouts or how she is. And now, with the news of John on top of it all," she broke into tears. "I don't know what I shall do!" I pulled her into my arms, the tears beginning to stream down my own face as well. All was not as peaceful and beautiful here as I had expected it to be.

* * *

I had been in Gettysburg for a few weeks now. John Barnes had come and helped me open up the house. He tried to do as much as he could, but I assured him that I wanted to do it. The work would give me something to keep my mind off all the sorrows and troubles that lay before and behind me. I struggled daily with the memory of how I had treated Nathan. I had been so wrong to treat him as if he was a criminal. After everything he did for me, to never be able to tell him, to thank him, to let him know how I felt now ... it tormented me. I read through our family Bible daily, intentionally looking for verses about forgiveness. I needed to know I was forgiven. I know I could never be forgiven by Nathan now, but knowing that God forgave me, that gave me the strength to go on. In the meantime, I tried finding clues and traces of where Amy might be. I had to be very careful though who I talked to and what I said so as not to uncover her identity in the process. Eventually, I did learn what units were recruiting about the time that she had disappeared. Tracing their whereabouts might be more difficult, but at least I had a lead now. I could pretend I was only trying to find my husband's or brother's unit and perhaps that way I could find her and convince her to come back home. Everything needed to return to how it was.

It had been a long autumn day. The leaves on the old oak tree were a beautiful hue. A breeze tossed the fallen leaves around my feet as I went out to finish up the work for the day. My hair was in a disheveled bun at the back of my head, and loose strands blew around my dirt smudged face. The apron I had pinned around my blue calico was also covered in flour and dirt smudges from the day's chores. Shadow nickered at me from the fence as I gathered several late vegetables from the garden that Mr. Barnes had kept for us. The sun was setting on the horizon painting the sky beautiful shades of red, orange, gold and pink. Putting the basket down, I went over to a fence board that had fallen once again. Lifting the heavy log up, my hands brushed up against the rough wood. I wiped at the bloody blister I had created from working on the fence line earlier that day. Tears sprang to my eyes as my mind reverted once again to the memories of this place with my sister and parents. Tears flowed for everything that was before me: the strain of trying to locate my sister, the decision of whether I should go back to help in the war effort, the pain of what was behind me, the mistakes, the fears, the battles … the friends I had lost … mostly, the friends I had lost. I wiped at the tears and mud on my face. Using my apron, I dabbed the blood on my hand. Lifting the vegetable basket, I turned to go back to the house. Shadow nickered once again, his head turning southward down the road. Hearing a jingling of reins and the thumping of hooves coming nearer, I wiped again at my face, hoping to get inside before someone saw me like this. The hoofbeats came nearer and then stopped short. Hearing the rider dismount, I stopped in my tracks as well.

"Elizabeth," a husky tone softly spoke my name.

My eyebrows drew together inquisitively. I slowly turned around. All time seemed to stand still, the breeze died, the leaves stopped rustling, the noises of nature dissipated. Everything around me became a blur. Surely it was another vision, another dream I was having. For ten feet in front of me, there stood Nathan, holding the reins of a black horse. He wore a blue uniform … an officer's uniform … not the old dirty one he had worn in the prison camp. His face was thin and pale, not tan with the strong jaw he had once before. Yet, he pulled off his hat, revealing the same thick, black hair he had always had. Was it him? He was thinner, but those eyes were still the same sharp blue that had met mine so many times before.

Dropping the basket and letting the contents spill onto the ground, I took hesitant steps toward him. Stopping and then walking, afraid that if I came too close he would vanish. Once I was inches away from him, I cautiously reached up to his cheek. The warmth of his face met my hand, and he was still there.

"It is you … but how?" I breathed, barely able to get the words out. Nathan dropped the reins and hat he was holding and I threw myself into his opening arms. Sobbing gently, I whispered, "I'm sorry, I'm so sorry. Please forgive me." His strong arms held me close as he stroked my hair.

"Of course I forgive you," he whispered gently. After a long moment, Nathan pulled me back at an arm's length. The cold blue eyes stared into mine, then he said softly, "Do you trust me now?" A long pause ensued as the eyes searched mine, then Nathan cupped my face in his hands and whispered, "I told you I would come back, didn't I?" After another pause, the slightest smile came over the ever-serious face. I nodded softly, not knowing what to say, the tears flowing freely down my face. Before I knew what was happening, Nathan came down on one knee before me, and there under the crimson autumn sky, near the tasseling grasses, among the whispering breeze, a request was made.

THE END

The story will continue with the sequel *Beyond the Fields of Fire* expected to be released in 2024.

About the Authors

Jessica Elam

Jessica Elam is a young Christian woman living in the rolling hills of Indiana. The American Civil War is one of her greatest passions and she visits National Battlefield Parks as often as she can, particularly Gettysburg. Jessica enjoys her job as the office manager at a local hardware store in town. She also loves writing, traveling, hiking, and spending time with her friends, family, and her Siberian Husky. Jessica wants to dream big, impact others, and live every day to the fullest.

Alexandra Elam

Alexandra Elam met and married her husband Lirim Haliti on a mission trip in Kosovo. They have two baby girls and dream about traveling to do mission work together one day. She deeply cherishes the moments of laughter that she shares with friends and family. One of her most serious mottos in life is, "You can never have too much chocolate." Alexandra is very passionate about history and inspiring others through the communication of writing and music.

Printed in the USA
CPSIA information can be obtained
at www.ICGtesting.com
CBHW021656040124
3045CB00007B/20

9 781956 867473